APRIL 20, 2015, BES[...]
Car[...]
Enjoy[...]
Paul Dillon

MW00886447

PRAISE FOR SIR CHRISTIAN DE GALIS AND THE FISH GRAVY

"Carl Ramsey is definitely a writer! He has a beginning that grabs the reader and keeps the action going. He understands 'show, don't tell' with lots of action and excellent dialogue. In addition, he keeps the reader guessing and wanting to know more."
—Nancy Polette, professor of literature for children and youth at Lindenwood University and award-winning author of *The Spy with the Wooden Leg, Angel in Fatigues, and POW: Angel On Call*

"A cleverly written story. The morals are not overly played...by unusually memorable but hilarious characters created by Mr. Ramsey. I give this a 5 star out of 5 star rating and look forward to the second installment in this series."
—Dr. Carl Werner, author and producer of *Evolution: The Grand Experiment* educational book and DVD series

"A playful romp into a mythic past that never was but should have been. The committed medievalist will delight in the fun of Ramsey's creation."
—Roberto Munoz, award-winning international filmmaker

"I think the whole book is a *masterpiece*."
—Paul Dillon, book illustrator, cartoonist

"I love your humor."
—Dr. Ray Rempt, Washington State–based physicist and Christian author of *Big Bang to Kingdom Come, A Season For All Time, Got Faith?,* and *Never Before...Never Again*

"Top-notch manuscript...very good at building suspense and dropping subtle clues...I love your writing style. I love this book."
—J. Taylor Ludwig, author of *It Was Never About Books*

"A must-read comedy at its finest."
—Dustin Murdock, high-school graduate, Saint Charles, Missouri

Sir Christian de Galis and the Fish Gravy

VOLUME I OF THE QUEST OF SIR CHRISTIAN

CARL E. RAMSEY

WESTBOW·
PRESS
A DIVISION OF THOMAS NELSON
& ZONDERVAN

Copyright © 2014 Carl E. Ramsey.

All rights reserved. No part of this book may be used or reproduced by any means, graphic, electronic, or mechanical, including photocopying, recording, taping or by any information storage retrieval system without the written permission of the publisher except in the case of brief quotations embodied in critical articles and reviews.

Illustrations by Paul Dillon

WestBow Press books may be ordered through booksellers or by contacting:

WestBow Press
A Division of Thomas Nelson & Zondervan
1663 Liberty Drive
Bloomington, IN 47403
www.westbowpress.com
1 (866) 928-1240

Because of the dynamic nature of the Internet, any web addresses or links contained in this book may have changed since publication and may no longer be valid. The views expressed in this work are solely those of the author and do not necessarily reflect the views of the publisher, and the publisher hereby disclaims any responsibility for them.

Any people depicted in stock imagery provided by Thinkstock are models, and such images are being used for illustrative purposes only. Certain stock imagery © Thinkstock.

ISBN: 978-1-4908-5670-4 (sc)
ISBN: 978-1-4908-5669-8 (hc)
ISBN: 978-1-4908-5671-1 (e)

Library of Congress Control Number: 2014918625

Printed in the United States of America.

WestBow Press rev. date: 11/20/2014

In memory of Patricia Craft, wife of fellow Marine and Grace Church, Saint Louis, pastor, Bill Craft. In the early days of developing this book, she devoted her time, talent, and encouragement to give it a firm foundation.

And to the following English professors at Concordia Teachers College, Seward, Nebraska (now Concordia University), who took a young Marine war veteran to the next level of literary excitement: Robert Baden, Doris Clatanoff, Stephen J. Korinko, James Nelesen (my faculty adviser), and Richard Zwick.

And to my nephews and nieces, blood related and church adopted, for whom I tried to write a good story.

And finally to Michael J. Miller, Sr. of Christian Family Guidance Center, Saint Louis, Missouri, who remains steady as a rock.

This was the beginning of the famous quests. They were
not made to win him fame or recreation...They were
his struggles to save his honor, not to establish it.
—T. H. White, *The Once and Future King*

TABLE OF THE FISH GRAVY SHOWS WHAT THE AUTHOR COOKED UP

ILLUSTRATED FISH GRAVY DISPLAYS WHAT THE ARTIST DISHED OUT

CAST (IN IRON, NOT STONE)

Companions of the Gravy
absolute worst knight at King Arthur's Round Table
his horse
his squire
his squire's horse (will be ladled out in volume 2)
his squire's packhorse (see his squire's horse)
a lady who looks harmless (until someone swings her the wrong way)
her horse
her maid
her maid's horse
her maid's packhorse
her grandson
an ancient archer (who is also a knight)
his horse
his squire
his squire's horse
his squire's packhorse
Unknown Bard (first name frequently appears in song books)
his horse (that died of fright)

Mercenaries-Not-So-Perilous from Navarre
Captain Sarito, a Navarrese mercenary commander
his men: Pedro, Cordero, Cisco, Aquila, Rogerio, Arrio, Bernardo,
Alvaro, Berto, Tulio, Currito

Supporting Characters (Some with Speaking Parts)
Myrddin, King Arthur's mysterious adviser who replaced Merlin
Meudwin, a medical hermit
Sir Mordred the Murderous, Knight of the Round Table and King
Arthur's secret son
Melehan, Sir Mordred's oldest son and squire
Melehan's younger brother (see his squire's horse)
Sir Dagonet, King Arthur's jester who isn't funny
Sir Erbin the Easygoing, an innkeeper
Heretoga, a Saxon commander
some of his men: Sarlic, Ator, Cearo, Acwel, Acwellen, Abeodan
a giant brown bear, with growling parts
Monster-of-Unheard-of-Savageness, with terrifying parts

FOREWORD BY NANCY POLETTE

Those of us who have gone down a rabbit hole, have climbed the mast of a plunging schooner with pirates hot on our trail, or traveled a yellow brick road with strange companions; those of us who have done these things know how narrow and bleak our lives would be without these mind-stretching adventures.

One of the world's great thinkers, Albert Einstein was an avid reader of fairy tales and fantasy. He has written: "The fairest thing we can experience is the mysterious. It is the fundamental emotion which stands at the cradle of true art and true science. He who knows it not, who can no longer wonder, can no longer feel amazement, is as good as dead, a snuffed out candle."

Imagination can illumine the real world and help us to make sense out of reality. If we question the validity of truly imaginative experiences, we need only recognize that the tears and laughter are indeed real.

Fantasy does help to shape great minds. Understanding real humanity, nobility of character, and the vitality of love that fantasy can bring alive is of far greater value rather than the counterfeit, superficial, remote, and plastic mannequins of the media world.

From the very first paragraph of Sir Christian de Galis and the Fish Gravy, the reader knows he or she is in for a rollicking adventure. The first line challenges the reader to develop an elasticity of mind. What is meant by "The worst choice is sometimes the best choice?"

Many dragons face us all in life today, and fortunate is the reader who has tilted with many on his or her path, and emerged victorious as we know Sir Christian de Galis will. Fortunate, too, is the reader who has won dragons to his side through gentleness and understanding. As we get to know Sir Christian and his companions, all of whom are far from perfect, we find the pervasive theme that gentleness and understanding will often win the day. What more important skills are needed by humanity! What better skill sharpener than exposure to meaningful fantasy.

Our schools have tended to overemphasize the "steam shovel" approach to learning. The "how to" or "first book" of atoms, magnets, automobiles, and pumpkin pies abound in classrooms and school libraries. In learning the construction of a bird's wings, we must not allow children to lose the awe that it does take flight. That same sense of awe is found in meaningful fantasy.

The real world is finite, but the world of fantasy has infinite possibilities. How could a knight be a wedding present to a king? Why would the worst knight in the kingdom be given a most important quest, when all expect him to fail? How can one be the object of one's own quest? And what does fish gravy have to do with anything? With a blend of magic, mayhem, and humor, these and many other questions are answered in *Sir Christian de Galis and the Fish Gravy*.

An important message in Sir Christian is "If only one will stand, that will be enough." Suggestions bombard us all to indicate that we are not that one. But Sir Christian shows us that it is in the heart of the simplest to be that one through trust, perseverance, and ultimate triumph.

Nancy Polette
Professor of Children's Literature
Lindenwood University

FOREWORD BY JIM TAYON

What a treat is this wholesome, tongue-in-cheek saga novel penned by my good friends Carl, as author, and Paul, as illustrator, which takes us back to the twelfth century and King Arthur and his Round Table! We also know US Marine Carl from his creation of monthly calendars on military history and Paul as commander of the St. Louis chapter of the American Ex-Prisoners of War, of which his late father was a member.

This fantasy gives new dimension to chivalry in Arthurian tales and legend, displaying comic narration as vivid images are built and we are led down a path under the weight of armor, chuckling behind open face mask and dragging our sword. We find delight in setting this work of folklore and mythology against the backdrop of a Welsh Triad found in medieval manuscripts: "Three things not easily restrained—the flow of torrent, the flight of an arrow, and the tongue of a fool."

James E. Tayon, P.E.
President and Cofounder
Franklin County Honor Flight

ACKNOWLEDGMENTS

This is one place the author gets serious. First, let me acknowledge my Lord and Savior, who empowered me to develop this story from a raw idea while reinforcing me with key contacts and helpers. Next, let me recognize those key contacts who gave extra help above and beyond their endorsements, especially Ms. Nancy Polette, who also wrote the first foreword; Mr. Jim Tayon, who took time from his busy schedule at Franklin County Honor Flight to provide an additional foreword; Ms. Judith Ludwig, who edited the manuscript under development for free twice; Dr. Carl Werner, who always had time to advise me over the phone; and the finest illustrator in Saint Louis, Missouri, Mr. Paul Dillon.

I wish to also thank Ms. Ola Martin, who donated an undisclosed corner of her basement (which I labeled the Bat Cave), where I have been able to display fifty-four-millimeter models used to develop characters, settings, and events in the stories of Sir Christian. This is where I took many of the photographs that were a big help in assisting Paul Dillon, the illustrator. The next major contributor was Ms. Kathy Baker Smith of Best Choice Bookkeeping & Tax Service LLC, who helped me establish Knight of the Fish Gravy LLC. I invite everyone to like her business's Facebook page, Best-Choice-Bookkeeping-Tax-Service-LLC.

I give special thanks to Ms. Kimberly Shumate of Living Word Literary Agency, who previewed the manuscript after three major revisions, providing invaluable advice that made the final product possible.

I want to recognize UK supporters, including Mark Watkins, British navy war veteran (of the Falklands), expert model builder, and Karaoke King entertainer. His excellent model products can purchased on eBay under markkaraokeking50 or on Facebook under Mac's Miniatures. Next, I also want to recognize a truly great contact, acquaintance, and encourager, Antoine Vanner, author of the highly moral and informative Dawlish naval adventures. I recommend everyone visit his site, www.dawlishchronicles.com. Its specialty is nonstop naval action in the late nineteenth century that never hesitates to explore the moral high ground. Antoine is a gift to the world of historical fiction. Next I want to acknowledge two wonderful young missionaries to the UK from Missouri, Nick and Sydni Brooke. For anyone looking for excellent missionaries to support, the Brookes should be reachable through their Facebook *like* of Knight of the Fish Gravy LLC (listed below).

I want to thank unlimited people (including my mail carrier) who applauded sample chapters and query recitations in public church rooms, parking lots, store lines, and bank lobbies and then went online and liked my Facebook page: https://www.facebook.com/pages/Knight-of-the-Fish-Gravy-LLC/1420460441523299 I thank them all.

Finally, I want to extend special thanks to Dr. Phillip Popejoy. If he hadn't challenged me to write comic dialogue after one of my satires appeared in his 2004 play, *In a Poet's Mind*, this book might not have been written.

Sir Christian de Galis and the Fish Gravy

A screwball comedy prayer adventure for all ages

CHAPTER 1

King Arthur's Round Table Honor Roll

Your name was finally added to
King Arthur's Round Table Honor Roll.
—Wade the Scholar, *Chanson de Chrétien*[1]

The worst choice is sometimes the best choice. Such was the case with Sir Christian de Galis, for thirty-plus years the absolute worst choice to do anything as a knight at King Arthur's Round Table. Jesters told jokes about him. Heroes avoided him. Bullies humiliated him. King Arthur got real tired of having him around. So what suddenly made him the best choice to go on a quest with the kingdom's scariest lady, who looked harmless?

It was March, the first month of the Arthurian medieval year AD 535. A forlorn figure facing west laid down a veterans' collection jar with his left hand, placed his right foot on a wooden bench, and called out to the air before him, "Lord Jesu, help me!"

Behind him came *thunk*, followed by *crash* and then *swoosh*, as if something had swung through the air before being sheathed like a sword. An eerie voice announced, "Cherrrry! Berrrry! Apppple piiiie! There's going to be a big surprise!"

---

[1]   Medieval French for *Ballad of Christian.*

1

The figure's foot slid off the bench, and he almost fell forward, but his left hand grabbed the bench side rail as the eerie voice continued.

"For Sir Christian de Galis, Sir Christian de Galis, and I presume you arrrre Sirrrr Chriiissstiannnn de Galiiiis!"

This was followed by an equally eerie, "Youuuuuu-heh-heh-heh!"

The figure answered, "Who might you presume to be?"

The eerie voice replied, "I'm an answer to all of your prayers!"

The figure replied with a shudder, "What are some of the other answers?"

"There aren't any today!" This was followed by another "Youuuuuu-heh-heh-heh!" and then a moment of silence. Then the voice sounded less eerie as it said, "Sir Knight, that poem was written by my grandson, Adragain; I added the rest. Wasn't that effective?"

It was so effective that the figure shook as if it were in an earthquake or an explosion in a small kitchen. In the meantime, the voice added, "According to my scrolls, you are indeed Sir Christian de Galis, one time knight in good standing at King Arthur's Round Table."

The figure froze as the voice continued. "It is also written in my scrolls that last November, after thirty-plus years of *merely* satisfactory service, your name was *finally* added to King Arthur's Round Table Honor Roll."

The figure now shook as if suffering from a cold chill.

"But then you offended King Arthur's fool Sir Dagonet and a host of others. Sir Dagonet got even by listing your name on a comic survey. The host of others got even by having their servants distribute it; they weren't well enough to do it themselves. It petitioned King Arthur's subjects to select him whose name shall be listed first on Sir Dagonet's new honor roll: Worst Knights at King Arthur's Round Table. And everyone knows what the word *worst*, in Sir Dagonet's vocabulary, also means—his other favorite word for someone he doesn't like: *dumbest*."

The figure froze almost solid as the voice added, "Sir Knight, I saw Sir Dagonet's survey making fun of your name on every town gate, church door, and bridge post between the winter court at Caerleon and Nauntes, the largest city south of here. Yesterday, I even read one on the Mawddach ferry, fastened just above the corral where everyone backs in their horses. I'm sure that's had an effect on your quest referrals—if you still get any."

The figure unfroze and spun around like a large fish on a strong string yanked by an expert fisherman. Instead of an eerie-sounding angler, however, the figure saw an eerie-looking woman watching him with one eye. She had the other focused on a lump resembling another large fish someone had dumped on the ground, except it wore a dented helmet and rusty chain mail links. She ambidextrously fastened a note near the hand that lay limply on the battered hilt of a sword.

The figure stared at the lump. "What happened to him?"

"He had a great fall as he prepared for a big spring. Isn't that amusing?"

Too forlorn to laugh, the figure asked, "What did you attach to his chain mail?"

"Words of guidance for his next great awakening."

"What if he can't read?"

Almost too fast to watch, she stepped over the lump and studied the forlorn figure with eyes looking deceptively young as she said, "I included a picture."

Her youthful look, which encompassed her entire person, was a commonly reported phenomenon in Arthurian Britain. In that enlightened time and place, almost everyone looked, sounded, and acted sixty, seventy, or even eighty or ninety years younger than thier biological age. But in the woman's case, she had a reddish tint in her brownish-blonde hair that didn't quite conceal her use of hair dye; this was one clue she might be an older woman. This was apparent despite her hair being partially hidden within the hood of her stylish dark red cloak.

If she had thought it appropriate to remove her hood, she would have revealed that her hair was fastened upward in an attractive knot. If she had removed her entire cloak, she would have displayed shapely, square shoulders above a feminine torso that looked athletic and youthful despite her elusive age.

The figure, on the other hand, was a muscular middle-aged knight who cared little for disguising his voice, his age, or his silver-white hair. He just looked forlorn in unwashed clothes, which included a blue patched cloak that blew mostly against him, but occasionally rose above him in the morning breeze. When it did the latter, the woman glimpsed a patched white cross on the back of his red surcoat, which looked equally patched.

This revealed even more detail to the woman's sharp, observing eyes. He possessed a youthful face that looked stressed from being harpooned and lampooned—by her—but she was pleased to see it looked neither undetermined nor weak willed.

The breeze lifted his cloak so that it floated above him like a banner of folded hands. The woman uttered a thoughtful "hmm" as she studied his remaining attire, which included a patched white cross also sewn on the front of his surcoat in a cheaper fashion than most Round Table heraldry she was familiar with.

She noted that his double-wrapped sword belt sagged on his left side. It was missing the long blade that should have hung within reach of his right hand. It also lacked the key-engraved sheath of a knife she was watching for. However, a tattered leather pouch—known as a scrip, or purse—dangled on the right by badly worn cords.

The sun rising behind the woman revealed them to be on the north side of an east–west road winding its way toward the Irish Sea. They stood on a short turn off near the leaning walls, battered gate, and dilapidated turrets of the Castle Perilous, which was located on the coast of North Wales—or Norgales, as it was called in King Arthur's time.

The Castle Perilous was once the home of the Lady Annowre, whom King Arthur had slain for the sin of sorcery during his early reign. But because of the subtlety and power of her evil ways, Arthur had required help from Sir Tristram of Lyonesse, the number-two

Knight of the Round Table, and Nimue,[2] the chief British Lady of the Lake.

This tall, slender woman was no evil sorceress like the late Lady Annowre, but King Arthur; his chief adviser, Myrddin; and Nimue all agreed she could be just as hard to get along with—and, at times, much scarier. She and Sir Tristram, on the other hand, never got along at all. She was a childhood friend of his abandoned wife, Isoud La Blanche Mains, daughter of King Howell of Brittany. This was also the tall woman's place of origin. She angled her position to stay out of the glare of the rising sun so that the knight could easily see her if he bothered to look very well.

"That survey was an unkind joke of Sir Dagonet," the knight blurted out as he peered back at her as well as he could. He rubbed his face with his left hand and, for a moment, considered saying nothing further. He hoped if he ignored her, she might think he was someone else and go away. Identity concealment was an acceptable custom among Round Table subjects. This was especially true when they met a stranger and even truer if the stranger behaved as disagreeably as this woman. He considered her arrival an annoying interruption that had nothing to do with his desperate prayer for help.

But then he breathed a heavy sigh, shrugged, and stopped rubbing his face. It occurred to him that she knew exactly who he was, and the way he mentioned Sir Dagonet and his wretched survey confirmed it. He said softly, "Yes, I am Sir Christian de Galis, Knight of King Arthur's Round Table, and that's hopefully a place where I retain some level of good standing. But it is very well known I have sat there over the years among many knights regarded more highly than me. And this is especially true of those fortunate enough to have their names entered on King Arthur's Round Table Honor Roll years ahead of mine."

He hesitated a moment and then added, "And I'm sure it's just as well known that last December I, uh, made a mistake that offended King Arthur's fool, Sir Dagonet—and a host of others."

---

2   *Nimue* is usually pronounced "NIM-you-aye."

The woman replied, "I am kinswoman to Myrddin, King Arthur's chief adviser. He informs me that all Round Table knights are regarded more highly than you, not just those listed before you on King Arthur's Round Table Honor Roll. That even includes Sir Dagonet, the fool.

"Also, between November, December, and January, you made more mistakes than the one that offended Sir Dagonet and the host of others. They were also on a higher level of impact than those the court scribes record on their scrolls as regular mistakes. That's because yours reached a magnitude they like to record as sensational mistakes. And," she added while giving him an interesting smile, "according to a saying coined by someone's scholarly squire, sensational mistakes are much more perilous than regular mistakes. This is especially true in your case, for yours have been perilous to every member of King Arthur's Round Table who hasn't died as a result!"

"What!" protested Sir Christian. "I didn't know that anyone—"

"Had died as a result? Well, maybe not yet; I said that to get your attention."

She had indeed gotten his attention, as well as a hostile look, as she presented him with another interesting smile.

"Sir Christian, in the previous months, you have offended every last living member of King Arthur's Round Table, not just the king's fool and court jester, Sir Dagonet. Accordingly, you are no longer considered a knight in good standing at the Round Table, which further disqualifies you from mention on King Arthur's Round Table Honor Roll. A month ago, at my kinsman Myrddin's recommendation, King Arthur had your name removed from the top of your Round Table siege[3] and the bottom of his Round Table Honor Roll. The siege stays at the Round Table, where it will hopefully be reassigned to someone less perilous to his comrades than you, but here's the latest copy of the Honor Roll."

---

[3] A knight's chair at the Round Table was called a siege; his name mysteriously appeared on top the moment he joined the Round Table fellowship.

She opened one side of her cloak, which, despite the wind, hung straight down, presenting a slender external look. But its internal side was unlike any cloak Sir Christian had ever seen. It bulged with pouches filled with scroll-covered wooden rods. Sir Christian wondered how the woman moved around in such a garment. Yet she maneuvered in front of him with an effortless swoosh as she drew one of those scrolls as smoothly as Sir Lancelot unsheathing his sword. She unrolled it in front of Sir Christian's astonished eyes and presented him with another interesting smile.

Sir Christian rubbed his eyes with his left hand and said, "You're pretty handy with that scroll."

She was also pretty fast with that scroll—and all the other scrolls in her cloak. They were designed to look harmless, but when necessary, she could draw any one of them faster than most knights could touch their sword hilts—which sometimes included Sir Lancelot. And she could swing it hard enough with either hand to smack an armored attacker unconscious—if she didn't drive him off first by tapping him on the top of his head, which, in front of groups of people, looked truly embarrassing.

Sir Christian rubbed his eyes again as the woman said, "The names of one hundred sixty-seven Round Table knights appear on this scroll, including all popular deceased members. But yours is officially gone, gone, gone. Please, take a look."

Sir Christian tried to ignore the weapon-like aspect of the not-so-harmless-looking scroll as he said softly, "My name is no longer on King Arthur's Round Table Honor Roll, and I am no longer a Knight of the Round Table in good standing. I didn't think my mistakes were that sensational."

Sir Christian peered closely at the scroll's bottom, where he used to see his name. Then he glanced up and down its two columns. Suddenly, he began counting with the fingers of his left hand. After his mouth crunched the same numbers more than once, he shook his head and confronted the lady. "There's something wrong with this scroll. It begins with sixteen kings and one duke. Then the knights are numbered one through one hundred forty-nine. But that adds up to one hundred sixty-six names. You said one hundred sixty-seven. Was someone else also removed from the Honor Roll? If so, I hope it was Sir Dagonet! Or is this scroll a fake?"

"This scroll is quite official. See King Arthur's imperial seal affixed just below where your name once appeared. You were the only one removed this year. If it's any consolation, Sir Dagonet has never been considered for mention on King Arthur's Round Table Honor Roll."

The knight perked up a little as he asked slowly, hopefully, and even a little vengefully, "Did you say *never?*"

"Yes, Sir Christian, I said *never*, which became a sore point with Sir Dagonet after yours made it. Before that, you were the unofficial, long-running, worst knight at King Arthur's Round Table, and even Sir Dagonet, the fool, was considered more prominent and less foolish than you. So when your name was added and his wasn't, Sir Dagonet hired the herald with the biggest mouth he could find."

"I remember that herald."

"Everyone remembers that herald. For three straight days, he hollered all over Camelot at five a.m., 'Hear ye! Hear ye! Hear ye! Sir Christian de Galis, recently added *to the bottom* of King Arthur's Round Table Honor Roll, is hereby proclaimed a genuine one hundred and sixty-eighth among equals!' The other Knights of the Round Table laughed for a whole week once they stopped yawning. Even crusty ole Sir Kay thought it was funny, and he seldom laughs at anything. As King Arthur's seneschal,[4] he's usually too busy listening to complaints about cold food, bad service, and anything else that goes wrong at the king's banquets."

---

[4] A seneschal was a medieval business manager whose duties included overseeing banquets.

"You're pretty handy with that scroll."

She paused and gave him another interesting smile before saying, "But as you pointed out, this copy of King Arthur's Round Table Honor Roll does contain a scribal error. Sir Merangis des Portz and Sir Gauuaine le Franc are both listed as number fifty-two.[5] They were savagely outraged when they found out. They declared their sacred honor compromised. Therefore, they each threatened to decapitate with a sword, impale with a spear, or trample under the feet of their largest warhorse (depending on which of them currently owned the largest and most ill-tempered warhorse) the very first scribe either of them happened to meet—and that's even if they happened to meet the wrong scribe. Only one thing prevented an all-out scribal panic: the fortunate fact that neither Sir Merangis des Portz nor Sir Gauuaine le Franc were physically well enough to carry out their threats. They were both incapacitated with body-shaking spasms and great abdominal pains. It was the aftereffects of something they ate at the last Christmas banquet." The woman paused and gave Sir Christian another interesting smile.

"Now, in the event those two specimens of unchivalrous knighthood ever do recover, it was deemed necessary to head off a general massacre of the scribal guild. Myrddin made it his personal priority to quickly track down the source of the error. But to his surprise, he discovered it was the work of his two most reliable assistants, Ordericus and Hubert of Hereford. When Myrddin confronted them privately, they each tearfully confessed that they had copied the scrolls while playing something new to Camelot called a card game. It's highly addictive, using a deck of fifty-two colorful cards, and was introduced to them by the same squire who coined the saying about the mistakes."

If the woman saw Sir Christian flinch, she didn't let on as she continued.

---

[5] A document known as *John Leyland's Assertion of King Arthure* contains such a list. The two knights mentioned above are indeed both listed as number fifty-two. Leyland was a celebrated librarian, scholar, antiquarian, and chaplain to King Henry VIII.

"It seems this squire who calls himself the Scholar is assigned to a knight who is frequently low on money. Thus, he is seldom equipped properly, fed properly, and is certainly not paid properly. He was getting desperate for a way to make up the difference, when he discovered directions for making the card game while studying an old monastery scroll.

"The Scholar must have a successful merchant in his lineage somewhere, because he cannily approached the two top scribes and talked them into signing a business deal that obligated them to do most of the work. Ordericus and Hubert each agreed to produce fifty-two decks of cards (there's something about that four-times-thirteen number), help test the rules, and assist the Scholar in marketing them to other scribes, squires, and even a few knights, lords, and ladies. In return, they would split the profits by percentage: ten, thirty, thirty, and thirty."

"Who got the first ten percent?"

"Whatever his other faults, this squire called the Scholar believed in tithing, which he was heard to say kept things on the high ground. It certainly worked, because the scribes proceeded with great gusto. They quickly helped the Scholar plan, design, and produce the necessary cards in packs the Scholar designated as decks. Then they began testing the rules, which is where the scribes—not the canny squire—got into uncanny trouble. There was no gambling involved in the Scholar's card game, just a lot of foolish shuffling and dealing of fifty-two cards. But unfortunately for Ordericus and Hubert of Hereford, the testing phase appealed to them so much that they began playing cards while copying scrolls. That's when they made their scribal error with the number fifty-two."

Sir Christian suddenly felt a body-shaking spasm along with a great abdominal pain of his own as he asked quietly, "Did you perchance learn from Myrddin the, uh, hmm, identity of this squire called the Scholar?"

"Myrddin only said that he's no longer in Caerleon, nor did he return to Camelot. Meanwhile, it was not convenient to correct the scribal version of the sensational mistake. Too many others have happened in this kingdom, the foremost being yours. Thus, for the moment, we must make do with the Honor Roll copies we have.

"For their own good, Myrddin temporarily reassigned Ordericus and Hubert of Hereford to manual labor. This was in place of their regular labor of copying manuals. Myrddin thought that a clever play on words, and everyone agreed, except Ordericus and Hubert of Hereford. That's because until further notice, they're part of the peasant crew that cleans out the castle gardé robe pits.[6] Everyone smells them coming, even when they're crawling back and forth on the lowest levels of the current court castle. But if Sir Merangis des Portz and Sir Gauuaine le Franc ever do recover, the scribes' sensational new aroma should keep them at a safe distance until things—ahem—blow over."

An extremely red-faced Sir Christian nodded as he glanced back through the Honor Roll. After another long look, he concluded, "It's true; my name's no longer here. Yet the unsavory sons of King Lot of Orkney remain listed. Backstabbing Sir Mordred the Murderous is still thirty-six. Attack-scabbing Sir Agravaine the Arrogant remains thirty-five. Snack-grabbing Sir Gaheris the Unheroic is hanging on at thirty-four. Skipping upward to where I used to find right-on-track-jabbing as well as bandit-nabbing Sir Gareth the Good—the only nice, decent, and truly courteous member of that Orkney clan—I see that he has been promoted to number nine, but his oldest brother—inflated, fact blabbing Sir Gawaine the Overrated—is now number three! Yet the late Sir Lamorak de Galis, famous and most natural third son of the late King Pellinore, was the all-time number-three knight at the Round Table and on King Arthur's Round Table Honor Roll!"

He gave the woman a puzzled look and said, "I don't see Sir Lamorak's name anywhere on this scroll. But you said only mine was removed. Is it possible those card-playing scribes made another mistake?"

The woman replied by giving him another interesting smile.

---

[6] Gardé robe pits were where the garbage and human waste ended up in the more sophisticated castles. Peasants normally cleaned them out twice a year.

CHAPTER 2

Just Like That

The one and only Sir Lamorak de Galis and me,
well, we were about to become just like *that*!
—Wade the Scholar, *Chanson de Chrétien*

The woman smiled again and said, "You were the only one removed from the Honor Roll *this year*. If you move your eyes down the list and look a little more closely, you'll see that Sir Lamorak's name was demoted to number twenty-nine."

"But he was King Arthur's all-time number-three knight!"

"Until he displayed unchivalrous conduct with a queen—and got killed."

Sir Christian nodded sadly as he reexamined the list. "Is that why Sir Tristram is no longer number two?"

"He displayed unchivalrous conduct with a queen who was married—and got killed. But the worst knave was Sir Meliagrance; he displayed unchivalrous conduct with a queen who was married and found it annoying when he wouldn't take no for an answer. He got killed, and his name was deleted from the roll, but not in the same year as you. Incidentally, the names of the three queens remain confidential."[7]

---

[7] To satisfy the curiosity of readers removed far enough in time, they are King Lot of Orkney's widow, Queen Margawse (also the mother of Sir Mordred via a trick she

"But everyone knows who they are."

"Nevertheless, no true knight is a bearer of such tales."

"In case any more of that unchivalrous conduct is going on with one of those queens?"

"Let's pray that it isn't."

"Or it just might tear the kingdom apart. I still mourn Sir Lamorak's fate. Are you aware that our names both end in *de Galis*?"

The woman braced herself as Sir Christian droned, *"de Galis* means 'of Wales.' Since Sir Lamorak and I are both from that teeny-tiny yet distinguished land—"

"Be careful, Sir Knight; we currently stand in that teeny-tiny yet distinguished land—and those castle walls may have teeny-tiny ears that can hear you."

But his teeny-tiny ears didn't hear her as he droned, "Surely our families were neighbors. Thus, when Sir Lamorak arrived at the Round Table years after me, I decided it was my sacred duty to break him in, and I made sure that I told him so in front of every famous knight I could find, and I know that gesture was appreciated. He was just too overwhelmed with shyness and gratitude to accept it—and me. Thus, he appeared to ignore it—and me—every time he walked past, as if he didn't see me very well. Why, I used to tell all of those other famous knights—the ones who gathered around to listen, that is—that just before he died, the great number-three Knight of King Arthur's Round Table, the one and only Sir Lamorak de Galis and me, well, we were about to become just like *that*!"

Sir Christian attempted to touch his two index fingers together, but his right hand held a spear in such a way that they stayed apart.

The lady watched his fumbling with another interesting smile. "Why, yes, Sir Christian, I'm sure it was just as you said. You and the great Sir Lamorak de Galis were about to become just like *that*!"

---

played on King Arthur when he was a young man); La Beale Isoud, wife of King Mark of Cornwall (not to be confused with Isoud La Blanche Mains, daughter of King Howell of Brittany as well as two-timing Sir Tristram's wife); and Queen Guinevere.

She pointed at his fingers that wouldn't touch.

Sir Christian gave up the attempt and buried his eyes back in the Honor Roll. After another long look, he said, "I was pondering when Sir Lamorak's favorite cousin, Sir Pinel le Savage, was removed from the roll."

"A year before yours was added. Unchivalrous conduct with a queen's apples using poison—that got the wrong person killed."

Sir Christian said, "He was just getting even with Sir Gawaine—"

"For getting even with Sir Lamorak for unchivalrous conduct with a queen—Sir Gawaine's mother—and he thought he got away with it until Nimue exposed him."

"How did Nimue find out?"

"Don't ever bring poison to a banquet where my grandson, Adragain, is on duty. He's only a page, but he's been carefully trained by me to observe everything and anything that goes on around him. Nothing gets by Adragain, especially after he prays. As Sir Pinel poured cinnamon sautéed with snake poison, plant poison, rock poison, dirty socks, rotten eggs, and sour milk over Sir Gawaine's favorite apples when he thought no one was looking very well, an innocent voice behind him announced, 'Cherry! Berry! Apple pie! There's going to be a big surprise!'

"Sir Patrice of Ireland shouted, 'Oh boy! There's a big surprise in those apples!' He nearly trampled Sir Gawaine as he bit into the closest one and gasped, 'This tastes bad enough to kill somebody!'

"Sir Gawaine didn't see him drop dead as he bit into an apple the poison missed and grumbled, 'I didn't get a surprise!'

"But Sir Pinel le Savage got one when he spun around and saw Adragain swinging a flask like a dead mouse. When he reached inside his cloak and found an empty pouch, he gave Adragain a look that could scare a bear, as he turned his hands into claws. 'You took my secret flask!'

"But neither bears nor claws ever scared Adragain who replied, 'Want me to take a different one next time?'

"Adragain dumped the flask inside a sack he'd borrowed from the castle herpetologist when he wasn't looking very well and then used it to scoop up a poisoned apple. There was a horrible hiss inside as the sack shook like it contained an earthquake or an explosion in a small kitchen. Then it went limp as a six-foot noodle. Adragain was heard to observe, 'After prayer, one still must check his sacks for snakes.'

"He hollered, 'I'm going for help!'

"And he dodged past a now truly savage Sir Pinel, who growled at Adragain, 'One of these days, somebody's going to apple your pie!'

"'Because the plural for *apple* is *apple pie*?'

"Sir Pinel wasn't exactly sure, so he hesitated for a moment. Then he lunged for my grandson with his giant, bear like arms and sneered, 'Knave of a prayer page, I'm going to tear thee into little petitions!'

"But Adragain has always been too alert, too smart, and much too quick to be captured by a vengeful oaf like Sir Pinel le Savage, especially after prayer. To repeat, nothing gets by Adragain, the prayer page, except the blundering arms of a non-praying klutz like Sir Pinel.

"Adragain swooshed past the knight like the messenger bird called a merlin as he rushed everything out of the banquet hall and straight to me—including the dead snake, which has since been preserved in the castle museum of natural history.

"As news of Sir Patrice's death spread along with his cousin Sir Mador's unchivalrous accusation of innocent Queen Guinevere for giving the banquet that almost got her killed, Adragain and I rushed everything to Nimue for examination by her experts.

"Hold this," she said as she pushed King Arthur's Round Table Honor Roll into Sir Christian's free hand with one of hers while using the other to pull another document from her cloak, this time even faster than Sir Lancelot drawing his sword. She didn't unroll it but swung it with a hissing sound past Sir Christian's head. She said, "Here is a copy of Sir Pinel le Savage's personnel scroll, including the apple episode, along with commendations to my grandson from King Arthur, Myrddin, and Nimue. Excerpts also appear on the scrolls of Sir Mador de la Porte and Sir Gawaine de Orkney, relating how Sir Pinel le Savage was publicly exposed for his deed, banished from the Round Table, and his name stricken from King Arthur's Round

Table Honor Roll. But before anything else could happen, he fled to this region."

"Why, yes," Sir Christian said cautiously, "that's exactly what happened. Until a month ago, I saw Sir Pinel every day in my inn's dining room—but only from a distance."

"Of three feet or less?"

The woman gave him a truly interesting smile. "Sir Christian, despite the cautious way you speak of Sir Pinel le Savage, I believe you remain his active acquaintance."

"Based on what?"

"You're holding his favorite spear in your right hand! I recognize the banner!"

"It's his second-favorite spear! I borrowed it last year when he wasn't looking very well!"

"You also weren't looking very well. The orange-gold cross on its banner clashes with the cheap white ones embroidered on your surcoat. As a former Knight of the Round Table in good standing, couldn't you afford a better seamstress? The square shape of the banner instead of the regulation swallow-tail pennant for plain knights also says you've promoted yourself to Sir Pinel's former rank of bannerette, knight commander." The woman shook her head and clicked her tongue.

In a non-ambidextrous manner, Sir Christian shook King Arthur's Round Table Honor Roll at the woman with one hand and Sir Pinel's second-favorite spear with the other as he demanded, "Who are you?"

"You took my secret flask!"

CHAPTER 3

A Lady Who Looks Harmless

Meantime, I travel around the realm as a lady who looks harmless.
—Wade the Scholar, *Chanson de Chrétien*

Sir Christian demanded once again, "Who are you?"

"I belong to a select corps of ladies and damsels who serve as special liaison between King Arthur; his senior adviser Myrddin, my close kinsman; and Nimue, the British Lady of the Lake. My main assignment requires me to wear this cloak full of scrolls while I deliver messages and assist knights, especially ones who pray for assistance. Meantime, I travel around the realm as a lady who looks harmless. However—" She pulled the cut half of a silver penny from her cloak, tossed it high into the air, and, with a swinging swoosh as it descended—*whack*—belted it even higher and almost out of sight, with the wooden rod poking from the rolled-up end of Sir Pinel's scroll. She waited a long, slow minute until it descended again. Then she caught it gracefully and dropped it back inside her cloak.

Sir Christian said, "What is that supposed to prove?"

"Whatever it needs to prove."

Sir Christian thought it proved that this so-called lady and her cloak full of scrolls looked as harmless as a tornado traveling around the realm with a thundercloud full of lightning bolts. He said quietly, "I've never seen you at King Arthur's court."

"There's much you have never seen at King Arthur's court. That's because you never learned to look at things very well. But if you developed the eyes of an eagle, which can see directly into the sun, the novice in our corps would be hard for you to notice. She's carefully trained to blend in while performing her main assignment, which is to record everything and anything that anyone in King Arthur's court does. She reveals herself to a knight *like you* only if she decides—"

"What?"

"You need to notice something you aren't capable of noticing on your own."

Sir Christian didn't know what to notice about that. He shook his head and peered back into the Honor Roll.

"Sir Christian, don't deny it. Through the ways, means, and methods of our corps, we know you remain acquainted with the perilous poisoner Sir Pinel le Savage. That's not, however, why I seek you today."

Whatever her reason was for seeking him today, Sir Christian was sure he didn't want to find out, just as he was sure she couldn't be an answer to any prayer he had ever prayed—at least not in his right mind. After another look through the scroll, while the lady looked through him, he remembered how he had gotten rid of the laundry lady who'd followed him around one of the inns. He gave this lady a sly wink. "Say, they don't call Sir Pinel *the Savage* for nothing. At breakfast, he crammed pancakes into his mouth with fingers dripping honey, grease, and butter. But that's nothing to what he did at other meals. He ran over any guest who got between him and the main dishes that disappeared into his mouth—like a food cart going down a mudhole! Then he washed everything down with rose water from those bowls you rinse your fingers in! *Slurrrrp!* When Endaf, the head kitchen knave, complained, Sir Pinel said such habits created in him the look of youth, health, beauty, and power. When Endaf said he was creating shortages for the other guests, Sir Pinel demanded,

'What shortages?' and chased Endaf away with the knife he uses to pick his teeth. Now, that's a downright nasty blade and somewhat rusty. It makes my teeth hurt right now to think of some of the things, including boot mud, that Sir Pinel used to scrape loose with its ugly, pitted, jagged, edge."

He stopped when he noticed a leopard-like intensity in the woman's glare. This reminded him that discussing another knight's lack of etiquette was also a lack of etiquette.

He attempted to cough politely as he replied meekly, "Despite a few recent mistakes, I don't understand why my name was removed from King Arthur's Round Table Honor Roll like those of Sir Pinel and Sir Meliagrance. On the other hand, the four sons of King Lot got away with murdering Sir Lamorak because they and King Arthur are just like—"

Thunk! Crash! He never heard the first swoosh of something flying past his head like a sword. But a second swoosh made him pause. Then he felt a cold chill, and that was when he did notice something very well. The woman was holding the extra thick wooden rod poking out of Sir Pinel's scroll inches from his head. She looked ready to swoosh it a third time in such a way that would smack him across the road, while being hard enough for the blow to be felt through a thick helmet—which he wasn't wearing. But she lowered the scroll and said softly, "Sir Christian, look behind you."

He turned and saw a second lump of scales lying on the ground with a head inside a dented helmet and another pair of hands limply clutching a battered sword.

The woman opened her cloak and slid Sir Pinel's scroll back into its pouch with another hiss, resembling the swing of Sir Lancelot's sword. She brushed unseen dust from her hands, her cloak, and, in another lightning move almost too fast for the eye to follow, the tips of Sir Christian's split ends.

"Looks like another great fall after someone planned a big spring."

The woman pulled another note from her cloak. She tapped Sir Christian's head with it as she stepped past him to fasten it to the fallen warrior.

A rechilled Sir Christian asked, "How many of those papers do you have?"

"As many as I need."

The woman lightly stepped back as she pulled King Arthur's Round Table Honor Roll from his hands, rolled it up, and slid it back into its pouch with a subsequent hiss.

After brushing more imaginary dust from her hands, her cloak, and, with another swoosh almost too fast to follow, an unexplored section of his split ends, she drew a scroll larger than the previous two put together. She unrolled just enough to show him the title calligraphy, which she read loudly enough to be heard inside the castle: "The Personnel Scroll of Sir Christian de Galis!"

She glanced at him with one eye. "That explains in detail how his sensational mistakes cost him his place on King Arthur's Round Table Honor Roll, plus his status as knight in good standing at the Round Table. Thus, he found himself categorized with the perilous poisoner Sir Pinel le Savage and the late criminally infatuated Sir Meliagrance of Gore."

She gave him another interesting smile. "Now, whatever caused a Knight of the Round Table with thirty-plus years of satisfactory service to be grouped with such as them? But first, let's ask a more basic question: How did someone like you become a Knight of King Arthur's Round Table in the first place?"

"I was a wedding present," he answered meekly, "the last of one hundred knights presented to King Arthur when he married Guinevere, daughter of Leodegrance,[8] king of Cameliard.[9] King Leodegrance announced to the wedding guests that we were thrown in with the Round Table as a last-minute wedding bonus."

"Are you sure you weren't the booby prize? Regardless, my question was rhetorical, because I wanted to hear what you would say—and how you would say it. But to repeat, I know all about you

---

[8]   Pronounced "Lee-O-duh-gruntz," with the accent on the second syllable.

[9]   Pronounced "Kuh-MIL-lee-yard," with the accent once again on the second syllable.

and those other ninety-nine knights of King Leodegrance. According to Ordericus the scribe, the tune 'Ninety-Nine Barrels of Ale by the Wall' was inspired by that band of bunglers during King Arthur's wedding feast."

"Ordericus repeated rumors spread by King Arthur's unfair fool, Sir Dagonet. His new knights from Castle Cameliard never did anything excessive with barrels of ale by any wall. Such behavior would not have been tolerated by King Arthur or King Leodegrance. But I do remember that a few of them did act a little rowdy. After all, it was a wedding feast, and knights will be knights."

"Especially if they're one hundred bozos dumped on King Arthur's court courtesy of Castle Cameliard. Sir Dagonet or no Sir Dagonet, I heard from more than one reliable source, including Queen Guinevere's lady's maid, housemaid, horsemaid, handmaid, parlormaid, chambermaid, laundrymaid, milkmaid, barmaid, nursemaid, as well as her kitchen knaves, stable boys, a part-time half-blind cabbage gardener who was on vacation, and the minstrel who wrote that song."

"What minstrel who wrote that song?"

"They call him Unknown Bard!"

"Because his father's first name was Unknown?"

"I meant *the* Unknown Bard."

"Because he's named after another bard that no one wants to know?"

"He merely uses the name."

"The same way unknown ladies merely use—"

Swoosh!

He ducked the lightning-fast scroll that once more whizzed by his head only to hear another *thunk* behind him, followed by another *crash.*

The woman swept past him to attach another note to an armored lump on the ground.

"Someone doesn't like you, Sir Knight," she said, watching him with one eye as she focused the other on brushing more unseen dust from her hands and cloak, but this time, she bypassed his split ends as she refocused on something to the side. She droned on as though nothing had happened.

"The Unknown Bard, known for much more than music, said several of those knights—as in all ninety-nine of them—got more than a little rowdy. They didn't exactly cross the line of the waterproof letter-box container; nevertheless, they pushed all boundaries to the last parchment edge."

"What a non-rowdy description."

"Not according to King Leodegrance once the celebration ended and the damages were cleaned up. That's when his first-knight champion Sir Bertholai along with his entire Privy Council got rowdy as they congratulated the king all the way back to Castle Cameliard about the clever way he unloaded his worst underachievers onto his new son-in-law, King Arthur. For despite the longevity everyone displays in this realm, one-third of those knights were long past retirement. They could barely walk, ride a horse, or swing a sword. Another third looked barely out of diapers to become pages. The final third should have been discharged with medical disabilities. Sir Christian, where does that leave you, as King Leodegrance's final selection to that prize crew?"

"King Leodegrance presented me to King Arthur as his most polite knight, whom he said never failed in courtesy defined by the laws of chivalry."

"He never heard you describe rusty-knife tooth picking in front of a lady. Although, knowing King Leodegrance the way I did, he probably meant you were too polite to scare anyone who was dangerous, especially with a knife you once carried."

When he didn't respond, she said, "Let's cut to the joust. King Arthur was obligated to feed, lodge, and pay annual salaries of twenty pounds to all one hundred useless members of your group. And he didn't dare turn any of you down. That would risk offending his new father-in-law, who helped him win his war of accession.

"So until the day they retired, died, or were slain by accident, most members of that Cameliard hundred ate, drank, slept, made merry, and also made sure they collected their Round Table salaries on time. But even so, one of them had to—"

Occasionally ride forth to attempt a deed, thought Sir Christian. That generally lasted until the Cameliardian thought of an excuse for getting out of it. Then he would ride like mad back to Camelot, where, once safely across the drawbridge, he would cause an alarm, start a panic, or pretend nothing had happened at all. In the latter case, he almost always tried to stay inconspicuous by hiding out in the castle kitchen. To minimize embarrassment for the rest of the Round Table, King Arthur would think up an excuse to find him while visiting the cook. When he finally cornered the Cameliard knight, usually licking day-old icing spoons by the cake mixes, King Arthur would seize him by his arm (instead of his throat, as he was tempted). He would say, "What a surprise, finding you in the kitchen dessert section. But since you are available, let's hear the outcome of your quest. You came back so early it surely went well. Just whom in the name of heroic deeds, Arthurian justice, and legendary quests did you capture, slay, or rescue this time?" In almost every case, the Cameliard knight told the king he'd turned back after he got lost, had horse trouble, or, worse yet, the weather was bad. To keep the peace with his father-in-law (and ultimately his wife, Queen Guinevere), Arthur would diplomatically concede the following: "I'm sure you'll do better next time." Then, as a Christian king, Arthur quickly left the kitchen before he was tempted—just because he was mad—to behead the not-so-sensational knight with a loud, swinging—

Swoosh!

The woman leaped past him with a swinging scroll in each hand, yelling, "Cut to the joust, Sir Christian! Cut to the joust! Bandits! But don't slay anyone!"

"Because that be our task!" announced a six-foot grizzled bear of a bandit swinging a tarnished secondhand sword as he bore down with a leer on Sir Christian.

Who responded with unusual animation, swinging Sir Pinel le Savage's second-favorite spear as he shouted, "Over your dead—I mean maimed—"

"Don't do that to them either!" cried the woman as she double-thunked a second bandit, who discovered with his dented head that he had never previously assaulted a lady quite like her.

As he hit the ground with a *thud*, she said, "Remember that's it's always better to pray than to slay."

"Then why is her knight swinging a spear?" asked a third bandit, rushing on her with a spiked club.

"Maybe he thinks we don't agree with her!" said a fourth bandit, raising a bow at close range.

"Prayer, mercy, and forgiveness always work better than murder, mayhem, and mutilation," the woman said while performing a two-step side step, allowing her synchronized scrolls to land a smoothly executed *ca-thunk-thunk!* As both bandits plopped, increasing dented chain mail totals on the ground by two more lumps, she added, "It also saves money on helmet repairs!"

In the meantime, Sir Christian got Sir Pinel's second-favorite spear caught in the loose chain mail cowl of the first bandit.

"Unsnag me, thou knavish knight of an unfair fighter!" the villain screamed. His face turned red as he flopped like a fish on the end of the spear's long pole, now shouting, "Employ not such tricks, lest I do to you something terrifying!" But only his face looked terrifying—and extremely red—as the spear became more and more enmeshed in a loose part of his chain mail, keeping him and Sir Christian apart as well as preventing them from getting close.

Thunk! Thunk! Thunk! The woman's copy of Sir Christian's personnel records in one hand interrupted the careers of three more bandits as her other wielded, not waved an exhaustive dissertation on "Ambidextrous Archery for Damsels" at their leader.

He yelled with outrage, "It be wrong for a woman to fight like a man!"

"That's why I fight like a woman! Surrender before I knock thee silly with documentation!"

That's when Sir Christian unsnagged Sir Pinel le Savage's second-favorite spear with such force that he spun around and leveled the bandit leader with a loud *ka-chunk*, meanwhile making the first bandit land on his head with a loud *ka-thunk*.

With his free hand Sir Christian rubbed his eyes and then his ears as the woman smoothly sheathed the scrolls and then went from lump to lump, attaching notes as she counted, "Two! Four! Six! Eight! Who did we annihilate? Yay, bandits!"

"Milady, aren't you afraid someone might hear you?"

"Because there's a possibility someone else might attack us?"

A scary glee in her eyes thoroughly chilled Sir Christian as she added, "Eight plus three thunked earlier makes a nice haul of eleven. Now, let's remember to pray that they be delivered and set free from their evil and avaricious ways."

"But what if they don't want to be delivered and set free from their evil and avaricious ways, especially after they wake up and start hungering and thirsting after revenge?"

The woman brushed more unseen dust from her hands, her cloak, and, once more faster than lightning could fly, another new section of his split ends. "Oh, don't go worrying about their hungering and thirsting. They'll be much more interested in being delivered and set free from their evil and avaricious ways. They just don't know it yet."

"Because they're still unconscious?"

She shrugged. "And they haven't seen the incentive I provided. But like the earlier bandits, once they experience their next great awakening, the papers I attached to their chain mail will give them just the right motivation to perform a deed that is most useful—and somewhat noble."

"But what if they don't want to perform a deed that is most useful—and somewhat noble?"

"Trust me." The woman gave him a truly scary look. "They'll want to do it."

"Even if some of them can't read?"

"That's why I included a picture. Incidentally"—she reached down, snagged a panache lying on the ground, and hummed as she swooshed it back and forth under his nose—"this fell out of your cloak during the fight. Is there something you want to tell me about why you're carrying a helmet plume that belonged to the psychopathic murderer, kidnapper, and bandit chief Sir Breuse sans Pitie?"

"Huh-choo! I mean no!" He seized the plume and stuffed it back into his cloak.

"Well then, Sir Christian," she said perusing his face with a thoughtful look, "it seems you have demonstrated some integrity to King Arthur. You became an accepted member of the Round Table, accumulated thirty-plus years of satisfactory service, and just fought ferocious bandits with superior numbers. So how do you find yourself in more trouble than Sir Pinel le Savage, Sir Meliagrance of Gore, the four evil sons of King Lot of Orkney, and Sir Breuse san Pitie combined? The answer is that with the exception of Sir Breuse, who likes to attack wedding receptions, family reunions, and that sort of thing, they have never been perilous to more than one or two people at one time. But you, on the other hand, have been perilous to everybody—the king, the queen, the knights, and even the peasants who milk cows, breed chickens, and grow flowers! And that's all within a hop, skip, and a horse ride of King Arthur's domains!

"So, Sir Christian, just what did you do to make yourself so perilous?" She looked at him semi-sweetly as she once more drew his scroll. With a sudden swoosh, she swung it past his head again. But this time, there was no one behind him to thunk.

CHAPTER 4

So Perilous

What did you do to make yourself so perilous?
—Wade the Scholar, *Chanson de Chrétien*

The woman repeated, "What did you do to make yourself so perilous?"

"What did you do to become an answer to all of my prayers?"

"I know every mistake you have ever made."

"That sounds like the answer to one of my enemy's prayers."

Thud! A war arrow from the castle ripped through the bench by Sir Christian.

"That may be one of them now." The woman resheathed the scroll and pulled the arrow loose; then carefully attaching one of her papers to the shaft, she fired it back with the bow dropped by the fourth bandit.

"Aiieee!" rang out from the top of a crenelated wall, followed by *thump!*

"Didn't allow for the wind," the woman said with a frown. "At least it didn't sound mortal."

"Wouldn't want you wasting one of those papers," said Sir Christian.

The woman nodded. "The fate of the kingdom might depend on it."

She propped the bow against the unconscious owner and peered up at the castle. Then she glanced at Sir Christian. "Also, what did you do to make Castle Perilous so perilous?"

"Besides attract you, nothing to deserve another arrow."

Thud! The war arrow bearing the woman's paper flew back and splintered another board on the bench.

Sir Christian shouted, "It doesn't count if it's the same arrow!"

They took cover beneath a leaning wall, between a cart and a pot hovering on a hook over smoldering coals. Sir Christian peered back at the shaft. "It seems no one looked at your note. Did you send it to the right person?"

"He screamed loud enough. But if anyone looked at it, it wouldn't be coming back."

The woman screamed, "Aiieee!" She threw an object that landed away from the wall with a thump. She smiled at Sir Christian. "Let's see how the castle guards answer that one."

Thud!

Sir Christian tugged at an arrow pinning his cloak to the cart. "They didn't believe you." When the arrow finally came loose, he tossed it to the woman. "And it's on a day that they have more than one arrow to shoot, and I already owe the clothes menders more money than I can collect by begging. What do we do next?"

She snagged the latest arrow, dropped it on the ground, and— *wham!*—nearly dropped Sir Christian next to it as she belted him with his scroll.

"Aiieee!" he yelled as he staggered as if he were in an earthquake or an explosion in a small kitchen.

"Make them think you're dead!" the woman cried as she pulled back the scroll and threw another object that landed away from the wall with a loud thump.

"And they'll be closer than they think!" Sir Christian moaned as he pushed Sir Pinel le Savage's second-favorite spear against the ground to help him regain his feet. With his left hand, he rubbed an embossed head bruise that resembled the great seal of Camelot as it appeared on his scroll. He shot the woman an unfriendly look.

Her eyes didn't shoot back because things had grown quiet enough for her to once more unroll the scroll. But this time, she went well past the title calligraphy. She scanned the document intently yet still managed to keep one eye focused on him and the other on anything else that might be coming their way from the castle. Meanwhile, she efficiently unrolled, rerolled, and then unrolled more of the scroll. When she reached the part she wanted, she stopped and repeated, "What did you do to make yourself so perilous? I come to the events of last November."

Sir Christian, wondering if the next arrow would be more perilous than the events of last November, observed, "You went pretty far down that scroll before you came to last November!"

The woman replied, "The first part of this scroll is an account of your regular mistakes, thirty-plus yards—I mean *years*—of them."

Sir Christian nodded to move her on to the next painful point before something else with painful points arrived—such as more arrows. At the same time, he argued, "You said I accumulated thirty-plus years—"

"Of satisfactory service—that is correct, Sir Christian. It was not exceptional or legendary—just satisfactory. I ask you this: How does someone perform just satisfactory service at a place like King Arthur's Round Table for thirty-plus years? The answer is simple. Your thirty-plus years of accumulated mistakes reveal you to be an anomaly, an unexceptional Knight of the Round Table. Here's a comment from your last liaison review: 'Jesters told jokes about him. Heroes avoided him. Bullies humiliated him. King Arthur got real tired of having him around.'"

Sir Christian warily watched the castle as he asked, "Who wrote that—Hildegard the Hard-Hearted?"

"You know Hildegard?"

"I hope not! But my name was finally added to King Arthur's Round Table Honor Roll."

"Let's clarify. After thirty-plus years of just satisfactory service, your name was finally added—*to the bottom* of King Arthur's Round Table Honor Roll."

"What does my name appearing at the bottom prove? The Round Table is round because all member knights are considered equal."

"Sir Christian, ask any crew—medical, logistical, or even recreational—who cleans up after a tournament just how equal those Round Table knights actually are to each other. Your own loss-loss joust record is a case in point, as well as reinforcing how just satisfactory your Round Table service has been."

"I protest. During those thirty-plus years, I know I performed services listed higher than just satisfactory. For one thing, I was frequently referred to at the Round Table and back in Cameliard as that most polite knight of King Leodegrance."

"And to whom did you appear so polite—visiting Huns who just sacked Sarmatia? Or was it Saxon pirates who match you in uncouth table manners? Come to think of it, either of them would have found you amusing. Especially the first time they heard you describe another knight's tooth-scraping habits in front of a lady. What do you say to that, Sir Knight of the Most-High Politeness?"

"Ask King Leodegrance how polite I am."

"I can't ask King Leodegrance how polite you *aren't*, because he died last summer. As his most-polite retainer, weren't you most-polite enough to attend his funeral?"

Like a well-aimed boar spear, she pinned Sir Christian to the leaning wall of Castle Perilous with that one. Preoccupied with dodging scrolls, arrows, and her remarks, he'd misremembered the deceased status of King Leodegrance. But after a brief pause, he shook his left index finger at her, almost like the head of a snake. (See why pointing is so impolite?) He just remembered he had been asked to serve as special pallbearer at the king's funeral. And the request had come from no less a person than Queen Guinevere herself. It had almost slipped his mind because he didn't actually go through with it. On the way to the casket, he tripped over Sir Pinel's second-favorite spear after he got it caught in the famous tapestry of the flag raising on Castle Cameliard (said by some to be the single most noted event during King Arthur's war of accession). Fortunately, no one saw the big rip he left right next to the flag. When he yanked the spear free, the force caused him to fall backward as he got his legs tangled around the shaft, and he hit the floor with such a crash that he sprained his ankle. The queen's request was still written up in the royal chronicles. It was also recorded how he had attended the funeral on only one leg. He made quite an impression as he hopped around, especially when his moans, groans, screams, and cries had been seen as signs of grief for King Leodegrance. Everyone was impressed, except the scribe, Ordericus, who recorded that Sir Christian had a silly accident. Sir Christian still thought his painful presence at the funeral was one example of a time he rendered higher than just satisfactory Round Table service. And he performed it for no less a person than the father of King Arthur's queen.

Before he could say anything further, the woman whacked his finger with a downward smack and then swooshed the scroll upward, but instead of tapping his head, she yelled, "Duck!"

"I can duck without help!" he yelled as he crashed into the cart on his way back to the ground, but his words were drowned by another *thunk*, followed by an even louder *crash* behind him.

She smiled down at him as she pulled back the parchment part of the scroll, which now contained a head-shaped crease. She smoothed it and then once more resheathed it like Sir Lancelot's sword as she stepped over Sir Christian to fasten a paper to an unconscious castle guard who had forgotten his helmet.

Sir Christian once more pushed against Sir Pinel le Savage's second-favorite spear to slowly and painfully rise to his feet. That's when he noticed the outline of the Great Seal of Camelot throbbing on the head of the guard. He said, "Milady, it doesn't pay to go bare-headed around you. But I suppose we didn't sound dead enough."

"You looked dead enough. For that matter, so does he. I hope I didn't hit him that hard. Meantime, cut to joust, Sir Christian! This castle has hidden sally ports, and I think I need to finish your sensational mistakes—"

"Before we meet more guards who think they need to finish—"

"Hopefully no one but you. Regardless, I must repeat: What did you do to make yourself so—"

Thud!

She studied the latest quivering arrow. "Perilous to anyone near you."

She backed up, holding Sir Christian's scroll so that only she could read it. When he stood on his tiptoes and strained his neck forward to see, the woman backed up farther. So he shrugged and settled back as she said, "I begin with the events of last November, starting with your first sensational—"

Thud!

The woman shook her head as Sir Christian's cloak absorbed still another arrow. "During King Arthur's campaign against a pirate fleet of Jutes, Anglos, and Saxon, an unexpected wind on a day when there was no wind blew a spark from a cartload of burning incendiaries into a nearby cauldron. *Kawoom! Kaboom! Karoom!* A blast shot skyward like the lid blowing off a volcano. It was heard halfway to Navarre in one direction and all the way across Ireland in the other. According to Ordericus the scribe, it really lit things up along the Humber.

"It also really lit things up in the camp of the Jutes, Anglos, and Saxons, who were so surprised, so terrified, and so singed that they surrendered en masse to King Arthur's equally surprised and terrified but slightly less-singed knights—but not before your fellow Cameliardians tried to surrender to the Jutes, Anglos, and Saxons. Fortunately, the Jutes, Anglos, and Saxons insisted on surrendering first. What did you do?"

"I dove under a cart."

"Apparently not the one that lit things up."

She gave him a semi-sweet look and continued. "Cheldric the Younger, overall Saxon pirate chief, told King Arthur he thought the world had ended, and his well-roasted host agreed. But the world didn't end—although, in the vicinity of the Humber, it sure looked like it. There were fallen trees, scorched earth, and ashes floating in the air almost everywhere. Everyone on both sides felt too sick, too sore, and definitely too singed to do anything except moan, groan, and roam—for a few feet only—around the camp in pain. Thus, the world did indeed come to an end for a few days around that part of the Humber.

"And whatever was in those floating ashes, it took the temper out of any metal it touched, as well as ate large holes through leather, cloth, and wood. King Arthur's men had to replace spears, swords, knives, arrows, chain mail, and even plate armor. That doesn't begin to count saddles, belts, shoes, shields, and surcoats.

"The shock wave also flattened the Abbey of Beale, and floating sparks burned down seven hectares of the Sauvage Forest. Angry inhabitants of both went in together on a team of greedy lawyers who submitted a bill to King Arthur, demanding royal government compensation. That case is still in litigation.

"Older Round Table knights said they were reminded of the Dolorous Stroke. Sir Christian, you look like an older Round Table knight."

"That's because I am an older Round Table knight!"

"Were you reminded of the Dolorous Stroke?"

"The one that occurred when Sir Balin stabbed King Pellam with the, uh—"

"Spear of Longinus![10] Yes—according to Merlin. Do you think he was protecting someone?"

Sir Christian said nothing, so the woman continued. "Yet his account, which also describes how the Dolorous Stroke wiped out the population in three shires, is the official version included in all court chronicles. It was likewise said to be heard halfway to Navarre in one direction and all the way across Ireland in the other."

She tapped his cloak. "Sir Mordred swore the Humber blast was caused by something in a dolorous camp cauldron you left unattended. He demanded you be held responsible for all damages, including a

---

[10] This was the spear that pierced Christ during the crucifixion. The traditional name of the Roman centurion who used the spear was Gaius Cassis Longinus (which was also the name of Caesar's assassin, commonly referred to as Cassius).

special monetary restitution to him for one of his men-at-arms who vaporized near the incendiary cart.

"King Arthur agreed with Sir Mordred that you were probably responsible, but the blast allowed him to win a decisive, although hardly painless, victory over Cheldric, especially after the Saxon chief repeated what his father, Cheldric the Elder, did when Arthur defeated his earlier invasion. He gave King Arthur all of his captured gold and silver in return for an agreement to sail away. So there was more than enough loot to pay for things that needed to be replaced—that time.

"On what seemed to be a whim, King Arthur declared you a national hero, released you from any liability, and gave you a parade through Camelot, where people cheered, applauded, and showered you with flowers. At the entrance to the castle, he presented you with a gold key, a gold medal, and a brand-new purse of gold coins. Finally, at a special gathering of the Round Table—for those who were well enough to attend, that is—he added your name to the bottom of his Round Table Honor Roll, and as an additional honor, he commanded that you serve among the other battle heroes at the upcoming Caerleon Christmas feast. All of that, by the way, was over the objections of Sir Kay and Sir Mordred. It's worth noting in this instance that Myrddin sided with King Arthur.

"Now then"—the woman tapped his arm with the scroll—"whatever was responsible, a cartload of prepositioned incendiaries, probably for use as a signal fire, can't possibly be powerful enough to re-create something like the Dolorous Stroke. So what did you leave simmering in that camp cauldron?"

"I left nothing simmering in that camp cauldron. I put out the fire beneath it before King Arthur ordered the attack."

"Something wasn't out. What was in that cauldron?"

"Only something my father recorded in a scroll before he disappeared. It's a special food condiment known as—fish gravy."

"Fiiiisssh graaaavy." She pronounced the words extra slowly as she tapped him again with the scroll while unrolling it further.

CHAPTER 5

Fish Gravy

Hmm, it seems this fish gravy is a catalyst
for complications—yours.
—Wade the Scholar, *Chanson de Chrétien*

"Fiiiisssh graaaavy," the woman repeated, "which brings us to your second sensational—"

Thud!

"Don't they ever shoot at you?" Sir Christian asked as he struggled to remove the latest arrow pinning his cloak to the cart.

"They know better. Back to the joust—didn't something called fish gravy get a kitchen knave into big trouble on the thirteenth day of the Christmas feast?"

"My father's scroll said fish gravy contained a big surprise. So that's what I told the knave he would give King Arthur's guests— once I talked him into serving it."

"You talked him into serving King Arthur's guests a big food-poisoning surprise!"

"The knave mistook my father's food condiment for unsweetened pudding—and added sugar when I wasn't looking very well."

"Sir Christian, do you look very well on days that you're healthy?"

He frowned and tried to move them on to the next painful point as—*thud!*—another arrow hit, followed by "Aiieee!"

Sir Christian didn't see another arrow pinning his cloak to the cart as she shouted, "Sir Christian, look behind you! It's a trick!"

He spun around, tripping but swinging Sir Pinel le Savage's second-favorite spear like windmill arms as he smacked another guard cold. The woman quickly fastened a note to him as she shook her head and asked, "Where were we?"

"Still outside the castle!"

She glared at him.

He glared at her as his foot prodded the guard. "Where we were talking about Sir Kay's kitchen knave—until I fought this knave!"

Her look eased to a smile as she said, "He doesn't look very well."

She added,"Niether did Sir Kay's kitchen knave when he was dragged screaming, pleading, and sobbing to clean out the castle gardé robe pits. But why did sugar mixed with your father's fish gravy mainly make those banquet guests sick? Nevertheless, a larger medical staff than the one on the Humber was required to treat this debacle. Even now, it's nursing Christmas guests with body-shaking spasms, great abdominal pains, and other symptoms a knight of the most-high politeness should never mention—at least not in public.

"And the Caerleon banquet hall resembled another place where it looked like the world ended. Nothing burned up or blew up—but the other damages caused King Arthur's seneschal, Sir Kay, to spend a fortune on cloth merchants, tailors, curtain and tapestry reweavers as well as carpenters and even masons to replace stones that turned to powder with a magical-sounding *poof!*"

"Uh, yes."

"Sir Kay received so many complaints for not supervising the Christmas feast better that he offered to spit you on his sword like a pot roast. But his own body-shaking spasms and great abdominal pains didn't leave him enough strength to spit three inches in front of his helmet. So he uttered ugly threats about your future, impossible observations about your past, and some unbelievable suggestions on how smart your parents weren't—until King Arthur got tired of listening and commanded that Sir Kay go to his castle, go on a quest, or at least go to his chamber and go to bed."

"Sir Kay went to his chamber and went to bed as soon as his kitchen knaves—"

"Who couldn't find a place to hide!"

"Were dragged screaming, pleading, and sobbing to clean up after the Christmas Feast."

"Which, thanks to you, ended three days earlier than the traditional fifteen. Do you realize this may cause a change in the calendar? It started church scholars debating if people should only celebrate twelve days of Christmas. The Unknown Bard even composed a song with the new number that's become so popular that church choirs plan to sing it at Easter, and veterans want to use it to collect money during the summer."

Sir Christian nodded sadly. "I've hummed a few bars myself— something about a game bird in a fruit tree while the seneschal hires more help to support the feast."

"Which he couldn't afford to do if you were involved. Fortunately, opposing theologians must be near an agreement, because the last I heard, they stopped excommunicating each other."

"Yes, milady, but there's nothing I can do about that. Meanwhile, after the Christmas feast days—those we actually celebrated, that is—King Arthur called a special meeting of the Round Table where he announced to the knights—"

"Those who were actually well enough to attend, that is," she pointed out.

Once again, he nodded sadly. "That the Christmas—"

"Fiasco!"

"Was declared an accident."

"Like the Humber?"

"Milady, the Humber was declared a victory."

"Not by the medical staff that was dragged screaming, pleading, and sobbing to treat an overwhelming, not to mention utterly disgusting, army of screaming, pleading, and sobbing patients! Hmm, it seems this fish gravy is a catalyst for complications—yours. It makes you incident prone as well as liable for sensational mistakes.

Yet it's only a recent source of your troubles. When did you first discover its dolorous delights?"

"On my last—"

Thud!

"Birthday—as in October," she noted, examining another one of his scroll's footnotes as he noted another arrow pinning his cloak to the cart—beneath his foot.

"Uh, yes," he said as he extracted the latest war-tipped shaft from his shredded cloak. "On that day, I fell on my knees and prayed for Jesu's help so hard—for the first time in years—that I shoved a table into a shelf of old scrolls, making one roll off—"

"And land on your head?"

He refused to say where it landed as he demanded, "What's this all about?"

"I'm an answer to all of your prayers!"

And she gave him a look that made him determined to watch for every other possible prayer answer—as soon as he could stop watching for arrows. To keep her distracted, he said, "A sudden wind in a room of my father's manor, where there's seldom any wind, caused the scroll to unroll to the fish gravy recipe, as recorded in my long-lost father's handwriting."

"Sir Christian, after reading a recipe in a room where the shelves, the scrolls, and even the wind are abnormal, did you consider further prayer before turning it loose on the innocent Round Table?"

"I noticed nothing particularly perilous."

"More accurately, you noticed nothing particularly at all."

His face grew so red that for a moment, he said nothing particularly at all. So she unrolled the scroll further. "Now for your third—"

Thud!

Sir Christian pulled the latest arrow from his cloak—this time, leaving slightly more holes than material—as he grumbled, "Can we speed this up before I catch cold?"

"Or have to buy a new cloak without money? I'll summarize. Your third mistake was somewhat sensational, although its consequences weren't perilous to anyone but you and your horse. But on top of everything else, it thoroughly annoyed my kinsman Myrddin.

"King Arthur, for reasons known only to his graciously royal self, attempted to smooth things out between you and the other knights. But Sir Mordred, whom nobody really likes, suffered from an unusually bad case of those body-shaking spasms and great abdominal pains. When he finally walked with a limping shuffle, he got right into your face without receiving criticism from anyone, because after the Humber campaign and the Christmas banquet, nobody really liked you either. That's when he dared you, on the honor of your Round Table knighthood, to charge on horse in full plate armor through a thatch-walled cottage."

"Milady, some of us have been known to charge on horse in full plate armor through a thatch-walled cottage during battle."

"For which there have been numerous complaints from people still living inside. Regardless, you accepted this challenge, and after your subsequent crash through the thin thatch walls, you and your horse slid through an opening in the even thinner thatch-covered floor—like a food cart going down a mudhole."

"That's one of my lines."

"If it wasn't good, I wouldn't use it."

She tapped his arm with another *swoosh* of the scroll and then pulled it back to brush more imaginary dust off of it, her cloak, and, with still another lightning move too fast for the eye to follow, another unexplored section of his split ends.

She said, "Myrddin passed by that cottage just in time to hear you—drop in. When he peered down the hole and caught a mouthful of whatever you and your horse were splashing around in—provided by the gardé robe pit cleaning crew, who, ever since the Christmas feast sewage overflows, truly loathe you—he was tempted to leave you down there. But he felt sorry for your horse. It took him, three engineers, and Sir Kay's kitchen knaves, who once again had to be dragged screaming, pleading, and sobbing, an entire afternoon to hoist both of you out of there.

"That twelve-foot hole contained enough goo to bury you and your horse and have some left over for a monument—if it ever dried. With Sir Mordred's backstabbing reputation, did it occur to you to look for traces of something murderous outside that cottage before you charged?"

"Sir Mordred dared me in front of every Knight of the Round Table still well enough to stand up. No true member may back down from a Round Table challenge under those circumstances."

"Maybe they should start. Recent Round Table mortality totals attribute half of all accidental death to such dares in front of other Round Table knights."

She gave him another intense stare before she continued. "Then Myrddin—"

"Treated bruises on me and my horse, and I had to replace all of my equipment and clothes, which disintegrated after they stopped attracting flies and started killing them. Please don't mention the archery lecture where Sir Agravaine the Arrogant made me yawn until I dislocated my jaw. When Myrddin made the loathly damsel pop it back into place, I heard drooling saliva jokes for weeks."

"I didn't know about that one—fish gravy again?"

"Yes."

"Did anyone have to replace anything this time?"

"Do you really want to know?"

She decided she didn't as she replied, "And Myrddin wouldn't see you?"

"Yes." Sir Christian's voice grew unusually low.

"He sent the loathly damsel instead?"

"Yes." His voice grew even lower.

"Myrddin only makes the loathly damsel help knights he doesn't like."

But Sir Christian wasn't listening as he took a long deep breath before he asked softly, "Uh, once again, what is this all about?"

"As an answer to all of your prayers, I require your services for a quest."

She gave him a look with her focused brown eyes that reminded Sir Christian of a similar look he had once seen in the eyes of his most ferocious manor cat. It had just cornered a clumsy field mouse in his stable.

CHAPTER 6

Questing for Food
and Supplies

Questing for food and supplies is better than
standing around with a second-favorite spear.
—Wade the Scholar, *Chanson de Chrétien*

The woman realized her stare had become one level shy of terrifying intimidation, which was how it affected most people, including famous Knights of the Round Table. She caught herself and suddenly tried to appear soft and reassuring. She was well aware her smile sometimes started like a cat scaring a cornered mouse, but before long, it might evolve into the look of a hungry she-leopard, unsheathing claws in her eyes as she cornered an elephant-size ox that didn't want to die. Such a stare wasn't completely useless. On a recent journey through the mountains of Navarre, she used it to drive off a thirteen-hundred-pound brown bear. One cold afternoon, the mountainous beast had risen up before her after she had ridden around the trunk of a large fallen tree. It appeared dangerously underfed and just as dangerously interested in selecting her and her horse as a main course solution. That's when she pulled back the hood from her head so that the creature could see every detail of her face. Then she unloaded on the mountainous beast an equally mountainous dose of her most ferocious and intimidating harmless-lady eyeful. The unhappy bear had responded with a shaky, frightened growl as it backed away with a confused look on its face. Then it slowly turned around and growled piteously one more time before it had run off on what looked like another desperate hunt for berries.

Sir Christian looked ready to back away like that bear until he hit the castle wall. Following another loud *thud*, he thought he had smacked his head, until he pulled another arrow out of his cloak. After muttering an unprayerful impoliteness about the flanking curtain-wall towers, he responded in his own attempt at a shaky growl, "You require my services for a quest after—"

Thud! Thud! Thud!

He pulled another arrow from his cloak and stared at two that had just missed as he said to the woman, "In my thirty-plus years—"

"Of merely satisfactory service," she reminded him.

"No one has ever shot that many arrows at me. Why, right before you arrived, me and the castle guards were about to become just like—"

Thud!

He pulled still another arrow out of his cloak as she said, "Why, yes, Sir Christian, I'm sure it was just as you said. Right before I arrived"—she stared up at the nearest tower for effect—"you and the castle guards were about to become just like—"

Thud!

Followed by a loud rip as she plucked the latest arrow out of his remaining cloak and waved it under his nose. He smacked it out of her hand—and looked tempted to do so more smacking. But this didn't faze her as she said with another one of her smiles, "Aren't you glad I arrived right when I did—as an answer to all of your prayers?"

"Are you sure you aren't an answer to the prayers of whomever sells arrows to the guards?"

"He's the sheriff's fletcher, whom I'm sure merely issues them, but there's merit in your thought because the castle guards are firing an unusual amount of arrows at you."

"But not at you!"

"But have you noticed that they always just miss you?"

Thud! Thud! Thud!

Such a stare wasn't completely useless.

"But not my cloak," Sir Christian muttered as he pulled three more arrows out of the remaining shredded material. "One might think it contained one of those new-fangled Far Eastern compass magnets."

"Archers shooting from Castle Perilous must have orders not to hit you."

He yelled, "Ouch!" as an arrow grazed his arm.

"Too close to a vital spot. Incidentally, that last arrow didn't hit you with the usual loud thud. Do you think your arms are growing soft?"

He felt tempted to see if her arms were growing soft, when she added, "But neither does someone pulling their bow strings want you going on a quest with me."

"As an answer to all of my prayers?"

She gave him a spiritual smile.

He gave her an unspiritual glare. "Milady, I don't want to go on a Sunday hike with you, much less a quest. I've decided to await the next answer to all of my prayers, which hopefully will arrive with a lot less arrows from well-wishers. So I suggest you leave and"—he pointed at the scattered collection of unconscious chain mail lumps on the ground, which were not being shot at from the castle—"beg, borrow, steal, or at least rent something to drag those ferocious recruits for a useful and noble deed away with you. Meantime—"

He attempted to signal the castle by waving Sir Pinel le Savage's second-favorite spear, only to hear a sarcastic announcement from a crenelated wall: "In the name of our teeny-tiny yet distinguished land—"

"Sir Christian," the woman warned, "I think the guards may have changed their minds about missing your vital spots!" She prepared to tackle him as a dozen bows twanged, but the wind suddenly shifted and blew so hard against Sir Christian's legs that they became tangled around the shaft of Sir Pinel's second-favorite spear, making him hit the ground with a crashing moan. He heard the arrows hiss harmlessly overhead as the wind picked up even harder, preventing further archery from the castle.

Once again, Sir Christian slowly regained his feet by pushing Sir Pinel le Savage's second-favorite spear against the ground as the woman said, "Let's take advantage of the wind blowing in our favor and cut to the joust! I found you outside this last-place excuse of a fortified dump—"

"Because I'm stuck here!"

"Saying prayers for Jesu's help that I heard while seeking you."

"You're not Jesu!"

"Were you expecting him to arrive in person?"

"I wasn't expecting someone like you!"

"Who were you expecting?"

He thought for a moment before he soberly shook his head. "I'm not sure, but here's my side of the joust. Sir Dagonet's survey made me such an embarrassment to the Round Table that King Arthur banished me to this one corner of his realm that he never likes to revisit and where he said the morale was already so bad that I couldn't make it worse. I was commanded not to return to court until further notice.

"But first, to help pay for the Christmas damages, he suspended my Round Table salary, confiscated my family assets, and seized everything he awarded me after the Humber. That included my gold key, my gold medal, and my purse full of gold coins, except he let me keep my brand-new purse as an object lesson."

The woman stared at the dilapidated object barely clinging to his belt. "That may be an object lesson, but it was brand new closer to the resurrection of Jesu."

Sir Christian frowned as he answered, "At my last inn, someone switched purses when I wasn't looking very well."

"As I said earlier, do you look very well on days that you're healthy?"

Once again, he nodded to get them to the next painful point as he said, "Using coins I found under King Arthur's chair when he wasn't looking very well, I eventually reached this shire with my horse, arms, equipment and, the secondhand armor on my back. And things haven't gone very well for me here. For the last three days, I have stood outside this gate, soliciting for charity with one hand and local knight errantry work with the other."

"Well, Sir Christian, give some credit to your prayers to Jesu for helping solicit—me. I'm no distraction, and you can forget all about charity. However, listen carefully because the directive I bring you has been approved by King Arthur himself. I am authorized to seek out and employ you as a fully equipped Round Table knight."

"I'm not fully equipped."

Smack!

She pulled back her scroll as he frowned while rubbing his arm. She said with a smile, "When you are, that won't hurt! Then you'll help rescue my grandson, Adragain, from Saxon pirates. With everything else going on and with everyone else not going on, King Arthur, with Sir Lancelot's cautious endorsement, referred you to me as my best choice."

"Are you sure? As in—sure? All your talk about prayer aside, you made it sound like I'd be your worst choice."

"According to Sir Lancelot, the worst choice is sometimes the best choice. He still won't ride into battle next to you and threatened to switch sides if he saw you anywhere near him. But he agreed with King Arthur that you're the best available knight for this quest. Without crossing their fingers—I looked—they told me you respect a lady's honor, won't violate her social boundaries, and would be—"

"Hungry enough?"

"Yes, but more important, they said you would be well enough."

Sir Christian was also desperate enough, as well as so hungry that he wasn't sure how much longer he would be well enough. At the moment, especially after the different fights, he thought he could barely hold Sir Pinel's second-favorite spear—leaning against a tree, slumping next to a cart, or even slouching across a bench. But he was convinced there was a catch in this offer somewhere. This strong-willed, disagreeable woman gave every indication she would be one sensationally scary quest companion, the kind only mentioned in whispers in King Arthur's late-night court as a damosel savage. There was a saying among older Round Table knights that it was safer to face the Monster-of-Unheard-of-Savageness in a cave corner blindfolded (with poorly fletched arrows) than to go on a quest with a damosel savage. This woman had mentioned her grandson, which meant she was a dame, not a damosel (another way of saying damsel), but she certainly seemed more than a little savage. He asked in another attempt at a squeaky growl, "What if I'm not interested—in spite of the fact you might feed me?"

"My dear Sir Christian, I promise to feed you things that provide a new definition of the word *food*."

Sir Christian shuddered so hard at the possibilities that he backed into the castle wall with a super *thud* as she expounded. "But let's say you refuse—what then? How much longer can you hold a second-favorite spear while dodging first-favorite arrows outside this last-favorite slum? Therefore, look at me as the most likely—or, if you will, most unlikely—answer to your prayers and possibly those of someone else. Otherwise, I might not have found you in time."

"For what?"

"That's not open for discussion. Hear me now, Sir Christian de Galis, Knight of the Fish Gravy. I am none other than Lady Britta de Brittany, close kinswoman to the honorable Myrddin the Magnificent, lord and leader of—hmm, that's not open for discussion either. I'm also most honorable liaison between him, his Britannic Majesty, Arthur, high king of Britons, Bretons, and other assorted nations (of which the complete list is also not open for discussion), as well as her extreme brilliance, Nimue, chief British Lady of the Lake (whose business is likewise not open for discussion). But you may call me Britta. Now, before the arrows once more start flying, let me pull Myrddin's latest Round Table knight errantry application forms."

She smoothed Sir Christian's scroll once more, carefully rerolled it, and, with another hiss like the swing of Sir Lancelot's sword, slid it back into her cloak.

Sir Christian slid Sir Pinel's second-favorite spear against the castle wall, where, as he watched sadly, it continued sliding downward until with a soft *thud* it wedged itself behind the hanging pot whose contents he had been experimenting with.

The woman appeared not to notice as she reached inside her cloak and drew three scrolls as if they were Saxon knives. The parchment edges looked sharp enough to cut steel as she unrolled them, in fact she used one to whimsically cut a notch in a leaning board before she said, "Ordericus and Hubert of Hereford completed these forms just before they were dragged screaming, pleading, and sobbing to clean out the castle gardé robe pits. You'll still be impressed with the watermark they centered at the bottom. It's that famous episode in the life of Sir Lancelot where he was held captive in the dungeon of Sir Meliagrance for one whole year. Yet he maintained daily discipline and dignity—"

The woman suddenly stared at the closest copy—"by playing cards with his guards? Hmm, I don't remember that being in the story of Sir Lancelot. No matter—the forms are embossed with the king's seal and, thus, remain official."

She pushed the nonsharp edges into Sir Christian's hands before she pulled pen and ink like another pair of knives.

"You can really draw with that pen, Brittle."

"Britta!" she cried as she threatened to draw on him with the pen. "Sir Christian, please read, sign, and initial all three copies of this simplified Round Table knight errantry contract. Per our mutual agreement, it eliminates all responsibility on my part to reimburse you with any salary, gratuity, per diem, or performance bonus. It further states that you will merely work—"

"Did you say *merely*?"

"Yes, Sir Christian, which doesn't mean barely—for food and supplies I deem necessary to provide."

As Sir Christian stared open-mouthed, she emphasized, "Questing for food and supplies is better than standing around with a second-favorite spear. It's also the best I can offer. For reasons also not open to discussion, this quest has been classified as personal business, not crown. That requires me to pay initial costs with limited startup money and then operate on what has been designated a shoe-latchet budget. That's partly because King Arthur has no money to spare—thanks to that gift you distributed at Christmas—and partly for other reasons not open for discussion.

"Now, bear with me on contract details. It temporarily reinstates you as Knight of the Round Table in good standing. It further states you may achieve full and permanent reinstatement, conditional upon your successful completion of the specified quest within the normal, acceptable time limit."

"Brittle—"

"I am Britta, not Brittle!"

"Uh, yes, of course, you're not Brittle, and I'm not good at remembering names. So, uh, Britta?"

Britta nodded.

"Did I hear you say I may achieve permanent reinstatement at the Round Table?"

"Yes, Sir Christian, which means your name may once more be added *to the bottom* of King Arthur's Round Table Honor Roll."

For the first time, Sir Christian looked at the woman with interest. He muttered to himself softly, "Maybe she is an answer to all of my prayers."

"I sensationally am!"

He nodded as he softly read the title calligraphy: "The Quest of Sir Christian."

"Catchy title, don't you think? Could be an epic tale by an inspired author."

"As opposed to the Quest of Sir Gawaine, the Quest of Sir Gareth—"

"Or any of those other one hundred sixty-seven more-famous Knights of the Round Table that you landed in the hospital without benefit of swinging sword, spear, or club!"

He nodded again as he examined the fine wording at the bottom: "The acceptable time limit for a quest is still a year and a day?"

"It's traditional."

"Brittle—"

"I'm not Brittle! But you may be if you call me that again!"

She smacked the pen into one of his hands. As he winced and shook it, she said, "Please sign and initial below the dotted jousting spear!"

"Yes, Britta, but isn't a year and a day outdated for modern knight-errantry work? A peasant can limp from Castle Perilous to Camelot in five days. Do we really need that much time to rescue your grandson?"

"For the sake of Adragain, you, and everyone else involved, I hope not. The traditional time limit is retained on all quest documents redesigned by Myrddin's scribes."

Sir Christian read through some more of the fine calligraphy and scratched his head. "I don't remember the old quest contracts being quite this involved."

"Knighthood at the Round Table is an ever-moving arrow target. Nothing routine ever remains the same for long, although changes are more noticeable to someone who has been absent for a spell— because they've been *banished*. Do you accept?"

"Do I have a choice?"

"Between me, King Arthur, Saxon pirates, and castle guards shooting more arrows at you when the wind dies down—not really. But regard it as an answered prayer to redeem your circumstances. One could add it's almost a way of rescuing yourself by rescuing another."

Sir Christian meekly glanced back through the documents and said, "I accept." He sighed as he signed and initialed all three copies.

Britta neatly took back one copy for her records and another to be filed later with a notary. She opened her cloak and, using a trick she learned from the Knight of the Two Swords, slid both into their pouches with a swooshing hiss.

She watched silently as Sir Christian struggled to stuff his into the aging pouch.

"Now," she said with a sugar-sweet smile, and it could be very sweet when she wanted it to be, "here's the first of the supplies I deem necessary to provide."

Britta pulled a large sack from her cloak and shoved it at him.

"You haven't washed recently. So puh-lease anoint yourself with these liquefied perfume spices. As official lady of the quest, I will ride behind you, slightly downwind."

Sir Christian stared at the sack, which contained a giant flask with a tight cork stopper. "I don't know what to say."

"I do. You will immediately apply these spices to yourself and your clothes, especially what remains of that cloak. The formula contains a wonderful mixture of musk, cloves, nutmeg, cardamom, and various secret ingredients also not open for discussion. But it's just what you and everyone standing close to you need—"

She paused to sniff, cough, and hold her nose before she said, "Immediately! Otherwise, I refuse to provide you with slices—as in bread, cheese, meat, and the like—at mealtime. Nor will I stand, sit, or ride anywhere near you when the wind blows—in any direction. It's time for Sir Christian to smell like a knight. I'll make you look like one—whew!" She held her nose tighter. "Later! When you're finished, follow me down that road to the east, where I'll be waiting past the first tree line."

She now gracefully and firmly turned her back on him and walked away.

Damosel savage, dame savage, or just plain woman savage, her annoying style finally had Sir Christian a little captivated but also aggravated and irritated. For a moment, he stared thoughtfully at his fingernails gripping the sack. Then he shrugged as he removed the flask from the sack, popped the cork, and took a sniff. Misty fumes floated out of the flask's neck. He noticed there was something gaseous about it, although it did seem primarily a fluid. But before he saw very well what he was doing, he dumped half of the contents on his clothes, especially his cape. He was soon covered with enough fumes to wake Sir Agravaine the Arrogant from one of his naps, even if the attack scabber was snoring on the other side of the room through the loathly damsel's latest first-aid lecture. Sir Christian shrugged again as he placed the half-empty flask back in the sack and fastened it to his sword belt. What he failed to see very well, however, was that his clothes, particularly his cloak, now gave off a fog-like mist that made him almost disappear—he was still too dazed from his misfortunes combined with his potential new fortune. Despite limited visibility, he grabbed the charity collection jar he set down earlier, but shook his head as he rattled out one brass farthing, one wooden button, and a broken chain mail link he got from a friendly barbarian. He dropped them next to the unconscious bandit with the bow as he looked east and prayed, "Lord Jesus, help and protect us all!"

He raised Sir Pinel's second-favorite spear as an unexpected wind smacked it against the hanging pot, showering its contents on everything behind. The stones on the castle violently disappeared with a gigantic powdery *poof* as archers re-aiming their bows lost their footing and plunged downward—none of which Sir Christian noticed, as the wind just as suddenly died down. Oblivious to what lay behind and placing his hopes on what was ahead, for once he wielded, not waved, Sir Pinel le Savage's second-favorite spear in the midst of his own cloud as he began a shuffling trot to catch up with Britta, who had just disappeared behind the tree line. This was necessary because she always walked faster than most people and certain breeds of horses.

CHAPTER 7

Steady as a Rock

> Yet despite disabilities, he's steady as a rock.
> —Wade the Scholar, *Chanson de Chrétien*

Britta walked past a freshly fallen tree into an area that looked as if it had been hit by a bigger tornado than the one she brought. The ground between abandoned cottages was strewn with weapons, equipment, plunder, and chain mail lumps, with one unconscious warrior hanging from a tree, a second spread-eagle on a thatched roof, a third sprawled in a doorway, and the limp legs of a fourth poked from a stone well.

In the midst of this mayhem, looking neither treed, sprawled, spread-eagled, well stuck, nor even well struck, a medium-height archer flexed rippling arms and broad shoulders as he prayerfully held on to the right side of a large, modestly equipped warhorse. A similar but slightly smaller horse stood on the left of the first.

Sensing Britta's approach, the archer released the horse, which nudged its companion. They moved quietly into fresh-looking grass, where, in a disciplined manner, they took turns nibbling. One bit off a choice grassy tuft and chewed while the other horse watched. Then they switched.

The archer turned toward Britta with brown eyes matching hers. But they peered from a face as blank as the sides of the helmet touching his shoulder length chain mail.

Nothing else about him looked blank. His long, powerful arms, clad in worn yet stylish blue sleeves, stretched out of a studded brown leather vest called a gambeson, in which he moved as rapidly as Britta in her cloak. His right hand now grasped the hilt of his long-bladed sheath knife, and his left brushed the bow stave protruding from a customized holster. Both weapons hung from crisscrossed leather belts supporting a bag of war arrows on his right hip. Below the waist, he wore off-white trousers tucked into brown boots that matched his belts. All of this had the look of non-blank speed.

His right ear pointed like an arrow at Britta as she announced, "Uncle Sir Cecil! I located our quest knight, Sir Christian de Galis!" She whispered, "I don't find him inept, as some believe. The axiom 'There's always more to see than one thinks one sees' certainly applies to him. Like the Corps of Liaison, methinks he pretends to be harmless—but in an unusually subtle way. If one judged him merely by reputation and appearance, one might truly believe he is the absolute worst knight at King Arthur's Round Table. But if that were so, how does he survive? In a lopsided fight against bandits, in which we prevailed, I surely saw him execute Lancelot's lunge and Galahad's gambit. We'll learn his secret as we prune him, groom him, replume him, and then give a little room to him as we prepare to raise him for our plan like a good—"

She never said *morning mist*, as she looked to the west and was hit by a cloud thicker than any fog she had ever gotten lost in. It blocked out the sun, hiding an even thicker cloud covering the collapse of the castle. As the closer cloud's nearest edge slightly dissipated, Sir Christian de Galis materialized in front of Britta like some sort of ghost. But the ability to walk with ghostly gracefulness didn't materialize with him as—*thunk!*—he tripped over the fallen tree where Sir Pinel's second-favorite spear sliced off a branch.

Sir Christian's left hand grabbed at a closer limb, but then his right plunged the razor-sharp tip of Sir Pinel's second-favorite spear between Britta's feet.

"Whoo! Wee! Ouch!" drowned out the spear's *thud* as Britta avoided being pruned by leaping to a safe distance. Angrily batting mist from her eyes, she choked on her first full whiff of Sir Christian's spice-saturated clothes, particularly his cloak. In a rare moment of her life, she swallowed a shriek along with fumes from the mist as she shouted, "Sir Christian! I told you to anoint yourself with those spices, not take a bath!"

"You said no spices, no slices at mealtime."

"I know what I said! But keep using spices like that and you'll eat extra-small slices at mealtime to offset the cost of resupply!"

With hands almost swimming as if she were in lost a flood, she batted more fog from her eyes, which for some reason only dissipated toward the east and the archer. After a long moment, she shook her head partly clear as she said slowly, evenly, and a little more loudly, "Sir Christian, please say hello to Uncle Sir Cecil!"

Sir Christian nodded as his left hand pointed the spear in a safe upward direction (except for any bird passing close overhead). He turned his right hand toward the archer. "I'm glad to meet you, Uncle Sir Cecil."

Uncle Sir Cecil removed his right hand from his knife and thrust it three feet in the wrong direction, where he vigorously shook it up and down in the misty air.

In a voice almost as loud as Britta's, Uncle Sir Cecil announced to the blank space in front of him, "I'm most glad to meet you, Sir Christian! Most glad indeed! Are you truly Knight of the Fish Gravy?" Then, in an even louder voice, he said, "Where are you?"

Sir Christian whispered toward Britta, "Brittle?"

There was the *swoosh* followed by the *thud* of a scroll smacking Sir Pinel le Savage's second-favorite spear. "Sir Christian!" she announced, "you will address me as Britta!"

"Brit-ta, not Brit-tle. There! I think I got it right!"

"You need to get it right a little sooner next time!"

Sir Christian nodded to move them a little sooner to the next painful point as he whispered, "Britta, is your uncle blind?"

"No, Sir Christian!" she announced patiently, firmly, and loudly. "Despite the ironic meaning of his iconic name, which means blind, Uncle Sir Cecil is not blind! So there's no need to whisper! Or shout!" She added as she lowered her voice. "He's just a little nearsighted—and a little farsighted."

"In both eyes—or does he have one of each?"

Her scroll looked ready to smack one of Sir Christian's eyes, but she restrained herself as she continued calmly. "With a blind spot—somewhere in front of him. And he's a little hard of hearing—in his left ear only. And he has a slight sinus problem—in one nostril, but not even he knows which one for sure. Hopefully it can't smell you. Yet despite disabilities, he's steady as a rock."

Sir Christian looked at Uncle Sir Cecil, who didn't appear as steady as any rock he had ever seen. Uncle Sir Cecil continued to shake not only his right hand but also the entire right side of his body. He went up and down and up and down—and he continued to do it all in the wrong direction.

For the sake of a peaceful quest with Britta, Sir Christian gave Uncle Sir Cecil the benefit of any doubts he still retained. He decided the archer might indeed be an example of a rock that remained steady while the ground went up and down—as in an earthquake or an explosion in a small kitchen.

Britta grabbed Sir Christian's right hand in hers and said, "Let me bring you two together."

She carefully but only semi-sweetly guided his right hand into Uncle Sir Cecil's until she gently folded them together, almost as if in prayer. She gave a slight nudge and released them so that their hands finally shook, and to Sir Christian's relief, Uncle Sir Cecil stopped shaking everything else.

"Like I said before, I am most glad to meet you, Sir Christian," said Uncle Sir Cecil loudly but also politely as he released the knight's hand. "I'm most glad indeed. I've heard all about your fish gravy—with my good right ear, that is. Thus, I wouldn't mind seeing that amazing stuff—with what remains of my poor old eyes, that is. And I know I would find the smell most stimulating—with my nostril that still sniffs, that is. I do hope that becomes possible. Now then, my honorary title is Uncle Sir Cecil the Steady. However, most folks call me plain ole Uncle Sir Cecil. You can too, if you like. I really am sorry about my eyes, left ear, and whichever one of my nostrils no longer sniffs. But they began shutting down when I reached sixty. Now, I think that was ten—I really mean fifteen—well, maybe it was more like fifty-five or so years ago. You know, I'm at that age where I'm not really sure how long ago anything was anymore. But I still perform lots of certified archery work."

"Certified archery work! But how can you see to shoot?"

"I pray before I shoot."

"While others pray that you don't?"

"Oh ho! You told a joke that doeth good like a medicine."

"I hope it makes you feel better than I do."

"In my condition, I don't feel much of anything. But to answer your question, whenever I grab my bow—"

"And try to aim it!"

"I don't see well enough to do that anymore. But as I started to say, whenever I grab my bow, people fall on their knees in all directions and begin to pray—out loud—in unison. To my good right ear, it sounds like I'm going to church."

"For a funeral—or are they praying that you don't hit them instead of the target?"

"Sir Christian, I only hit people who are the target."

"How do you know, if you can't see them?"

"I can see them, just not very well. However, I make it a rule to never shoot anyone without proper guidance, especially prayer. That's why I'm called the prayer archer!"

Sir Christian said softly to Britta, "Your uncle can't see very well, and he's—"

"The prayer archer!" Britta proclaimed as, with a *thud*, her scroll once again belted Sir Pinel's second-favorite spear. Sir Christian staggered to stay on his feet as she added, "Which makes him my quest archer of choice!"

She swung the scroll like a swooping eagle around his head as she said, "Before I go further, let me establish this rule: when Uncle Sir Cecil is present and the conversation is about him, he will be included! You will never discuss Uncle Sir Cecil in front of Uncle Sir Cecil!"

Standing still enough to avoid a scroll swing that might cripple, Sir Christian noticed the glint of leopard claws emerging from Britta's eyes. He quickly spoke toward Uncle Sir Cecil's good right ear. "My apologies, Uncle Sir Cecil—the Steady."

"Simple Uncle Sir Cecil is just fine. Otherwise, that's all right, Sir Christian, quite all right."

Uncle Sir Cecil groped around until he found Sir Christian's right hand again, and he gave it a friendly tap as he added, "But you had better listen carefully to Britta if you're going on a quest with us. Else you may not get along very well—with her. I no longer have the eyes to verify, but I don't think you want to face that stare of hers. Did you know it scared a bear off a mountain?"

Britta looked ready to scare the legendary Monster-of-Unheard-of-Savageness off of a mountain, until she stopped swinging and said loudly, "Dear ole Uncle Sir Cecil, everyone knows you're not blind. You're just a little hard of seeing and a little hard of hearing and a little hard of smelling. Otherwise, you're just as steady as a big ole rock, especially after you pray."

She tapped one of Uncle Sir Cecil's arms with the scroll affectionately. "Sir Christian will get a chance to see."

Sir Christian protested, "But what will Uncle Sir Cecil see?"

Britta flashed her leopard-claw eyes so quickly that he immediately amended his question. "What I meant to say was, Uncle Sir Cecil, what will you see or hear?" He discreetly stopped himself from saying, "We'll forget the smelling part."

Britta retracted her eyes and gave Sir Christian another interesting smile as Uncle Sir Cecil said, "While having a nice morning prayer, I watched the horses while Britta watched for you."

Sir Christian said, "Are you sure the horses weren't watching you?"

The larger warhorse, which was a mighty stallion, turned his head and gave Sir Christian an intensely focused and curious look. For a moment, the horse almost smiled at Sir Christian—like Britta. The stallion concluded with a horse snort, turned his head toward the smaller mare next to him, and communicated something that made them neigh in unison. The interaction almost appeared to Sir Christian to resemble some kind of horse laugh. It seemed as if the horses were telling jokes about him in horse language. Sir Christian didn't know if he found that annoying or unsettling, but it wasn't funny to him. That's when he noticed the other surroundings, with dented chain mail lumps lying everywhere as well as on everything, including roofs, doorways, and trees. He also noticed the large fallen tree he had tripped over didn't lie anywhere near its stump.

He asked, "What in the name of the Monster-of-Unheard-of-Savageness did all of this?"

"I didn't notice a monster," said Uncle Sir Cecil, thoughtfully squinting. "Why, does someone look devoured?"

"No, but several armored warriors look unconscious, just like everyone else who gets too close to Britta and her wild-woman war club scrolls. But she was with me. Also, how did one knave land six feet off the ground in a tree? And then there's that fallen tree whose trunk—"

"Used to be in the ground over there," said Uncle Sir Cecil, pointing in the wrong direction. "Or was it really over there?" And he pointed in still another wrong direction. Then he shrugged and said, "I don't remember where that tree stood attached to its stump. Is that important?"

"Not as much as it seems abnormal—even for a quest."

"Then you'll fit right in," said Britta, resheathing the scroll like Sir Lancelot's sword before pulling out more notices.

Sir Christian pointed at the chain mail lumps and the toppled tree as he asked, "Uncle Sir Cecil, did you do all of this?"

"Before or after I prayed?" Uncle Sir Cecil grinned as he patted his mount with folded hands.

Sir Christian suddenly pointed at Uncle Sir Cecil's destrier, who also seemed to be grinning—for a horse. "Uncle Sir Cecil, surely it wasn't—him?"

"He isn't called a warhorse for nothing," Britta said as she tossed a notice-wrapped rock to the warrior on the roof. His body winced as the stone landed on him with a soft *thud*.

Britta shrugged. "Didn't allow for the wind."

"Second time today," said Sir Christian.

"I didn't throw it that hard," she said. "And I wasn't trying to hurt him."

"I'd hate to see him if you were," said Sir Christian.

"I wouldn't do a thing like that," Britta said as she moistened her finger and held it up. "Because then he couldn't help us."

Sir Christian said sarcastically, "Perform a deed that is useful—somewhat noble deed?"

"That's right," she said as she warmed up before delivering a lightning-quick upward underarm toss. This was followed by a clang as a notice-wrapped rock landed in the hanging helmet of the warrior in the tree.

"I win lots of prizes at shire fairs," she said as she tagged one leg of each man sticking out of the well and the doorway. "It supplements my shoe-latchet budget. Speaking of which, Sir Christian, where do we collect your horse, armor, weapons, and other equipment? We can't afford to replace them."

Sir Christian let go of Uncle Sir Cecil's right hand, which he was happy to see didn't resume shaking, and pointed farther to the east. "I left them at the large travelers' inn one mile down that main road."

"The one with the slime pit on the outside and the knave pit on the inside?"

"That's the place."

"With a destination like that, what are we waiting for?" Britta grabbed the reins of the slightly smaller horse, once again not looking back at Sir Christian as she turned and started on foot toward the inn.

Sir Christian called out, "Britta, can't we ride the horses to the inn?"

Still not looking back, she shook her head. "One of them would have to carry double, which I never allow when questing on a shoe-latchet budget. On the other hand, two of us could ride while the third walked. But I don't think you could keep up."

She almost disappeared down the road as Sir Christian shouldered Sir Pinel le Savage's second-favorite spear, and Uncle Sir Cecil grabbed the right side of his horse. They started after her in what almost resembled a pursuit. But they had gone only a few steps, when Sir Christian whispered into the ancient archer's good right ear, "Uncle Sir Cecil the Steady?"

"My boy, plain ole Uncle Sir Cecil will do just fine."

"Of course, Uncle Sir Cecil. Are you also only working for food and supplies?"

Uncle Sir Cecil did not break his stride, which matched Britta's. This was in spite of his disabilities and partly because of his well-trained horse. He answered without breathing hard, "I suppose it might look like that. I am part of her family, however, having served Britta as bodyguard since she was a little girl. Thus, I mostly work for a share in the family profits."

At that moment, a vision of Britta's ageless, oval-shaped face materialized out of foggy mists in Sir Christian's semi-foggy mind, and it occurred to him that there was something attractive about her—in a hard-charging, bear-scaring, obnoxious lady sort of way. This was despite her crown of hair that didn't quite conceal its use of hair dye. She admitted that she was a grandmother, which implied that she wasn't a young Arthurian woman. The way she thunked bandits unconscious with a library scroll, frequently faster than Sir Lancelot swinging his sword, suggested that she wasn't an old Arthurian woman either. Sir Christian couldn't help asking, in a conspiratorial sort of way, as he worked hard to keep up, "Uncle Sir Cecil, just how long ago was that?"

Britta, who had gotten so far in front of them that Sir Christian had trouble seeing her, suddenly reappeared with her horse in front of his face.

"Sir Christian!" she boomed loudly enough to deafen his ears even more than Uncle Sir Cecil's.

Sir Christian instinctively blocked her hands from reaching his neck with Sir Pinel's second-favorite spear. But she stood her ground before him as she proclaimed, "You are Knight of the Round Table in good standing—even if only temporarily reinstated! Therefore, you must be aware that any discussion that hints at a lady's age or a warrior's wage is proprietary information! On an official Round Table quest, that can be grounds for dismissal!"

"Does that mean you won't feed me today?"

Britta looked ready to feed Sir Christian to the Monster-of-Unheard-of-Savageness. But instead, she counted backward from twenty, breathed slowly, and said, "Sir most polite knight of Castle Cameliard, quit showing less taste than your father's fish gravy!"

She then breathed even more slowly before she attempted to add in a nice way, "Sir Christian, it is said at court that a knave who discusses a lady's age or a warrior's wage will discuss *anything*. On an authorized Round Table quest, we must be more discreet than that. One never knows who may be listening nearby."

She then attempted to give him a friendly smile. But Sir Christian saw the sharp tips of unsheathed leopard's claws lingering below the surface of her eyes. He wisely shut up.

CHAPTER 8

Another Sensational Mistake

Methinks his sensational surprise has caused
another sensational mistake.
—Wade the Scholar, *Chanson de Chrétien*

The group of three, leading two modestly equipped horses, proceeded up the road to the east. Under Britta's direction, they intended to collect Sir Christian's horse, armor, weapons, and other equipment at his recent stopover and home, the notorious Inn of the Knight Perilous. Then they would go to Britta's camp.

But when they got within a quarter mile, Sir Christian became agitated. He quickly walked forward a few steps. He turned left and walked sideways a few quick steps. Finally, he turned completely around and stopped in front of Uncle Sir Cecil, dead center in his blind spot. Sir Christian turned sharply again and whacked Uncle Sir Cecil across the gambeson with Sir Pinel le Savage's second-favorite spear. The razor-fine point missed Uncle Sir Cecil's left shoulder.

For once, this made Uncle Sir Cecil unsteady. He stumbled and almost fell backward. But with natural, catlike agility, using reflexes developed during unexpected battle situations, he jumped lightly forward and landed gracefully on his feet with a soft clinking from his helmet's chain mail. Fortunately for Sir Christian and the quest, Uncle Sir Cecil took this near stabbing in stride and gave Sir Christian an easygoing smile. But because of his poor eyesight, he didn't see Sir Christian almost run him through again. Sir Christian then dropped Sir Pinel's second-favorite spear while he struggled to maintain his own balance.

With a fresh wind blowing away instead of toward them from Sir Christian's cloak, the two modestly equipped horses watched everything patiently and calmly. They took all of this in horse stride and gave Sir Christian easygoing horse smiles accompanied by bemused neighs.

Sir Christian didn't get a horse smile, a bemused neigh, or anything easygoing from Britta. When she saw he just missed Uncle Sir Cecil twice with the razor-sharp tip of Sir Pinel le Savage's second-favorite spear, the glint of razor sharpness reappeared in her eyes. She looked ready to give him another leopard-claw, bear-scaring, obnoxious-lady eyeful.

Sir Christian watched the glint in her eyes carefully as he cleared his throat. "Britta, before we get closer to the inn, I have a small confession to make."

"How small?"

"Small enough."

Seeing Uncle Sir Cecil safely on his feet and Sir Pinel le Savage's second-favorite spear safely on the ground, Britta retracted her eyes. She nodded for Sir Christian to continue.

"I haven't been back to my inn for three days."

"No wonder you smelled sour and disgusting."

"I may not be able to go back to my inn at all."

"Pray, continue."

"A month ago, Sir Pinel le Savage left the inn, leaving me with no one to borrow money from. I soon got behind on my bill. When I suspected the innkeeper was about to put me out, I approached him privately, and when I got his attention—which, when he saw it was me, took a long time—I assured him that I was still Knight of the Round Table in good standing and that this was only a temporary situation. So he continued to let me stay. But after several more weeks of feeding and housing me for free, he became more and more annoyed every time he saw me without money. That's when he directed Endaf, his head kitchen knave, to only serve me food after everyone else in the inn was finished. That included the lady's maid, housemaid, horsemaid, handmaid, parlormaid, chambermaid, laundrymaid, milkmaid, barmaid, nursemaid, kitchen knaves, stable boys, and even the part-time half-blind cabbage gardener. I soon was eating very little. The inn's food of the day was almost always gone before any dish got to me. On days when the inn was busy, I ate less than the head cook's stray dog, Gilgamesh.

"Out of desperation, I began visiting the stable to sneak meals from the bag of dry oats and beans that feeds my horse. That is to say, I was eating the same dry oats and beans as my horse; I wasn't actually eating out of his bag.

"My horse never ran low on dry oats and beans, because the innkeeper kept his feed bag filled to the brim. He wanted my horse in prime shape in case I grew hungry enough to sell him. To rub my situation in further, the innkeeper frequently sent Endaf to the stable to feed my horse fresh carrots and apples in front of me. So—"

"Sir Christian, please cut to the joust."

"Britta, my horse resented sharing his food with me. In fact, he resented sharing his food with another horse. He acquired that attitude in the stables of his original owner, Sir Egglame de Moated, a knight notorious for teaching horses to only look out for their own manger. With that conditioning in his background, my horse kicked me whenever I reached for his bag of dry oats and beans. In fact, just the other day, he nailed me a good one that left a large bruise on my upper right leg. Would you like to see it? It's just above the kneecap. That's because I tried to squeeze past—"

And he tried to squeeze too close past Britta who side-stepped and yelled, "Sir Christian! Please cut to the joust!"

"Britta, here comes the joust." For emphasis, Sir Christian reached down to pick up Sir Pinel le Savage's second-favorite spear. That was when he noticed that Britta had planted her right foot firmly on the wooden shaft.

He stood up, smiled weakly, and said, "There are a dozen Navarrese mercenaries staying at the inn. They're renting a large upstairs room above the ground floor, where I was now forced to sleep with the traveling herdsmen. One afternoon, as I hung around the kitchen, trying to talk Exmore, the head cook, out of a few leftovers—an old cabbage husk, an extra-stale bread trencher, or even a day-old icing spoon to lick by the cake mixes—Endaf, the head kitchen knave, walked in. He swept past me as if he didn't see me very well—and I know he did—and told Exmore that the Navarrese just signed a lucrative mercenary contract with the sheriff of Castle Perilous. They planned to celebrate with a lavish banquet in the inn's main dining room. But to enhance the condiments, they were looking for someone to prepare a fish sauce similar to something they called garum[11] back in Navarre. It would serve as a crowning touch on their bean and rice dishes.

"As soon as I heard, I stopped licking the latest day-old icing spoon and handed it back to Exmore. He wasn't expecting the messy end and got real mad when he wiped his hands on his clothes. He gave me the no-more-leftovers-for-you look, but I was already on my way out of that kitchen—"

"Like a bird who spotted a worm!" declared Uncle Sir Cecil.

"And I ran up the narrow, winding stairway to the floor with the mercenaries' room. I stopped outside the door, which looked badly scarred from being constantly hit with heavy trunks. That's where I heard voices singing a catchy Spanish song on the other side. I listened for a moment and recognized it as a popular tune by a Spanish acting family that I, uh—"

"Attempted to rescue from Sir Breuse sans Pitie?"

Sir Christian stared at Britta as she said, "You never know when one of our novices is watching and—"

---

[11] Garum was a popular fish sauce and universal topping that dated back to Roman times.

Swoosh! Britta swung a scroll past his head, which Sir Christian for once saw coming and ducked. Then he glanced over his shoulder. Once again, however, there was no one standing behind him to be thunked. But Britta's backswing thunked him on the return as she indicated with a follow-up shake of the scroll for him to cut to the joust.

He gave her a glare and replied, "Sir Breuse didn't like the happy ending to their musical play, *Job and the False Witness*, which—"

"You can tell us about another time. Once again, cut to the joust!"

"The music of the Spanish family was being sung so well by whoever was on the other side of that door that I couldn't help tapping my foot in time for a moment, but then I remembered why I was there and pounded on the wooden door panels. The voices inside stopped, and I heard whispering. After one very long minute, I heard the scraping sound of a barricade being pushed away from the other side of the door. It opened a crack, and a weasel-faced individual who looked more like a pickpocket than a soldier poked his head out. When he didn't recognize me, he pointed a rusty-pitted knife in my face that closely resembled the one Sir Pinel le Savage used to pick his teeth. It even bore traces of the same boot mud. I didn't realize there was more than one of those nasty things around. The weasel-faced soldier looked ready to pick my face with it—which would have been painful because it looked awfully dull, just like Sir Pinel's—until I uttered the magic word *garum*. His eyes suddenly grew wide. Meantime, he looked me and my clothes up and down, giving the impression he was memorizing the location of every valuable I carried—that is, if I still had any valuables to carry. Then, waving the rusty point of the knife inches from my eyes, he muttered something over his shoulder to someone prodding him with a giant spear. I didn't understand the reply in Spanish Navarrese, but after the weasel-faced soldier jerked and yelped something that sounded like 'Ouch!' (which must be the same in every language), he slowly opened the door and motioned for me to enter. Without lowering the knife, he rubbed his bottom with the other hand as he performed the amazing feat of escorting me while walking backward past the giant spearman. Weasel Face tried to distract his tormenter with glares, while his free hand tried to lift the warrior's belt purse. But the spearman plunged the spear with a *thud* between my guide's feet. With a wicked smile, he removed the spear, covering Weasel Face's feet with a cloud of splinters.

"Other soldiers in the room acted like this was normal as they also looked me over for anything that they could steal. Meanwhile, Weasel Face gave angry stares to the giant spearman as he guided me around chests, bundles, and other piles of assorted loot until he presented me to his captain. This individual, looking more like a pirate than the Saxons, lounged on a throne-like stool, playing with a jeweled knife that looked just like one I used to see hanging on the belt of Sir Palomides the Saracen. I didn't realize there was more than one of those blades in circulation either. The captain was not as large as the spearman, but he possessed one of the cruelest and most pompous faces I had ever seen. When he suddenly turned his head and stared across the room at the giant spearman, the larger man trembled as he presented arms with his giant spear—while Weasel Face smirked. It was to this captain that I made my little offer."

"And just what was your little offer?"

"In return for seven shillings,[12] plus an advance dish of beans and rice, I offered to prepare for his men's banquet a wonderful batch of—"

"Fish gravy."

"Yes, Britta, which I assured them would taste like the Navarrese version of garum, only ten times better."

"Sir Christian, does trouble look for you, or do you look for it? Think back to all the recent trouble fish gravy got you into at the Round Table. Could you possibly have considered leaving well enough alone and avoided it for a time?"

"Britta, I was desperate, and I was getting hungry for something more filling and juicy to sink my teeth into besides dry oats and beans, especially while I tried to avoid being kicked every night by my horse. I also thought, after some experimentation, that I had

---

[12] Seven schillings equals one hundred dollars in 1950s American money.

discovered a successful way of preparing my father's fish gravy recipe. So after some haggling in which the weasel-faced soldier waved his nasty knife in my face the whole time, I collected my fee from the Navarrese captain. This included all seven shillings in advance—just in case."

"Of what?"

"Why, Britta, just in case."

"Sir Christian, doesn't seven shillings seem an exorbitant amount to charge anyone, even a cruel and pompous mercenary captain, for gravy?"

"But, Britta, this is no ordinary food topping, sauce, or condiment—it's *fish gravy*, made with a secret ingredient discovered by my father. I found it all recorded in his long-lost scroll. I convinced those Navarrese that once they smothered their beans and rice with it, they would be in for a sensational surprise they would remember the rest of their lives."

Britta glanced at Uncle Sir Cecil, who was listening thoughtfully with his one good ear. As he studied Sir Christian's face with his limited vision, an amused grin spread across his face. He whispered to Britta, "Methinks his sensational surprise has caused another sensational mistake."

An amused grin likewise spread across Britta's face as she patted Uncle Sir Cecil's right hand. She spoke into his good right ear. "It's the latest in his series."

Uncle Sir Cecil whispered, "Do you think he does them deliberately?"

Britta whispered back, "Before this quest is over, we'll find out."

"What?" demanded Sir Christian.

Britta replied, "Whatever we need to achieve the object of this quest."

Uncle Sir Cecil said, "Sir Christian, in most inns we visit, the going price for one serving of gravy is a half pence. I did hear once of a special salmon sauce that went for eight pence, but it came with the whole salmon."

But Sir Christian wasn't listening to Uncle Sir Cecil as he muttered to Britta, "In short order, I described to those Navarrese the virtues of fish gravy. It got them salivating so much that they couldn't wait to rush downstairs with me to visit the kitchen. That's where their captain held a short but savage consultation with Exmore, during which he scared him a little, twisted his arm a lot (the head cook wore a sling for the next week), and even threatened him with his backup knife that looked just like one I saw hanging on the belt of Sir Breuse sans Pitie. That's when I was served the most delicious bowl of beans and rice I had tasted in months, if not years. I gobbled it down so fast that I thought I had inhaled it.

"Then I told the captain what supplies I needed from Exmore's storeroom. His men practically trampled the frantic head cook as he barely prevented them from kicking in the kitchen's supply-room door. They almost ran over him again as they carried out sacks of ingredients over his objections. The weasel-faced soldier pointed the rusty-pitted knife in Exmore's face the whole time. Meanwhile, the captain accepted my offer to cook them an immediate sample of fish gravy. I led everyone like an excited mob to the inn's main dining room, where I mounted a large cast-iron cauldron over a portable stove. After I built up a fire that was hot enough, I started cooking. Because they're Navarrese, whom I believe are cousins of the Spaniards, I used a new kind of fish. I substituted red herring for salmon. Then I threw out some of these herbs and spices, and I threw in some of those herbs and spices. I doubled the olive-oil content. Finally, I threw in just a dab of my father's secret ingredient, which I diluted according to a note I found on the bottom of his long-lost scroll."

"Which said?"

"What?"

"The note you found on the bottom of your father's long-lost scroll."

"The diluted ingredient would provide an extra-big surprise."

"Nothing else?" asked Britta.

When he didn't reply, Britta shook her head as she and Uncle Sir Cecil said, "Hmm."

Sir Christian said, "That sounded like *yum*, which the mercenaries uttered in anticipation, as the initial fish gravy results smelled absolutely wonderful. Each pair of mercenary messmates became so excited they fought with each other over who would get the first ladle. They finally decided it with a knife-throwing contest. The winner would be the one who came closest to hitting a pine knot on the far wall of the dining room."

"Who won?" asked Uncle Sir Cecil.

"Nobody really did. With the exception of the captain, who only watched, none of those mercenaries seemed to know anything about knives except how to steal them. I may not notice some things."

Britta nodded in agreement.

"But I've always had a thing for knives. Five blades, resembling those carried by Sir Pinel le Savage, Sir Sagramore le Desirous, Sir Grummore Grummursum, Sir Hector de Maris, and Sir Lionel de Ganis, got stuck in the ceiling. The next four, looking like blades I saw hanging on the belts of La Cote Male Taile, Sir Nerovens de Lile, Sir Epigrinis, and Sir Harry Fise Lake, missed Gilgamesh, the kitchen dog, by the thinnest dog hair before tearing large holes in the kitchen door. A knife resembling Sir Mador de la Porte's hit a cloak rack, and winner by default went to the mercenary who pinned the cap of Endaf, the head kitchen knave, to the far dining room wall, although nowhere near the pine knot. Now his blade looked like the one carried by Sir Dodinel le Savage. Starting with the winner by default, in mercenary grab-grub order, they greedily ladled globs of grayish fish gravy from the big, hot cauldron to cover their bowls of fresh beans and rice, after which they could hardly wait to sit down and dig in with gusto."

"And?" asked Britta with a smile of amused anticipation.

Sir Christian's eyes showed panic, shock, and unbelief as they produced the largest tears Britta had ever seen on the face of a seasoned Knight of the Round Table. He said somberly, "Britta, the results that originally looked and smelled so wonderful turned horrible. After a few satisfying chomps, every last mercenary came down with a bleached face, body-shaking spasms, and abdominal pains. They looked worse than Sir Mordred the Murderous, Sir Agravaine the Arrogant, and Sir Dagonet the fool at King Arthur's last Christmas feast.

"One by one, they moaned and groaned, and a few even foamed. But they were in too much pain to roam as they doubled over and spilled fish gravy all over themselves. This created noxious smoke, and every last one of them soon had holes appearing throughout their clothing, leather belts, and even some of their cheaper armor. The weasel-faced mercenary rose from his bench and attempted to walk. But after a few jerking steps, he had a spasm that tripped him so hard, he lunged forward, spilling his ladle into the fire beneath the cauldron. Instantaneously came a loud *Kawoom!* The room shook like it was in an earthquake—"

"Or an explosion in a small kitchen?" asked Britta.

"The inn's dining room was a lot larger than a small kitchen," Sir Christian replied painfully. "On a good day it was known to seat a small army. But a smoking gray fish gravy glob whizzed across it like it was shot out of a bombard, and actually hit that pine knot."

Britta said, "No subsequent *kaboom-karoom!* Your father's long-lost note showed you how to dilute fish gravy that much?"

"But not as much as I thought," Sir Christian said as he moved them on to the next painful point. "Britta, grayish fish gravy globs now began whizzing everywhere, hissing, smoking, and generating noxious fumes on everything they touched, even if the item wasn't flammable. They eventually caused bigger holes in the walls, doors, and furniture than the knives. Fortunately, they missed tapestries and curtains. They also missed the rushes spread around the floor. The dining room was short on them that day, or else a brush fire might have burned down the entire building. They also missed the man-size wooden platform over a hole in the middle of the dining room floor. But a shock wave toppled anyone in the room still standing, as well as launching guests on the front porch into the slime pit, where some disappeared—"

"Like a food cart going down a mudhole?" asked Uncle Sir Cecil.

Sir Christian answered Uncle Sir Cecil's good ear. "You know that line?"

Uncle Sir Cecil nodded as he replied, "If it wasn't good, I wouldn't use it."

Britta asked, "Just how bad of a fire did it cause?"

"Fortunately, not one that went out of control. The kitchen knaves smothered the flames with buckets of sand and water kept available for such emergencies. Also, the weather was wet outside, which helped. But when those mercenaries finally noticed all of the holes spreading through their clothes, leather belts, chain mail, and cheaper armor, they almost went out of control."

Britta asked, "Why almost?"

"None of them could stand up. They suffered from such severe abdominal pains that they rolled around on the floor while they uttered ugly threats about my future, impossible observations about my past, and some unbelievable suggestions on how smart my parents weren't."

"What happened to you?"

"When Weasel Face tripped, I dived under a table."

"Like the cart on the Humber?"

He nodded as his face turned fish gravy gray.

Britta asked, "What about the innkeeper?"

"He was gone. But when he returned that night, he almost erupted like a volcano!"

"With billowing clouds of fish gravy?"

Sir Christian nodded as Britta added, "Did he threaten to spit you on his sword like a pot roast?"

"If I don't pay for all of the damages to his inn."

"And just how do you plan to do that?"

"Is this where serious prayer may be the best option?"

Uncle Sir Cecil said, "This is where serious group prayer may be the best option."

Britta nodded and asked, "What happened next?"

"The innkeeper drafted a damage-control list on a scroll thicker than the one you carry with my personnel record."

"That is indeed a long scroll," agreed Britta.

"And he didn't fill it with big, long letters but he cheated by using the shortest fonts he could find. Then he took unfair advantage of the situation in other ways. In addition to dining room damage to his tables, chairs, and walls, he listed clothing damage to his lady's maid, housemaid, horsemaid, handmaid, parlormaid, chambermaid, laundrymaid, milkmaid, barmaid, nursemaid, kitchen knaves, stable boys, and even the part-time half-blind cabbage gardener, who was visiting his aunt in the next shire. Then he included bedbug holes in the bedrooms. I don't remember fish gravy causing the inn's bedbug holes. Finally, he listed smoke damage because he said the entire inn smelled like the aftermath of a Saxon fire-arrow assault, which made it reminiscent of some conditions at Caerleon and the Humber but maybe not quite as bad—except for one other thing."

"What was that?" asked Britta.

"The innkeeper also included his entire vegetable garden. He said fumes seeping through the dining room walls spoiled the edibility of everything growing within fifty feet of the inn in all directions. That included carrots, cabbages, parsnips, onions, long beans, short beans, string beans, broad beans, green beans, peas, asparagus, lettuce, and artichokes."

Uncle Sir Cecil said, "You haven't mentioned fruit trees."

"The innkeeper ran out of scroll before he got to them. But he threatened to start a new one if I don't start finding him some money."

Britta said, "Hmm."

"The innkeeper said something much worse, but offered to reduce my bill if I signed over to him ownership of my warhorse."

"Hopefully you didn't," said Britta.

"Hopefully I didn't," agreed Sir Christian. "At least I hope I didn't—hopefully." He rubbed his head again and frowned.

"Sir Christian," Britta said, "that all sounds too familiar. But one thing puzzles me. Your father's fish gravy exploded on the Humber and at the inn. But why did banquet guests mainly get sick at the Caerleon Christmas feast?"

Sir Christian shrugged. So Britta motioned for him to once more cut to the joust.

"The kitchen knaves slowly, painfully, and strenuously lugged the mercenaries on stretchers up the narrow, winding stairs to their room. But as they did, they kept tipping, tripping, and ripping the mercenaries against the narrow walls. Then the knaves entered the mercenaries' room, where they banged the warriors around some more as they stumbled over and around the various chests, bags, and piles of captured loot.

"The mercenaries were laid up in their room for the next week, during which time their moans and groans grew so loud and annoying that many travelers refused to stay at the inn longer than one night. This made me even more unpopular with the innkeeper, who gave me the no-more-equipment-for-you look, if I didn't quickly find a way to pay him for the damages.

"That's when a mysterious hermit arrived. After he showed the innkeeper the moon-shaped half of a cut silver penny, he entered the mercenaries' room and took over nursing them. I later heard from the lady's maid, housemaid, horsemaid, handmaid, parlormaid, chambermaid, laundrymaid, milkmaid, barmaid, and nursemaid— the only people in the inn still kind hearted enough to slip me bread crumbs and icing spoons when Exmore and Endaf weren't looking— that the hermit possessed a special ointment. When he applied it to the mercenaries, it healed their burns and bruises right up. But it couldn't do much for their internal pains. For that, the various maids said the hermit kneeled down and prayed."

Britta said, "A hermit's prayer can change many things, including the hearts and minds of those mercenaries toward you."

Sir Christian said, "The only thing that changed in the hearts and minds of those mercenaries toward me is where they to plan to stab me the next time they see me."

"Ouch—I mean, that's unfortunate," said Uncle Sir Cecil.

Britta said, "Sir Christian, you suggested prayer as an answer. Didn't you pray this morning for Jesu to send you help?"

Sir Christian nodded nervously.

"Well, didn't he?" she asked with a smile.

Sir Christian looked at Britta and Uncle Sir Cecil for a long, slow minute before he nodded and said, "The hermit left when the mercenaries became well enough to stand. The Navarrese didn't know quite what to make of him or even if they should look for him. But they certainly knew what they wanted to make of me."

"A pin cushion," observed Uncle Sir Cecil.

Sir Christian painfully nodded. "Only the first time they emerged from their room they appeared very thin, very bleached, and very weak. They also wore ill-fitting clothes that looked stolen from the inn's clothesline. Because of their physical weakness, the first few times they saw me, they backed off to just within earshot. There they uttered more ugly threats about my future, more impossible observations about my past, and even more unbelievable suggestions on how smart my parents weren't.

"That was until three days ago, when their leader—the cruel, pompous, and unforgiving brute they call Captain Sarito—snuck up behind me. He tapped my shoulder until I turned around. Then he pulled out a freshly sharpened knife that looked like one I saw hanging on the belt of backstabbing Sir Mordred the Murderous. He waved it in my face and then tossed it so hard that it whizzed like an arrow across the road. With a *thud*, it pinned a falling leaf to a freshly cut stake piled high with wood that one sees at an execution for someone nobody likes. Captain Sarito gave me an ugly smile as he pointed at the knife, the leaf, and the wood around the stake."

Uncle Sir Cecil asked, "Was Captain Sarito aiming the knife at the leaf, the stake, or both?"

"I don't know. At least he wasn't aiming at me—yet. He coldly crossed the road and removed the knife from the stake in such a way that it left a big, heart-shaped hole. He crumbled the leaf to dust as he gave me an uglier smile that included the no-more-safety-for-you look. Then he coldly strode back to the inn's front porch, whistling a mournful tune while waving the knife in my direction.

"As Captain Sarito disappeared inside, Endaf, the head kitchen knave, wearing clothes so full of holes they looked like cheese from the Swiss (he couldn't afford to replace them until I repaid the innkeeper), called from the inn's balcony, 'Sir Knight of the Fish Gravy in no one's good standing, I heard Captain Sarito say his men whistle that tune before a battle where they don't take prisoners.'"

"Sir Christian," said Britta, "I've never heard of mercenaries going into a battle where they don't take prisoners. Holding them for ransom is the biggest way they make extra prize money."

"Britta, maybe these Navarrese are new to the mercenary business. Their country is next to Spain, which currently isn't known for exporting soldiers, and half its population does speak Spanish. Before meeting these Navarrese, I thought the only thing people did in that small but distinguished land was run once a year with bulls and hunt large bears, when they weren't eating olives and oranges. Now, I do have fond memories of the Spanish actors I rescued."

"Attempted to rescue," Britta reminded him.

"Attempted to rescue," Sir Christian acknowledged. "I think they came from somewhere nearby, but it's in Spain."

"Sir Christian," Britta said, "don't forget the best warhorses come from Spain. Plus, how do you know that the Navarrese weren't using the word *poisoner* in their revenge song instead of *prisoner*?"

Sir Christian looked very uncomfortable as he said, "Britta and Uncle Sir Cecil, my horse, armor, weapons, and personal equipment have been impounded by the sheriff of Castle Perilous. His men locked them in the inn's stable until I pay the innkeeper the entire list of fire damages. So I vacated the inn for a few days while I worked out a solution."

"Which included standing outside the Castle Perilous, waving Sir Pinel le Savage's second-favorite spear!"

"Britta, as Knight of the Round Table in good standing—"

"Former Knight of the Round Table in good standing."

"Former Knight of the Round Table in good standing," he acknowledged. "I wielded Sir Pinel le Savage's second-favorite spear. I didn't wave it."

"With that mismatched banner-and-surcoat combination, I'm sure it looked like a lot more waving than wielding, which I'm sure made an impression on any passerby who needed a knight errant and only saw you—"

"Wielding!"

"I'll concede wielding versus waving. They saw you wielding a spear with that banner." She pointed at the offensive cloth fluttering on Sir Pinel le Savage's second-favorite spear. "Which doesn't match that outfit!" She pointed at the cheaply embroidered white crosses on his surcoat.

"You saw me wielding that first *that* while wearing that second *that.*"

"Sir Christian, when I found you outside the Castle Perilous, I saw a lot more than you think I saw. But cut to the joust! Do you realize you may be much more perilous with fish gravy than you ever were with sword, spear, knife, and horse? What if we take you just as you are to the Saxon pirate camp? I could stand outside one of their secret gates and shout, 'Drop your weapons, all you bloodthirsty Saxons, and put your hands up! Now, please turn lose my grandson, Adragain, before Sir Christian de Galis of the Round Table attacks you with his fish gravy!'"

Uncle Sir Cecil, who at times could barely hear a war arrow thud with his one good ear, laughed so hard that he bent over and brushed the ground with his helmet top, which was an amazing physical feat for someone his age. The action caused the tip of the helmet to acquire a distinct dirt smudge, which Britta noticed, and with a tidy woman's touch, she wiped it clean with a cloth she pulled, with another lightning swoosh, from a cloak pouch.

Uncle Sir Cecil never noticed as he said, "Sir Knight of the Fish Gravy, in your own special way, you are most perilous! See what a sensational mess you have gotten yourself into! However, I think you, Britta, and I can recover your horse, armor, weapons, and other equipment. We surely don't want to face the Saxons with just you and your fish gravy. Agreed, Britta?"

But Britta only looked thoughtful and said, "Hmm!"

Sir Christian said, "Britta and Uncle Sir Cecil, twelve vengeful mercenaries said something that sounded like 'Harm!' They're waiting for me—I mean us—back at my inn, where I think they want to test some freshly sharpened razor-edged weapons on me—I mean us!"

Britta snapped her cloth as she also snapped out of her thoughts and playfully poked Uncle Sir Cecil with one of her fingers. She and Uncle Sir Cecil smiled knowingly at each other, as if they were sharing a very funny inside joke.

"Don't be concerned," Britta said to Sir Christian. "Between you, Uncle Sir Cecil, and me, we shall have them off-balance, outnumbered, and surrounded."

She removed her right foot from the shaft of Sir Pinel le Savage's second-favorite spear as, with another swoosh of her cloth, which was actually a rather nice scarf, she signaled Sir Christian to pick it up.

"Oh, and, Sir Christian," she added, "please remember you are once again in service as Knight of the Round Table, even if only temporarily reinstated. Therefore, when not facing an enemy, keep the sharp end of that spear pointed in a safe direction. That's straight up, as in the direction of heaven, where I don't want you accidentally sending one of us the next time you trip."

She and Uncle Sir Cecil smiled knowingly at each other again as they took the reins of their horses and prepared to resume their fast-moving stride down the road. But Britta stopped suddenly and asked, "Sir Christian, if you were out of money, who paid the head cook for your fish gravy ingredients? Did it come out of your seven shillings?"

"I still have the seven shillings, which I intend to hang on to."

"So what did you do?"

"After the mercenaries lugged my supplies past the frantic head cook, I, uh, told him to wait a few days before sending them an invoice with a special event surcharge—to cover repairs to his door. After all, it was for their banquet."

"That they didn't have. So how much did the cook invoice the mercenaries?"

"Another seven shillings. My father's improved fish gravy recipe required high-quality ingredients."

Britta and Uncle Sir Cecil smiled at each other as they shook their heads again. Uncle Sir Cecil observed, "I think we better have that serious group prayer."

"That will make Sir Christian feel better," said Britta.

Sir Christian said, "How will it make you and Uncle Sir Cecil feel?"

Britta just smiled as Uncle Sir Cecil reminded him, "In my condition, I don't feel much of anything."

Following those supplications, which became a truly effective group prayer, they started once more down the road toward a showdown with any mercenaries awaiting them at Sir Christian's inn.

Meanwhile, their two modestly equipped horses attempted to remain calm and keep everything in stride, but they began sniffing curiously at the air that started blowing toward them from Sir Christian's cloak. Every so many horse clops, one of them turned its head toward him and his cloak with sensational interest.

This made Sir Christian eye the horses almost as nervously as the road to the inn. He followed with Sir Pinel le Savage's second-favorite spear positioned between him and them. He also kept it pointed toward heaven, where the breeze wielded—not waved—its bannerette like praying hands as they advanced toward the Inn of the Knight Perilous.

CHAPTER 9

The Results of Being Merciful

*Do you truly think the results of being merciful
to him would be so negative?*
—Wade the Scholar, *Chanson de Chrétien*

A short distance to the east stood Sir Christian's recent home and notorious knave pit, fantastically known to the locals as the Inn of the Knight Perilous. Its north-side porch and balcony overlooked an equally notorious slime pit positioned in the center of the thirteen-foot-wide dirt road that ran from the western sea past the gate of Castle Perilous before it disappeared with a *poof* into the old Roman road called Watling Street. This latter was approximately thirty miles, as the crow flies, to the east.

When a road crew failed to fill in the slime pit, a merchant complained that similar pits were appearing on roads throughout the shire, allowing unfair use of the law called groundage, which entitled the local ruler to confiscate as salvage any merchandise inside a cart if one of its axles touched the ground. That was when he disappeared into one of the pits—like a food cart going down a mudhole.

Across the road from the inn, a field had been cleared that was large enough for six hundred men to drill. On the field's edge by the road, a long, sharpened stake had been planted with sides that bristled with ugly splinters.

On this particular morning, which had all the makings of a most perilous day, eleven Navarrese mercenaries gathered on the inn's porch in a motley mob. Every one of them wore clothing that once belonged to someone else, even if it was the wrong size. They were also armed with weapons that once belonged to someone else. They waved them (not wielded—an important distinction) as they milled around their brutish leader, Captain Sarito. He was dressing down his most gravel-faced follower.

"Pedro, your new knife is not sharp enough! The test cut you made on this porch rail is a disgrace. See, the carved wood on this rail that once felt so smooth is now as jagged as a broken stick! So the blade itself must be jagged!"

Captain Sarito snatched the knife from Pedro and rubbed his thumb along the cold steel. Yet as he closely examined it, he noticed the edge felt neither jagged nor dull but gave every indication it was forged of the finest steel. It looked sharp enough to smoothly shave a man with a heavy beard.

"Ouch!" Captain Sarito cried as he shaved skin from his thumb with the blade's keen edge. He thrust the bleeding digit into his mouth and sucked noisily as he studied the knife even more closely. The name of the craftsman, Trebuchet, was engraved on the steel above the hilt, along with quotes on both sides of the long blade. Since he considered reading mainly fit for scribes, he ignored most of the writing and concentrated on the ivory handle. It was finely carved into the shape of a full-grown ram, with a face presenting a whimsical smile as its legs straddled an island it protected with its horns. Beneath its feet, the words *Isle of the Male Sheep* appeared as another example of fine engraving, which once again, he wouldn't read.

Captain Sarito was much more interested in how easy an island protected by any kind of sheep would be for his men to plunder or to at least give a good shearing. Thinking along that line, he returned the knife to Pedro and snapped the fingers on his unwounded hand as he cried, "Cordero, my most sheep like soldier!"

He stopped sucking his thumb and held it out to an individual who saluted him, looking more respectful than most of the others. Without expression or even acknowledgment of the salute, Captain Sarito watched as the soldier sheepishly yet carefully bandaged the wound. When the soldier neatly finished, Captain Sarito snapped the fingers on his good hand again, causing the man once more to salute before he stepped back.

Pedro chose this moment to speak defensively. "Captain, the jagged cut is not the knife's fault. It's Cisco's. He didn't keep the rail from shaking when I swung at it with the blade."

Cisco, his most weasel-faced follower, cringed. "Captain, I couldn't help it. Pedro swung the knife in such a way it might miss the porch rail but not me. Besides, see how flimsy this porch rail is?"

Cisco shook it back and forth several times as he added with disgust, "The last carpenter to work on this rail must have been asleep!"

But when Captain Sarito only stared, he whined, "Captain, I'm the one who lifted that knife from the old knight's belt when he wasn't looking very well. That was right after I replaced his brand-new belt pouch with my raggedy old one—after I filled it with scrap metal I lifted from the shire blacksmith when he wasn't looking very well. The foolish old knight never noticed a thing as he bragged how much his father's fish gravy tasted better than our wonderful garum. It serves him right that I stole his knife—and his pouch. I only gave the knife to Pedro after you ordered me to replace the one he lost in the tavern knife-throwing contest. Pedro never did learn to throw a knife very well."

"None of you learned to throw a knife very well," replied Captain Sarito as he retrieved the knife once more from Pedro.

"We're working on it, Captain. But it was Pedro who accused the Abblasoure archer of winning with a trick knife. When the archer argued that the only thing tricky about his knife was that he could throw it better than one of us could steal it, the resulting brawl wrecked every stick of furniture in that tavern. That's when forty guards with de Mentia, the name they give the local sheriff, broke down the remains of the front door and completely surrounded us. We were ordered to pay for all of the damages, including a hefty fine, or work like slaves in the local mines. After de Mentia cleaned us out, I barely cleaned him out—and his guards when they weren't looking very well. So why don't you make Pedro hold the porch rail while I swing the knife? Even though the blade is now his, I did all of the work to steal it."

"Cisco"—Captain Sarito addressed him patiently as if he were a child—"of course you did all of the work to steal the knife. But that's not what I really care about. As your captain, I don't care who stole the knife, I don't care who owns the knife, and I also don't care which one of you attempts to throw the knife, because—"

Captain Sarito threw the knife like a whizzing arrow into the rail by Cisco, where it quivered next to the soldier's hand after sticking with an ominous *thud*. This reminded Cisco and everyone else in the company that their captain knew how to throw one.

Pedro showered Cisco with splinters as he pulled it out, which earned a smile from Captain Sarito as he continued his lecture.

"I do care, however, who obeys my orders without question. Now, suppose one of my men would rather debate me when I tell him what to do with a knife. I might be forced to punish him severely for the sake of discipline. Surely you wouldn't want something like that to happen to you?"

Cisco hung his head and nodded meekly but not necessarily in agreement.

Captain Sarito pretended not to notice as he said, "Besides, as your captain, I'm the only one I allow giving orders in this company. Therefore, I order you, not Pedro, to hold the porch rail steady. Then if the knight's knife doesn't cut in a way that pleases me, you will be encouraged to steal Pedro a different knife—after you give me this one for safekeeping. Find another old knight who isn't looking very well and lift his. Only this time, find one that carries money in his pouch, not unpaid bills from the innkeeper's cook. You are in charge of scrounging, and it will keep you in practice."

Cisco hung his head slightly lower and nodded a little more meekly as Captain Sarito added, "Now, hold still while Pedro tests this knife with one good swing that will show just how sharp this blade really is. Then give me a report, along with the knife."

"But, Captain, what if Pedro slashes me instead of the rail?"

Captain Sarito shook his head like a condescending parent. "Cisco, if I only led soldiers like you, what could I possibly achieve? When I ask you to do something that looks painful, you reply with words like *slashes me instead of the rail.* What kind of an answer is that to a leader like me? Why can't you say something inspiring like 'No pain, no gain—to aide my captain get his fame'?"

Cisco hung his head even lower and almost seemed to grovel as he nodded more meekly. But deep inside, he thought Captain Sarito possessed no true understanding of how his men's pain contributed to his personal fame. For the moment, however, Cisco was too intimidated to do anything but keep his conclusions to himself.

Captain Sarito continued to share his own conclusions. "I need to lead soldiers who don't mind feeling a little pain—on their arm or anywhere else—for me. Otherwise, I could never hope to become a leader renowned for conquest in these foreign territories. I'd be forced to ally myself or, worse yet, intermarry with the Germans, the Saxons, the Danes, or even the British Celts. I would be forced to share with them greatness I only wish to share sparingly—with me first and then with my men."

He shook his head, believing he had made his point.

But Captain Sarito didn't really make his point until Pedro swung the knife one more time and missed the rail but not Cisco, whose arm he shaved like a bad barber.

"Aiieee!" Cisco cried as he waved his appendage—which was, fortunately, sliced only enough to be painful—in the direction of Cordero for a bandage.

Once again, Captain Sarito pretended not to notice as he stepped from the porch into the road. He looked west toward Castle Perilous, which was no longer visible because of something resembling a dust cloud, with abrasive particles starting to blow their way. He rubbed some from his face, which felt more irritating and annoying than the secondhand clothes he was forced to wear. Puzzled, he called to his lookout on the upstairs balcony, "Aquila, do you see any sign of that despicable knight?"

Aquila, who had been staring west at Castle Perilous for some time, rubbed his eyes hard when he no longer saw it and rubbed his face even harder when he began feeling the particles. He answered slowly, "I see nothing, Captain."

"Let me know the moment you see him. He must return to this inn sometime to claim his horse, armor, weapons, and equipment. Then we will repay him for the dishonor he caused us with his father's so-called fish gravy. We were still too weak when he left. But right now, we are strong enough to make him slowly and painfully pay."

Captain Sarito turned to his three largest men and watched with a cruel smile as they vandalized a corner of the porch with a variety of stolen weapons. It was difficult for him to tell which of them displayed the worst scars, tattoos, and gaudy jewelry, which clashed horribly with the secondhand clothing they had chosen to wear. But he didn't care as long as they obeyed his orders without question.

He addressed the tallest one, who had just split an ornate floorboard with the barbs on his eight-foot spear. "Rogerio, my number-one enforcer, what will you do to the Knight of the Fish Gravy?"

"Captain, I will rearrange his kneecaps with my spear shaft— like so!" With a growl, Rogerio ripped the spear loose from the floorboards in such a way that it left a large, shredded hole. Then he swung its weaver's beam of a shaft around his head before smashing it down on a large, expensive flowerpot. Fragments showered everyone on the front porch.

An annoyed Captain Sarito brushed pottery, flower stems, and dirt from the arm with his wounded thumb before he turned to the shortest of the three. This gruesome gnome of an individual practiced jumping up and down while attempting to knock insects out of the air with his club. He wasn't successful—with hitting the insects, that is—and Captain Sarito barely dodged one of the club's spikes. The captain frowned as he asked, "Arrio, my number-two enforcer, what will you do to the Knight of the Fish Gravy?"

"Captain, I'll jump up and down on his toes until he can't jump up and down on them, and then"—he twirled his club around his head with an overhand swoosh as he shouted even louder—"I'll give them love taps with this!"

Arrio missed more insects as he hammered the spiked end of the club into another expensive flowerpot. It wasn't the one he aimed at or even one that was near it. But with cruel satisfaction, he smacked the one he did hit like an elephant cracking an egg. Once again, pieces of pottery, dirt, and flower stems showered everyone on the front porch.

A disgusted Captain Sarito shook his head as he brushed more fragments off his arm with the wounded thumb as he turned to his third brute, a block-shaped individual who resembled granite holding up the side of a building. "Bernardo, my number-three enforcer, what will you do to the Knight of the Fish Gravy?"

"Captain, I will dot his eyes with his elbows."

"What if his elbows don't reach that far?"

"Captain, I will make sure his elbows reach that far—after I squeeze them like this!" And Bernardo flexed gigantic, bearlike fingers as he picked up the ornate flowerpot Arrio had actually aimed at. He crushed this masterpiece of floral pottery with his calloused hands until it shattered like another egg, once again showering everyone on the front porch with pottery, dirt, brush, and flower stems. But Bernardo wasn't finished until he squeezed the fragments that remained in his hands with a horrible crunching sound until they sifted through his fingers like fine dust. Those frightful digits looked more than able to rearrange Sir Christian's middle-aged elbows.

A now extremely annoyed Captain Sarito brushed a third layer of pottery, dirt, brush, and flower stems off his arm with the wounded thumb before he addressed the rest of his men, hoping there were no more flowerpots within their range. "Alvaro, Berto, Tulio, Cordero, and Currito, my other soldiers, are your preparations also complete?"

"Yes, Captain," said Currito. "We sharpened everything: our swords, our spears, our axes, our knives, and even our arrows, as well as additional swords, spears, axes, knives, and arrows Cisco stole from owners in the inn when they weren't looking very well. We also covered the stake we planted across the road with barbed splinters."

"You didn't waste money paying for that stake?"

"Captain, why should we waste money paying for something," Currito replied gleefully, "that we're only going to burn? But before we get that far, especially before we tickle the Knight of the Fish Gravy with the nasty splinters on the sides of the stake, let's tie his feet to the back of our largest warhorse, depending, of course, on which of us currently owns the largest and most ill-tempered warhorse."

"Currito!" Captain Sarito interrupted. "As commandant of this company, may I remind you that only I may own the largest and most ill-tempered warhorse."

"Pardon, my captain! I forgot! So do you want us to tie his feet to our second-largest and most ill-tempered—"

"Currito! My largest and most ill-tempered warhorse will do just fine, providing I'm riding it when the knight is dragged until he resembles gravy! Just remember that in this company, only I may be associated with what is largest and most ill-tempered."

"Yes, my captain, which is what I tell the men every time you pay them. It helps them remember how generous of a leader you truly are."

For the first time Captain Sarito nodded approvingly as Currito continued. "So, Captain, you drag the Knight of the Fish Gravy with your largest and most ill-tempered warhorse around the inn three times to warm up. Then we'll fasten him to the stake for heavy-weapons practice, which I—"

Currito drew his sword and with a horrendous *ca-smack!*—whacked still another expensive, ill-fated flowerpot. Once again, everyone on the porch got showered with dirt, pottery, brush, and flower stems, except Captain Sarito, who stepped behind Cisco as he opened his mouth.

Spitting, choking, and gagging, the weasel-faced soldier looked desperately for anything holding water to steal, which he solved by draining the nearest watering bucket, with floating stems, dead insects, and all. Checking to see if anyone was looking very well, he then slid the bucket inside his stolen shirt.

But the other soldiers were watching Currito smash still another flowerpot, which showered even more debris on everyone, except the captain, who this time jumped behind Pedro—who knew when to keep his mouth shut. After shaking the residual dust, stems, and other flowerpot debris off his sword, Currito sheathed it as he sneered with a wicked smile, "Am looking forward to. And now for the finale—if you so direct—we will light a fire under that fool of the fish gravy and slowly heat him up until he looks as sickening as the dish he served us."

"Currito," Captain Sarito said, "I salute you for thinking like me! Keep it up and I'll put you in charge of new recruits."

"But, Captain, since you've been in charge, we've never had any new recruits."

"Currito, that's because I'm still establishing my renown. When I get the military reputation I truly deserve, people will come in droves to glimpse all of us. Then there should be plenty of new recruits, and I will put you in charge. So I agree. We'll do all of those things to that foolish Knight of the Fish Gravy. But first, check his clothes for his ingredients. We can't allow them near any fire we ignite under him. Any further questions, my soldiers?"

"Your pardon, Captain," said Cordero uncomfortably as he finished tying a clean rag around the arm of Cisco. "Are you sure we need to get revenge on this poor old knight? I talked it over with Alvaro and Berto, and we decided this was just an accident. We also talked it over with the local padre, who prayed with us, which gave us much peace. He suggested we simply forgive the knight and ask him to repay us some money for the damages."

"This old knight has no money to repay us for the damages!" roared Captain Sarito. "Didn't you foolish ones see the patches on his clothes? Don't you remember the way he gobbled down the bowl of beans and rice we placed in front of him?"

"But, Captain, maybe if we ask him kindly, he'll return those seven silver coins you paid him," suggested Cordero meekly.

"As well as that other seven silver coins we were invoiced by the head cook for his ingredients!" roared Captain Sarito. "Shall we ask him kindly for those too? Rather, let's ask him unkindly! But it still wouldn't be enough to repay us for the damage he has done—not just to our money and equipment but also to our military reputations.

"I train you to be professional soldiers who fight for hire. What do you think will happen if word gets out that a bankrupt middle-aged knight laid up all twelve of us without consequences? Why, no ruler, noble, or warlord within six days' travel of this place will ever rehire us! We would be called fools and treated as a laughing stock everywhere we go! We might even end up begging for beans and rice like this Knight of the Fish Gravy! Enough! As captain, I know what's best for this troop. We will take our revenge on him—publicly!"

Cordero courageously spoke up one more time. "Your humble pardon, Captain. Do you truly think the results of being merciful to him would be so negative? On the other hand, we three feel no good will befall if we're unmerciful to him."

"Cordero! Alvaro! Berto! Enough! I don't pay you to feel! And I certainly don't pay you to hand out mercy! I only pay you to fight! And today you shall fight! And you will help us take our revenge on this Knight of the Fish Gravy! Enough!"

Cordero and his two companions nodded sadly as they hung their heads submissively. But inside their consciences, not one of them felt anything good would come from Captain Sarito's unforgiving decision.

Captain Sarito, on the other hand, looked at those three with disdain. He thought about how well they lived up to their names. He swore all three had sheep like attitudes that occasionally got in the way of his attempt to lead them and, when he saw fit, bully and push them around.

Eight of his mercenaries were easy enough for him to control, because they looked at life pretty much as he did. They acknowledged him as captain by virtue of his being the strongest and wisest in the ways of the world. Aquila, whose name aptly meant "eagle," had the sharpest eyes in the group and agreed with Sarito on his philosophical vision. So he operated as Captain Sarito's chief scout, spy, and lead crossbow archer. Pedro, whose name meant "the rock" (and whose face looked more like trampled gravel), and Cisco, whose name meant "free" (and whose face resembled a weasel), agreed with his philosophy on provisioning—or, as he called it, getting the most supplies at the lowest bargain prices, which, to him, almost always meant for free. So he put them in charge of weapons, equipment, and supplies. That meant when money was low, they had the job of scrounging for all of them. But they also scrounged when money wasn't low and they could pay. That was when Cisco, who was notoriously brainless and spineless in other ways, really lived up to the meaning of his name. Cordero, on one conscience-troubled occasion, had dared to say that in Cisco's case, *free* frequently rhymed with the word *thieve*. This remark had made its way back to Captain Sarito, who had threatened Cordero with a severe thrashing after subjecting him to humiliating insults in front of the other men.

Rogerio's name meant "famous spearman," Arrio's meant "warlike," and Bernardo's meant "brave as a bear." These three epitomized Captain Sarito's attitude and philosophy "Might really makes it right" and served as his bodyguards. They also operated as his designated enforcers. Whenever Captain Sarito needed thugs to lean on an opposing liege lord's subjects but didn't need everyone, he sent them. Bernardo, in particular, it was said, could outwrestle any thirteen-hundred-pound brown bear from his home mountains in Navarre. Captain Sarito's remaining recruits of like mind were Currito, whose name meant "to enclose," and Tulio, whose name meant "lively." They admired Captain Sarito and were primarily along for the adventure.

The remaining three mercenaries differed because they each possessed a bothersome conscience. Therefore, they often thought about things Captain Sarito would rather they left alone. He had only recruited them because he needed three more men, and he knew they had let themselves be recruited because they weren't sure how to find something better. As a result, he didn't like them and despised their names. Cordero, in complete innocence, had once told him his name meant "little lamb." He came from religious parents who had gotten the name from their local priest, who had convinced them that in the Bible, it was the name of a mighty warrior. Since Captain Sarito wasn't religious and avoided priests whenever he could, he wasn't sure he believed that. Rather, he thought "little lamb" sounded weak, if not downright sissyish for a soldier. He was extra hard on Cordero as a result. Captain Sarito had never met Cordero's parents, because they primarily associated with religious people, which, of course, excluded him.

Alvaro had told Captain Sarito his name meant "wisdom and justice," which he claimed his parents were known for back in Navarre. But Captain Sarito knew Alvaro's parents. He also knew that other people like himself, whom he considered to be the only truly wise and just people of the world, always took advantage of them. Thus, to him, Alvaro's name was meaningless, and he considered him just another sheep like Cordero. In Captain Sarito's opinion, they both needed someone to periodically shear them, and he concluded that person might as well be him.

Captain Sarito had laughed outrageously when he heard Berto's name meant "noble and bright." He was the son of an unemployed scholar in Navarre whom Captain Sarito thought was anything but noble or bright. Rather, he was unsuccessful and naive. Captain Sarito looked on Berto, the scholar's son, the same way as the other two. He was just a third sheep.

All of Captain Sarito's soldiers came from the same part of Spanish-speaking Navarre, where Sarito grew up as the son of a mighty man-at-arms who never quite earned his knighthood. His father was called old Sarito, which was Spanish for "old Caesar." Old Sarito liked to model himself after the original Caesars and saw himself as a potential conqueror waiting for the right chance to replace anyone in power, including his liege lord. Therefore, there was always something challenging, insubordinate, and usurping about him. This, of course, made his current liege lord, Count Sancho the Severe, mistrust him. But because of his strong personality and military prowess, his lord was willing to let him train the new recruits who came from the peasants—but nothing more. Old Sarito passed these characteristics on to his son, young Sarito, who never understood why they held back his father's promotion. But he knew their liege lord disliked him even more than his father. So when old Sarito finally died, the liege lord started breathing down hard on young Sarito's neck, wanting him to knuckle under to authority much more than his father had ever done.

That was when young Sarito heard of a passing mercenary company that had just completed service in King Arthur's war against the emperor of Rome. When the captain advertised for replacements, young Sarito approached him with a deal. He knew everyone his age in the local community, so he promised to get the captain all the new recruits he needed, provided he was placed in charge of them. When the captain agreed for lack of a better offer, Sarito ruthlessly went to work on his boyhood neighbors. He applied everything he had ever learned as his father's understudy in trickery, manipulation, and coercion, and in the end, he persuaded several dozen local recruits to join this mercenary company.

For the next few years, they fought small wars throughout Spain, France, Italy, and Germany—until one watershed day, when the mercenary captain was sensationally killed in battle. One soldier, who mysteriously disappeared the next day, said it was due to a military mistake made by the younger Sarito. The soldier also swore—and it was the last thing he ever swore—that Sarito had constantly challenged the late commander's judgment and decisions. When the survivors of the troop couldn't agree on a replacement leader—and most of them refused to serve under Sarito—the company disbanded. Some of them joined other mercenary companies, and others returned home. That's when Sarito gathered his eleven surviving neighbors and, through more trickery, persuasion, and bullying, made them organize a new company with him as their captain.

They spent another three years on mainland Europe, where the self-appointed Captain Sarito specialized in helping big nobles push around little nobles. He always considered that less risky and more profitable than the other way around. During one campaign, a soldier from an allied mercenary company made the mistake of telling Captain Sarito in front of his men that God wouldn't favor their cause if they continued that way. He mysteriously disappeared the next day. Meanwhile, Captain Sarito told his men that if there truly was a God, which he personally doubted, he was on the side of the big companies. Thus, Captain Sarito never signed them to a new mercenary contract until he first checked out which side in a dispute had the most men. Occasionally, he also checked out which side was willing to pay the most money—but he still never signed with the weaker side. He only wanted to know if its people looked wealthy and weak enough for easy looting.

Then they were hired to guard the stock of a Spanish wine merchant on its way by ship to Cardigan, in Sugales, or South Wales. During the voyage, when the wine merchant wasn't looking very well, Captain Sarito and his eight kindred-spirited soldiers severely depleted the stock. When the merchant finally noticed his unusually low wine levels, he refused to pay them their fee for protecting the cargo. However, Captain Sarito tricked the merchant into thinking the missing wine had been left behind in Spain.

Because this meant no free wine on a return voyage to Spain, Captain Sarito and his men deserted the ship in Sugales. He briefly considered signing them to a contract in nearby Gore when he met its dubious ruler, Sir Meliagrance, just before he met his fate with Sir Lancelot. Captain Sarito initially admired Sir Meliagrance as a kindred spirit, but luckily for him and his men, he quickly saw through Sir Meliagrance as one much more slippery than he ever hoped to be. He discovered that Sir Meliagrance only pretended to offer recruitment to him and his men but was really looking for foreign prisoners to populate his lands.

That was when Captain Sarito entered his men into an orchard dispute in Stranggore in which he almost bankrupted two contending nobles. He kept switching sides and raising his fees until one day, both enraged nobles caught on. They forgot their differences and joined forces, making open preparations to attack him. He took the hint and quickly force-marched his men out of the area. They headed to North Wales, or Norgales, where they got wind of a cattle dispute near the shire of Castle Perilous. But the disagreement was settled peacefully before they arrived. The feuding heirs might have heard they were on the way, along with their reputation for bleeding an area dry. Captain Sarito and his men supported themselves for several months with secret raids on nearby shires and traveling merchants, when they landed a lucrative mercenary contract with the sheriff of Castle Perilous. This also led them to their fateful encounter with—

"Sir Christian de Galis!" called out Aquila from the inn's balcony.

Captain Sarito's thoughts immediately returned to the present as he heard Aquila call out again, "Captain, I see Sir Christian de Galis approaching. But he's not coming from the west like we expected."

"What?"

CHAPTER 10

A Steady Archer
Never Misses

A steady archer never misses—when the right lady aims his bow!
—Wade the Scholar, *Chanson de Chrétien*

"What!" repeated Captain Sarito.

"He approaches from the east," said Aquila, "and he does it in such a way that no matter where we look, the sun will be in our eyes."

"When you returned from your predawn scout, you said he was standing outside Castle Perilous, which, unless a magician moved it in the last two hours, still stands to the west of us."

"Captain, he *was* standing outside Castle Perilous, which—" Aquila looked west and rubbed his eyes extra hard. "Captain, how hard is it for a magician to move a castle in two hours?"

"What!" repeated Captain Sarito.

"Not *what*, Captain, but *where!* The castle is no longer there!"

"Aquila, a castle doesn't disappear with a loud *poof!*"

"Loud poof, low poof, or no poof, Captain, this castle is gone! But the tree I hid behind remains. That's where I watched him wave, not wield—an important distinction—a secondhand spear in front of the gate. He gestured with it wildly as he talked to the thin air."

"Are you sure he wasn't talking to himself?"

"It looked more like he prayed to God for his luck to change."

"Aquila, only actions make our luck change."

"Captain, something has changed!" Aquila looked back toward the east. "And it may be more than a castle. Sir Christian approaches on foot with two strangers. One leads a horse. But the other"—Aquila rubbed his eyes extra hard in the glaring sunlight to make sure he was seeing right—"has a horse leading him!"

"What do they look like?"

"As best I make out"—Aquila squinted with extra effort to see through the glare of the sun—"the one led by the horse hangs on to its side like he can't see very well. Yet he is clad like an archer who shows no difficulty keeping pace with his horse and the person leading the other horse. Hmm, even from this distance, he looks as old as Methuselah, which makes him the first adult I've seen in this realm who doesn't appear thirty years old. If he truly is of such an advanced age, his eye trouble may include a blind spot somewhere in front of him."

"Aquila, how do you know things like that?"

"Captain," the lookout replied proudly, "I was taught by my father, who always said it was better to observe than to simply see. He also explained to me in great detail the science and mechanics of how eyes worked. In this subject, he was most passionate, having studied every known piece of knowledge written by Aristotle, Galen, and Pliny. He named me Aquila because he wanted me to have good eyes—like Aquila the eagle. He said that is the only bird that can see while looking directly into the sun."

"Then I suggest that you live up to your name, Aquila the eagle, and tell me more of these strangers you see approaching while looking directly into the sun."

Aquila nodded as he squinted into the glaring light. "Captain, the other stranger is a tall, slender woman in a dark red cloak with a covered hood. By its style and manner of subtle bulges, it must be full of pouches containing scrolls. Yet despite its size, content, and elusive weight, she walks smoothly, confidently, and aggressively. She is clearly the person in charge."

Aquila continued his difficult squinting, of which he was doing an excellent job under the circumstances, which further reflected his father's training. He was amazed at what he saw next.

"Captain, the woman has pulled back her hood, allowing me to see every detail of her head and face. It looks timeless, classically oval, and powerful. As I have observed more than once in this country, where people seem to live as long as trees, she may be as young as a girl or as old as a grandmother. But the reddish tint in her hair hints she is older. Yet she walks faster than most people and certain breeds of horses. In that way, she resembles my favorite grandmother, Maria, whom I hope is alive, strong, and well in our native Navarre."

Aquila was now so fascinated with the appearance of Britta that he failed to see his captain's growing impatience. He droned, "Captain, she's close enough to where I can perceive her minutest details. I'm certain she's using hair dye to make herself look younger. Yet for some reason, she doesn't look all that bad—I mean old—to me."

"Aquila! If you make one more report like that, I may doubt you can see into the sun like your namesake, the eagle! Castles disappearing! Mysterious strangers, one who can't see while being led by a horse, and the other who is an attractive older woman! I'm ready to replace you as scout and lookout with someone like Cisco!"

That was an insult, but there was nothing Aquila could do about it at the moment. Yet he would remember those words, and a chance might come later.

Captain Sarito gave him a severe look before he turned to his other men and said, "Everyone, get into position. What is about to happen will not take long."

Captain Sarito's ten mercenaries on the ground stretched out across the road like a secondhand clothesline. This caused snickers from spectators who began emerging from the inn, making Captain Sarito frown.

Meanwhile, his men blocked the entrance to the inn as they positioned themselves at standard military intervals, with enough space between each for effective sword swinging—or use of whatever weapon he liked to smack his opponents with.

The twelfth mercenary, Aquila, remained on the inn's balcony but with his finger off the trigger of his loaded crossbow. He did not raise it at Britta as he watched her almost hypnotically. She contained an element that puzzled and intrigued him. It caused a nagging thought in the back of his mind that he was seeing something strangely familiar. The feeling had to do with eyes, his pet subject of study; this woman's unusual cloak; and, of all things, a big brown bear. Then it came to him.

During the wine voyage from Spain to Wales, he became friendly with a Navarrese huntsman named Thibault. One day, while the ship wallowed extra slowly through an almost calm sea, Thibault invited Aquila to visit the ship's stern, where the huntsman showed him a canvas-covered cage fastened down with extra heavy cables. Thibault undid one corner of the canvas and carefully lifted it so that they could see inside. But he immediately stepped back as a gigantic brown bear lunged at them with a growling rumble. It battered the bars of the cage with gigantic claws that tried to reach through and lacerate them. There was a sharp crack as one of the bars weakened, but not enough for concern, although the bear's blows vibrated throughout the ship.

Aquila remembered hearing those same growling rumbles and battering sounds the day before. A Welsh archer who was escorting Thibault to the infamous Castle Abblasoure, where no one says *mass*, gave the other passengers a wicked smile as he said the sounds came from none other than the Monster-of-Unheard-of-Savageness. It supposedly prowled these waters this time of year, seizing and devouring sailors like an eagle grabbing fish. It also plucked bathers from the sandy beaches and swallowed them like turtle eggs.

He then stared unexpectedly at Cisco and let out a monstrous roar of his own. With a shriek, Cisco shot himself through the air like a catapult rock, where he performed an amazing ninety-degree turn while doing a somersault that landed him behind a group of wealthy passengers with a sensational *thud*.

Captain Sarito shook his head, saying the noises indicated a storm somewhere over the horizon. He roughly pushed his way through the passengers to shake Cisco in a manner reminiscent of the Monster-of-Unheard-of-Savageness. But he changed his mind when his henchman presented him with a sly, sleazy, and wicked smile while giving a thumbs-up to the Welsh archer. Then he slipped Captain Sarito several heavy purses he removed from the wealthy passengers while they weren't looking very well, including two from the unconscious merchant he landed on. Captain Sarito nodded as he slipped them inside his own cloak before he shook his head again and sneered, "I must have been mistaken."

Thibault and Aquila watched the bear lunge at them again and again in a manner that might have frightened the Monster-of-Unheard-of-Savageness. Finally, the huntsman slid the heavy canvas back over the cage, which quieted the bear down. He told Aquila he didn't want to get it too riled up, because he had been offered a handsome reward. All he had to do was deliver it, intact and undamaged, to Sir Arthfrel[13] of Castle Abblasoure in Wales. In return, he would receive as much money as he would get for ten ordinary bears from anyone else. It was an offer he couldn't refuse, but he was forced to take extra precautions. This particular brown bear had an unusual dislike for people and had already maimed one careless assistant who tried to pet it like a dog. The bear, who was unusually powerful for his breed, had then demolished his first cage by pounding it to pieces with its paws. Thus, Thibault had named him Battering Ram.

"Despite the bear's disposition, tremendous rage, and power," Thibault told Aquila, "I captured it in a most unusual way. It fled terrified down a mountainside in Navarre, when it slid into one of my bear pits—like a food cart going down a mudhole."

"That line gives a vivid description," said Aquila.

"If it wasn't good, I wouldn't use it," agreed Thibault.

"Do you know what scared the bear?"

---

[13] Bear king.

"A peasant said it ran from a woman in a dark red cloak after she stared at it. I didn't believe him until such a woman rode by and almost scared *me* with her stare—until she changed it into a harmless-looking smile that was even scarier. She saluted me with a scroll that she drew from her cloak faster than the average knight can touch his sword hilt. Then she sheathed it just as quickly and continued down the mountain. But while the bear sensed her presence, its rumbling growls became shaky moans and groans."

His thoughts returning to the inn, Aquila thought of the huntsman, the bear, and the woman as he looked down the road at Britta, who caught his eye with her own look that appeared harmless—and simultaneously not harmless. He almost dropped the crossbow as another thought nagged him. He remembered lessons his father had taught him about prayer providing another way to see. Aquila wondered what they were about to see as the result of prayers by the Knight of the Fish Gravy.

Britta prepared to show them from a short bow shot away.

She knew they had Captain Sarito's men off-balance and knew that they knew it, except possibly Captain Sarito, who, from what she could see, looked off-balance to begin with. She thought he was about to sink—or, as she liked to say, *think*—to his own level.

To seize this initiative, she and Uncle Sir Cecil had steered Sir Christian around the inn on a little-known forest path she discovered years earlier when they guided Nimue to the rescue of King Arthur from the evil sorceress Annowre.

Because they traveled at Britta's normal walking speed, which was faster than most people and certain breeds of horses, they approached the inn with the morning sun glaring hard into the eyes of their opposition.

Sir Christian unexpectedly yelled, "Hah!" on Britta's right. With a clink of mismatched armor pieces, whether he would admit it or not, he waved, not wielded—a truly important distinction—Sir Pinel's second-favorite spear in a circle around his head. Then he swung the razor-sharp point toward the Navarrese, except its square-shaped banner caught the only overhead tree branches in the area. Amid a shower of leaves and twigs, he turned around and around until he twisted the spear free. He fell backward as his legs tangled around the shaft. Then he quickly regained his footing and smiled weakly toward Britta—except he no longer saw her or anyone else. Behind his back, she said, "Sir Christian, you're facing the wrong direction."

He spun around and said, "I was confusing the enemy."

Britta stared at the Navarrese, who were staring at the hole Sir Christian had left in the overhead foliage, and said, "You were successful. Have you ever thought of going on a quest to trim tree branches?"

On her left, Uncle Sir Cecil couldn't see the enemy either, but he positioned himself so that his poorly-sighted, half-deaf, solo-nostril-searching presence didn't give anything away, as he appeared to look harmless.

The two horses had also been trained not to give anything away as they likewise looked harmless—unless someone got too close and they growled at him in horse-language. They stood patiently behind their riders, ready for rapid remount. But an alert enemy might have noticed they were becoming increasingly distracted by whatever was blowing past them from Sir Christian's cloak. Fortunately, they weren't facing an alert enemy.

Britta adjusted Uncle Sir Cecil's crisscross belts as she spoke into his good right ear. "I replaced your war arrows with a fresh bag of blunt tipped."

Sir Christian asked in surprise, "Britta, aren't blunt-tipped arrows only used for hunting small birds in high trees?"

"Sir Christian," she explained patiently, "Uncle Sir Cecil and I have adapted such arrows for our special use. In my normal role as liaison between Myrddin, King Arthur, and Nimue, the British Lady of the Lake, I travel around the realm while I deliver messages; assist knights, especially those who pray for assistance; and try to look harmless. That's because I and my retinue are sworn to protect, serve, and save from harm the humanity of this island, not eliminate it. Also, we are on an authorized Round Table quest, and the primary objective of such must never be the slaughter of anyone—including brainless foreign mercenaries. Besides, you started it. Those soldiers purchased your father's exorbitantly priced fish gravy because they desired something similar to their native dish of garum to eat on their beans and rice. So why should they suffer excessively for *your* mistake? Some pain and suffering may be necessary, however, to teach them a little lesson in forgiveness. But you, on the other hand, need to learn a little lesson on what to do with your father's fish gravy before you accidentally kill somebody with it. There's also more to see in this situation than you think you see. So have faith. Uncle Sir Cecil and I know what we're doing."

"Are you sure?"

"Are you?" Britta turned to Uncle Sir Cecil. "I have you pointed at the captain. His men are deployed in a standard infantry line to his left. Call out, and ask him if we may pass through their line in peace. If he and his men refuse, raise your bow for Stratagem B."

"Stratagem B?" muttered Sir Christian.

"Stratagem B," explained Britta, "refers to the first letter in the word *blunt*. It directs Uncle Sir Cecil to shoot the blunt-tipped arrows in such a way that those mercenaries are merely stunned. Based on the same system, we also have stratagem A."

"What's Stratagem A?"

"*A* represents the first letter in the word *awful*. That's when Uncle Sir Cecil shoots arrows from the warhead bag that are *awful* sharp. Stratagem A is only used on one of our quests as a last resort."

"And what do you consider a last resort?" pressed Sir Christian.

"A last resort is, well, a very last resort for anyone we use those arrows on. So even though we carry sufficient bags of arrows tipped for hunting and war, we mostly use them to scare enemies into avoiding us."

Uncle Sir Cecil nodded to Britta as he politely called to the Navarrese, "Sirs, may we pass through your line in peace?"

"I have you pointed at the captain."

Captain Sarito was in an ugly mood that day. It might have been because of the secondhand clothes in which he and his men appeared ridiculous. It might also have been because of the laughter he and his men heard from the people who continued to emerge from the inn and the surrounding shire—when they thought he couldn't hear them very well. Or it might have been because of the exorbitant price he paid Sir Christian for his father's fish gravy, plus the subsequent invoice from the inn's head cook. Whatever the reason, he wasn't thinking wisely or calmly when he replied. Maybe if he had counted to ten first, he would have said something less volatile, and the encounter might have ended another way. As it was, he said the wrong thing in the wrong way at the wrong time. "Ill-sighted knave of an ancient archer! You and the lady of the loathly hair may pass after you give us that even bigger knave of the fish gravy!"

Captain Sarito drew his sword as a signal to his ten men on the road. Rogerio brandished his spear. Arrio swung his club. Bernardo and the rest drew their swords. They advanced in a ragged attempt to move as one. But they still remained weak from fish gravy aftereffects. They also looked harpooned and lampooned from comments erupting from the crowd. The mob grew larger and even more boisterous as swarms of humanity continued to emerge from the inn and just about everywhere else in the nearby shire. Everyone hoped to see a good show, and the mercenaries, with their ill-fitting clothes, mismatched weapons, secondhand equipment, and arrogant attitudes, indicated that a rare performance was about to begin.

Captain Sarito attempted to respond to the tumultuous din of boos, catcalls, and hisses that he and his men were attracting. Trying hard to keep his sword from shaking as it pointed toward Sir Christian, he announced for all to hear, "Right is on the side with the most men!"

A voice in the crowd jeered, "So what keeps most men from doing what is right?"

Another voice added, "Right is also on the side of a lady who looks harmless!"

The crowd's remarks provided Captain Sarito with a perilous frown as his men continued their uneven advance toward Sir Christian.

In the meantime, Britta provided the mercenaries with a perilous look that wasn't harmless as she swooped her cloak across her horse's saddle. Slipping back behind Uncle Sir Cecil with war in her eyes, she spoke into his good ear. "He called you an ill-sighted knave!"

"I am an ill-sighted knave."

"And he said I have loathly hair!"

"I never noticed that you have loathly hair."

"You wouldn't notice if you could notice! But it's not as loathly as theirs is going to look! Quick, Uncle Sir Cecil! Before they seize Sir Christian! Raise your bow to offhand archer position!"

Someone near the inn yelled, "The archer's going to shoot!" There was a *thump* as the crowd prayerfully hit the ground—shaking it halfway to Navarre in one direction and all the way across Ireland in the other.

But it didn't shake Britta as she aimed Uncle Sir Cecil. "Your elevation is two notches up, and windage is three notches right. Your balance weights are adjusted. Start shooting left to right at the captain as I feed the arrows!"

There was a blur as she and Uncle Sir Cecil rolled like thunder flashing with lightning. *Thud! Thud! Thud! Thud! Thud! Thud! Thud! Thud! Thud! Thud! Thud!*

Captain Sarito and his Navarrese never knew what hit them. As they bounced along the dust, Britta couldn't resist looking up and giving Aquila a loud, "Youuuuuu-heh-heh-heh!"

She addressed Uncle Sir Cecil's good ear. "Go sideways left one half step, adjusting your bow one notch upward. When you feel the arrow on the string, hit the lookout on the balcony before he remembers his finger sits on the trigger of a loaded crossbow!"

There was a twelfth *thud* as an arrow smacked Aquila between the helmet and the eyes. He staggered backward before pitching headfirst over the balcony rail. Fortunately for him—but not anyone near the slime pit—he landed in it like a food cart going down a mudhole. A moment later, he reappeared smelling like a gardé robe pit, along with everyone he soaked. Then he gasped and collapsed over the pit's side.

Sir Christian waved Sir Pinel's second-favorite spear past Uncle Sir Cecil's neck as he exclaimed, "Twelve shots! Twelve hits! I've never seen shooting like that!"

"Neither have I," answered Uncle Sir Cecil, oblivious to the whizzing weapon. "I've had bad eyes for ten, I mean fifteen, or maybe twenty going on fifty-five years, I think."

"How does that make you feel?" Sir Christian asked as Sir Pinel's second-favorite spear whizzed by the archer again.

Uncle Sir Cecil reminded him, "In my condition, I don't feel much of anything."

"A steady archer never misses—when the right lady aims his bow!" Britta said as she whacked Sir Pinel's second-favorite spear away from Uncle Sir Cecil's shoulders with one hand while pulling her cloak back around hers with the other.

She grabbed the reins of her mount and said, "Let's find the innkeeper and pay the bill for Sir Christian's horse, armor, equipment, and weapons."

Turning her back on them, she headed toward the inn with her stride that once again continued to be faster than that of most people and certain breeds of horses.

Sir Christian, hanging on to Sir Pinel's second-favorite spear, and Uncle Sir Cecil, hanging on to the side of his horse, started after her in what once again almost resembled a pursuit.

As they passed the mercenaries, who were ungracefully sprawled in all directions, Sir Christian called to Britta, "What of them?"

Britta didn't answer as she drew the cut half of a silver penny and waved it at someone approaching. Sir Christian recognized the hermit who had nursed the Navarrese walking toward them with a stride that was also faster than that of most people and certain breeds of horses.

CHAPTER 11

Nothing Gets by Adragain

Nothing gets by Adragain, especially when he prays.
—Wade the Scholar, *Chanson de Chrétien*

The hermit also waved the cut half of a silver penny.[14] When he reached Britta, he matched his with hers, while his other hand pushed the razor-sharp tip of Sir Pinel le Savage's second-favorite spear upward toward heaven. "Where I don't want you accidentally sending me," he said cautiously to Sir Christian, "in case of—Aiieee!"

Sir Christian tripped over the nearest Navarrese, planting the spear butt hard into the hermit's nearest big toe. The hermit hopped around Sir Christian in agony, attempting to store his half of the coin as he addressed Britta while she calmly stored hers. "I pray that you're an answer to that knight's prayers!"

"Before he accidentally kills someone?" she asked.

Sir Christian, attempting nonchalantly to hold the spear in a safe position, grumbled, "I want to see the other answers."

Britta said, "They aren't available today!"

The hermit said amid gasps while favoring his foot, "You may wish they were when the shorthanded sheriff of Castle Perilous learns you laid up all twelve of his hard-to-find replacements."

---

[14] Note: In this story waving money around doesn't mean the same as waving a sword or spear.

Britta quipped, "Right after Sir Christian laid them up?"

The hermit moaned. "And right after he almost laid me up!"

Uncle Sir Cecil, with his good ear aimed like an arrow, said, "Then let's pray the sheriff disappears before we do."

"With a loud poof?" the hermit asked cryptically.

Britta gave the hermit an interesting look as she said, "It happens all the time in well-written stories."

The hermit ignored his pain as he stopped hopping to study her more closely. "Like a yarn an author may someday write about you?"

Britta gave him an approving nod as she asked, "What's your name?"

"I am called Meudwin."

"That means 'Blessed Hermit.' Was your father's first name Blessed?"

"Not according to my mother. I was given that name by the Unknown Bard, of whom I bring you word. He wanders in the wilderness near Cadir Idris."

"Does he look healed of his wounds?"

"He didn't sound like it. The last time he sang the local peasants locked their doors while their cows stopped giving milk, their hens stopped laying eggs, something weird happened to their sheep's wool, and his horse died of fright!"

Sir Christian interrupted. "Do you also bring word of someone called Adragain?"

"The prayer page?" Meudwin ignored the pain in his foot again as he studied Sir Christian from a safe distance. "I heard that last November he prayerfully discovered the Saxon camp on the Humber."

"All by himself," Uncle Sir Cecil proudly announced, maintaining his good ear like a pointed arrow in the right direction.

Britta nodded at Uncle Sir Cecil as she said, "If you ever plot treason with the Saxons, don't do it at banquet where my grandson, Adragain, is on duty. He's only a page, but he's been carefully and prayerfully trained by me to observe everything and anything that goes on around him. As they say, nothing gets by Adragain, especially when he prays. When a knave in unmarked livery slipped a treasonous message disguised as boot polish into the cloak of a guest when he thought no one was looking very well, an innocent voice behind them announced, 'Cherry! Berry! Apple pie! There's going to be a big surprise!'

"The knave complained before he disappeared—without a poof—'I didn't get a surprise!'

"But the guest got one when he checked inside his cloak and found real boot polish that was open! He never saw Adragain get his hands on the real message, but he saw his own hands get the real boot polish—black, gooey, and squishy—all over his clothes. Frustrated and ready to scream, he fled the banquet hall.

"Adragain waited a moment before he fled after him, unfrustrated and not screaming—but not before he planted the real boot polish message along with other clues. They allowed me and my retinue to follow when I couldn't find him after the banquet. Meanwhile, Adragain pursued what was now a well-polished guest all the way to the Saxon camp."

Meudwin said, "Thanks to Adragain's prayerful alertness, King Arthur and his knights would have attacked that camp and captured it intact if something hadn't gone—"

"Kawoom! Kaboom! Karoom!" announced Britta.

"Like the lid blowing off a volcano!" added Uncle Sir Cecil.

Meudwin nodded. "It was heard halfway to Navarre in one direction and all of the way across Ireland in the other. According to Ordericus the scribe, it really lit things up along the—Aiieee!"

Sir Christian was listening so intently that he tripped over another fallen mercenary, catapulting him close enough to jam Sir Pinel le Savage's second-favorite spear butt into Meudwin's second-favorite toe nail. The agonized hermit once more hopped around, yelling, "This knight would be less perilous at being so perilous—"

"If he wasn't so dangerous at being so perilous?" asked Uncle Sir Cecil.

Meudwin nodded more painfully than perilously.

"He's working on it," said Britta nonpainfully.

"With your help?" Meudwin asked Britta skeptically.

115

"She's working on it," said Uncle Sir Cecil nonskeptically.

Sir Christian asked quietly, "Any more news of this wonderful page of prayer called Adragain?"

Like an agonized dancer, Meudwin kept hopping, leaping, and shuffling his feet in case Sir Pinel le Savage's second-favorite spear butt plunged to the ground near them again. He managed to say with a moan, "Rumor says he's only ten years old."

"Fourteen," corrected Britta.

"He must be short for his age."

"He spends a lot of time on his knees."

"Like I'll be doing if Sir Christian jams my feet with that spear one more time! Fortunately, the blade's safely pointing toward heaven, where—"

Plop! A low-flying bird, confused by a sudden gust of dust from Castle Perilous, didn't see it.

Meudwin noticed that it was a stunned vulture as he shook his head. "Whatever his age, Adragain the prayer page is getting pretty famous around here. Last week, someone saw him slay a dragon. The week before that, someone else saw him do a catch and release on a giant. And the week before that, he was seen diverting a river that cleaned out the local lord's stables. Next week, he's scheduled to look for the seven lost treasures of Britain after he rescues a long-haired princess trapped in a tower. Meantime, he practices throwing coins across the nearest river."

Sir Christian said, "I thought Adragain was busy being captured by Saxon pirates."

Uncle Sir Cecil said, "When Sir Lancelot was captured by Sir Meliagrance, he was given time off to attend a tournament."

A scroll thunked Sir Pinel le Savage's second-favorite spear, but not hard enough to knock the point away from heaven. As Britta calmly resheathed her latest document, she turned everyone's attention to their fallen opponents. She addressed the hermit. "Meudwin, when the captain of these mercenaries-not-so-perilous recovers, tell him, 'A true warrior is polite to the disadvantaged and handicapped as well any persons they assist. Catch us if you can. The Lady of the Youthful Hair—who looks harmless.'"

Meudwin would have smiled at her message if he didn't have sore feet. But he raised his eyebrows in what looked like extreme pain when she whispered something into his ear and nodded toward Sir Christian.

Meudwin shuddered as he stared at Sir Christian with disbelief, shock, and a slight touch of horror. He painfully saluted Britta. He then turned his back after making sure his feet were two spear lengths from Sir Pinel's second-favorite spear and began examining the even-more-painful-looking men sprawled on the ground; this included tagging them on the arms or legs with notices.

Sir Christian looked at Britta. "Is that notice the same as your notice?"

"Complete with the same picture."

Sir Christian frowned. "What did you whisper to Meudwin?"

"That you are the kingdom's most perilous knight, who will stop at nothing to recover his equipment."

"Is that all?"

"Is that enough?"

Sir Christian frowned. "In my thirty-plus years—"

"Of merely satisfactory service," Britta reminded him.

Sir Christian nodded to move them on to the next painful point. "No one has ever looked at me like I was most perilous in that way."

"Sir Christian de Galis, knight of the all-powerful and most obnoxious fish gravy, something about you has changed."

This made Sir Christian rub his head. Meanwhile, a breeze blowing from his cloak toward Uncle Sir Cecil caused the archer to rub his nose as he tried to determine once again which of his nostrils sniffed. Behind them, the two modestly equipped horses, who knew perfectly well how their noses sniffed, whinnied as they caught the air not blowing from the castle and looked for a chance to move near Sir Christian. There they planned to do some serious rubbing of their own against his faded, overly spiced, arrow-shot cloak.

CHAPTER 12

It Wasn't Funny

Several guests declared his material tasteless and offensive
to their families, but worst of all, it wasn't funny.

—Wade the Scholar, *Chanson de Chrétien*

Britta approached the inn with her stride that continued to be faster
than that of most people and certain breeds of horses. Her companions'
attempt to keep up once again almost resembled a pursuit.

Britta briefly paused as Uncle Sir Cecil, striding extra quickly and
breathing extra hard, even for his amazing level of endurance, pulled
up on her left side. With an affectionate tap, she placed the reins of
her horse into his steady right hand. Then, with a signature swoosh,
she drew one of her largest scrolls and wielded it up and down in the
direction of the innkeeper. She recognized him on the east side of
the porch, gloomily shuffling his feet through wooden splinters from
the railing and floorboards, as well as shattered flowerpots that once
held his wife's favorite plants. He moaned as he shook his head, his
hands, and the apron fastened around his waist. He lifted the apron
and rubbed his face several times as he considered disasters brought
upon his inn by Sir Christian, the Navarrese, and the latest arrivals,
culminating in the lopsided twelve-arrow mercenary shoot-out.

This innkeeper was a retired knight known locally as Sir Erbin
the Easygoing because he tried to keep everyone at his inn happy,

at the same time, in an easygoing sort of way. This of course meant he seldom kept anyone happy at his inn at any time in any sort of way—and contributed to his shakiness. But it gave him one popular characteristic: he was always willing to return a favor. And he owed Britta a big one for the night she had stayed at his inn one year earlier, which was also the only night Sir Dagonet, King Arthur's dubious and, at that time, not-so-shaky jester, was a guest.

On that night, a commotion broke out in the dining room as Sir Dagonet, King Arthur's court jester and fool, insisted on telling a very low-level style of traveling-merchant joke. This was after several guests declared his material tasteless and offensive to their families, but worst of all, it wasn't funny. The least obnoxious included the following: "What's the difference between a traveling merchant and a dead snake? The traveling merchant still knows how to crawl." Or "What's the difference between a traveling merchant and a dead fish? One floats a loan, while the other floats alone."

Sir Erbin, who was already tired of hearing complaints about cold food, bad service, and anything else that goes wrong at an inn's dining room, attempted to intervene. From his place at the head table, he cried out in a shaky attempt at growling-voice authority, "I say—Sir Dagonet!"

The jester, who had snobbishly ignored Sir Erbin earlier in the evening, looked his way with a sneer as he slowly pulled back the hood from his head so that the innkeeper could see every detail of his face. "Youuuuuu-heh-heh-heh!" he yelled at Sir Erbin defiantly.

Sir Erbin wasn't wearing a hood, but he did have his signature apron fastened around his waist, which he continuously failed to remove when he tried to keep everyone happy. Instead, he lifted the apron nervously to wipe, unwipe, and once more rewipe his face. Then he shakily dropped it as he attempted to stare back at Sir Dagonet just as defiantly. In an even louder attempt at growling, shaky-voice authority, in front of all present, he threatened to evict Sir Dagonet from the inn if he told one more joke about anything at all.

In response, an angry Sir Dagonet announced that his jokes were tasteful enough for Round Table knights, such as Sir Mordred the Murderous and Sir Agravaine the Arrogant. Thus, they were more than suitable for the present company of Welsh clods and their families. Therefore, he declared himself mortally insulted, his Round Table honor demanded satisfaction, and he threatened to get it jester-style. As everyone's eyes rested upon him, he declared that he would list Sir Erbin's name on a comic survey he had just made up called Worst Innkeepers of the British Isles. He coldly added that the word *worst*, in his vocabulary, also implied his other favorite word for someone he didn't like: *dumbest*. Within the week, he promised to have that survey nailed to every town gate, church door, and bridge post between the winter court at Caerleon and Nauntes, the largest city south of Sir Erbin's inn. To emphasize, he waved a viperish finger in Sir Erbin's face, who prayerfully responded, "Lord Jesu, help!"

"How?" asked an archer from Castle Abblasoure, where no one says *mass*.

Behind him came the swoosh of something swinging through the air like a sword, which was followed by "Ow!" as a scroll smacked Sir Dagonet's finger into the table. Then it swung upward where—*kapow!*—it clobbered the jester's head in the most embarrassing way possible.

A spontaneous "Wow!" erupted from the diners in the room. Their eyes remained fixed on Sir Dagonet as he twisted sideways like a wounded snake and saw Britta peering nondescriptly at him after the fashion of her liaison corps. She gave him one of her more interesting looks and said, "Smile!"

Sir Dagonet responded with a murderous frown as he leaped to his feet, waving his serpentine finger at her, and said, "Now—"

"What?" Britta demanded as her scroll whacked Sir Dagonet's finger and head even harder.

"Ow!" he cried again. Shaking his finger and rubbing his head as they turned violent shades of purple, he screamed, "You're a lady magician trying to scare me with that scroll!"

"Oh no, Sir Knight of the Round Table, absolute lowest half!" declared Britta. "I'm a lady who looks harmless smacking you around with your Round Table personnel record!"

Moving faster than most people and certain breeds of horses (although horses seldom climb on tables, except maybe at Britta's manor during her family's semi-annual Armed Horses Day festival), she suddenly strode on to the middle of the table facing Sir Dagonet. She stopped swinging the scroll as she unrolled it to the title calligraphy, where she read loudly, "The Personnel Record of Sir Dagonet de Drag-a-net!"

"That's not my suffix!"

"It should be, the way your jokes drag like a net!"

Sir Dagonet's finger and face turned darker than a purple amethyst as he almost choked. On the other hand, Britta's face glowed as brightly as a diamond as she poked, "Did you know your look rhymes with 'almost joked'?"

Sir Dagonet's face almost smoked as Britta continued. "That shade suggests additional rhymes: *artichoke, someone croaked, okeydoke*. But where was I? Your personnel record, which includes, in detail, your position near the bottom of King Arthur's Round Table, with twenty-three footnoted assertions as to why your name will never be added to even one margin of his Round Table Honor Roll."

Sir Dagonet glared up at her. "Quit glaring down at me!"

"Isn't glare always in the eye of the beholder?"

Sir Dagonet sputtered up at her, "Now you're talking over my head!"

"Which I could do standing in a hole!"

"Don't talk funny to me!"

"That's your job—when are you going to start?"

Sir Dagonet looked up at her. "Now you're looking down at me!"

"Did you ever hear of taking the high table or even a highchair?"

"Now you're talking childish!"

"With you—not hard!"

Sir Dagonet's face turned so many shades that one couldn't tell which color was dominant, until—"Yellow!" Britta observed finally.

"Yellow what?" Sir Dagonet yelled back.

"Yell low enough so that no one hears you. It's also the dominant shade in your face, which brings us back to things that really are low—like you and your jokes!"

Sir Dagonet wasn't sure he understood exactly what she said, so he paused for a moment before he growled, "You won't take the high—whatever it is you're on—"

"It's called a table!"

"Against me for long!"

"If I wasn't opposed to gambling, I'd say, 'Want to bet?'"

The archer from Castle Abblasoure said, "I'm not opposed to gambling! I offer ten to one on a lady who looks harmless against a fool who doesn't sound funny!"

The dining room dissolved into chaos as more bets were placed while trestle benches and tables were pulled aside so that diners could see the outcome better.

Britta said to Sir Dagonet, "See how your brand of humor brings out the worst in people? It's also not very original. Here's a comment from your last liaison review: 'Jesters wrote jokes for him. Heroes wrote jokes for him. Bullies wrote jokes for him. King Arthur got *real* tired of hearing jokes that other people wrote for him.'"

"Who wrote that—Hildegard the Hard-Hearted?"

"You know Hildegard?"

"I hope not! And I don't want to know you! Meantime, you're going down!"

The archer from Abblasoure asked another archer from Abblasoure, "Do we know Hildegard?"

The second one replied, "I hope not."

Sir Dagonet furiously reached for his hood to pull it back from his head, when he remembered it already was pulled back from his head. He gave Britta his most intimidating jester-stare eyeful as he growled, "Youuuuuuu-heh-heh-heh!"

She said, "My *youuuuuuu-heh-heh-heh* is more powerful than your *youuuuuuu-heh-heh-heh*!" She removed her hood so that he could see every detail of her face as she unloaded on him a mountainous dose of her most ferocious, bear-scaring, leopard-claw-snarling, harmless-lady eyeful. Then she added, "Youuuuuu-heh-heh-heh!"

The result made the jester shake as if he were in an earthquake or an explosion in a small kitchen. With a confused look, he uttered a moan, fell over a bench with a groan, and then rolled backward head over heels twice onto a section of the floor covered by an extra-thick pile of fresh rushes. A loud, rumbling *crack* filled the air as Sir Dagonet and the rushes disappeared with shrieks through a fresh break in the floor!

"Like a food cart going down a mudhole," observed the first archer from Castle Abblasoure.

"Say, that's a pretty good line," said the second archer from Castle Abblasoure.

"If it wasn't good, I wouldn't use it," said the first archer.

A long moment later, everyone in the dining room heard a loud, squishy, gooey, subterranean *splat!*

Sir Erbin shakily wiped his face with the apron as he peered down the Sir Dagonet-size hole now gracing the center of his dining room floor. He couldn't see far, but somewhere down below he heard the jester slushing around in whatever had broken his fall. Sounding, smelling, and moving as if he had landed in a castle gardé robe pit that hadn't been cleaned in thirty years, Sir Dagonet uttered ugly threats about the innkeeper's future, impossible observations about his past, and some unbelievable suggestions on how smart his parents weren't.

He attempted to repeat the list with Britta, when everyone in the dining room heard his reverberated echo: "Who was that woman?"

"A lady who looks harmless," she called from the edge of the hole. "Who did you say was going down?"

A moaning reply echoed back up from the pit: "I'll have the last joke on you yet!"

Britta called back, "You finally said something funny. Better write it down before you forget!"

She heard angrier mushing and slushing down below as she asked Sir Erbin, "Did you know that pit was oozing beneath your inn?"

Sir Erbin replied in a voice that was finally not so shaky. "It's part of subterranean caverns which some say connect with the cave where Merlin disappeared. At one time, it was accessible through the hill below the inn, where its dry part served as an underground stable for the Romans. But its entrance was blocked by a landslide."

Britta added, "When the Dolorous Stroke caused a disturbance felt halfway to Navarre in one direction and all the way across Ireland in the other."

"That's what they say," said Sir Erbin with a surprised look on his face.

"And that's why I'm here," said Britta. "To investigate a connection between the Dolorous Stroke and this inn."

"The only connection I know," said Sir Erbin in a voice once more sounding shaky, "is that on the day of the Dolorous Stroke, a Celtic knight who began service as a fish cook during the reign of King Uther Pendragon was experimenting with something in the underground stable. He said the results would give everyone a big surprise—but he never reappeared after a landslide following the Dolorous Stroke gave him a big surprise."

Britta said, "The Dolorous Stroke was centered on the castle of King Pellam, which is nowhere near this inn. But my kinsman, Myrddin, thinks there may still be a connection."

"I wouldn't know what it would be other than coincidence. Meanwhile, the underground stable became sealed, but not completely due to cracks in the bedrock. Because the underground stable contained so much muck that could no longer be removed, it slowly built up gasses that seeped upward through those cracks into this dining room. That's when the previous owner sold me the inn cheap. Because of poor sinuses, I noticed nothing until customers complained, and some even refused to pay their dining room bill at sword point. That's when I hired multiple carpenters to seal off the cracks and block the smell, but the local craftsmen always worked like they were half asleep and never did a good job. I finally ordered an extra-large pile of fresh rushes placed daily over the largest crack and forgot about it until now."

At that moment, Sir Dagonet's unhappy squire, Hungwin—with the equally unhappy help of Endaf, the head kitchen knave, and three of his helpers, who had to be dragged screaming, pleading, and sobbing to the pit's edge—grabbed the inn's longest rope, which later had to be burned, and pulled the goo-dripping jester out of the subterranean smell-hole. Resembling the latest knave to be sentenced to the castle gardé robe pit cleaning crews, Sir Dagonet stumbled into the dining room—splattering walls, food, the floor, and more than one unhappy guest running for cover.

Sir Dagonet, looking ready to roar like the Monster-of-Unheard-of-Savageness, angrily searched the room for Sir Erbin and Britta, only to feel the padded tip of Uncle Sir Cecil's bow stave prodding his gooey chest. The ancient archer, protected by his insufficient sense of smell, pushed Sir Dagonet across the remaining floor and out the door, which Endaf slammed with a louder *thud* than a fat knight makes when losing a joust.

It was said that the jester was later forced to replace all of his clothes with whatever he could find on the inn's clothesline, which only contained dish towels that day. The next morning, he left the inn wrapped in a secondhand sheet he borrowed from a traveling herdsman, without visiting the dining room for so much as a crust of bread or even to try to get in the last joke.

In remembrance of that event, Britta tried to attract the innkeeper by wielding (not waving—an important distinction) her copy of Sir Dagonet's infamous scroll as she climbed the porch steps. But he was so busy shaking his head, his hands, and the apron with which he nervously wiped, unwiped, and then rewiped his face that he didn't notice when she stopped in front of him.

"Oh dear, oh dear, oh dear," he cried as he blew his nose into the apron. "What will I do when the sheriff finds out?"

"Tell him that everything is okay," she said.

"But everything isn't okay—uh, who's there?"

"The Lady of the Youthful Hair, who says that everything is okay."

When he didn't respond, she took the solid end of the scroll and went *knock-knock* on the shaky porch rail, almost making it fall over onto Sir Erbin.

"Who's there?" he gasped as he grabbed for something else to hang on to without dropping his apron.

"The Lady of the Youthful Hair, who says that everything is okay."

"The Lady of the Youthful Hair who?"

"Looks harmless."

"No lady of youthful hair ever looks harmless around this inn!"

"I'm the Lady of the Youthful Hair, who says that I look harmless, like I did last year when I saved your inn from Sir Dagonet."

"That Lady of the Youthful Hair didn't look harmless. Uh, where are you?"

"If you get your head out of your apron, you'll see me standing harmlessly in front of you."

"You don't sound like you're standing harmlessly in front of anything!"

He stopped wiping, unwiping, and rewiping his face as he got his head out of his apron. When he saw Britta standing in front of him, he muttered, "Oh dear, oh dear, oh dear. You definitely don't look harmless!"

Britta said, "Sir Erbin, I am a lady—"

"Who helped an archer shoot down all twelve of the sheriff's hard-to-find new men. And that was right in front of my inn, where it wasn't very pretty, it wasn't very funny, and it probably wasn't very legal—and it didn't look very harmless!"

"But it looked necessary—and harmless enough! Uncle Sir Cecil and I merely stunned the sheriff's new men. They'll get over it in a few days."

"But will my inn, or will the sheriff of Perilous, or will I when the sheriff of Perilous finds out it happened to his men in front of my inn? Oh dear, oh dear, oh dear. The sheriff was shorthanded when twelve of his men didn't return from the Caerleon Christmas feast, where it's rumored something not so harmlessly laid them up! The sheriff hired those Navarrese as emergency replacements just in time for Sir Christian to not so harmlessly lay them up—in my inn's dining room! When they were almost well, you and your trick-shot archer came along and not so harmlessly laid them up again! Oh dear, oh dear, oh dear! The sheriff of Perilous will not be pleased."

"Sir Erbin, I can handle the sheriff of Perilous. I know a few things about those road pits his men dig for Prince Idris II that I'm sure he doesn't want getting back to King Arthur. In the meantime, you owe me a favor, and everyone knows—"

The innkeeper answered sadly, "That I'm always willing to return a favor."

"And you owe me a big one for driving Sir Dagonet away from your inn last year."

Sir Erbin stared at her extra hard while she attempted to stare at him extra harmlessly—which she wasn't.

As she and Sir Erbin went stare for stare, she said, "This is the favor I want. In return for a modest fee from my shoe-latchet budget, release unto me Sir Christian's horse, weapons, armor, and equipment. He requires them to begin service as my quest knight."

Sir Erbin gagged worse than last year's guests at Sir Dagonet's jokes as he cried, "Modest fee! Quest knight!"

Britta hummed while drumming the scroll on a new section of porch rail until, with a climactic *crack*, she almost whacked it over onto Sir Erbin. She smiled as she hummed some more and said, "Doesn't this railing contain a nice musical tone?"

"If you like concerts that resemble a cattle stampede!" Sir Erbin cried as he barely kept the new section of rail from collapsing by grabbing it. He looked as if he were on a ship tossed at sea. He glared at her. "You don't come with a nice musical tone either! First, you insult me by offering a modest fee from your—what do you call it?"

"Shoe-latchet budget," she answered sweetly.

"Shoe-latchet nothing!" he answered sourly. "Which is what you're trying to pass off on me in exchange for Sir Christian's horse, weapons, armor, and equipment. And second, so that knave of the fish gravy can begin service as your quest knight. Aside from your modest fee being robbery against a law-abiding innkeeper, Sir Christian is the worst choice to begin service as a quest knight I have ever seen."

"The worst choice is sometimes the best choice."

"According to whom—the king of fools? Thank you very much for driving Sir Dagonet away from my inn last year. But I don't think I owe you that big of a favor."

"Think harder," she said as she drummed harder, in a manner that suggested the Monster-of-Unheard-of-Savageness sharpening its claws. "For you certainly do. You just don't know it yet." And Britta whacked the scroll against the rail so hard that it collapsed like a crash of symbols.

Britta, for once, looked sheepish as she said, "You need a better carpenter to work on your porch."

Sir Erbin yelled back, "And you need a better knight to go on your quest! That is, unless you brought an extra-heavy bag of gold! That's what I will accept as a modest fee from your shoe-latchet budget! Then I don't care what bozo you recruit as your quest knight, just as long as he does his bozo questing far, far away from my inn!"

"That sounds pretty far!" she observed.

"And it probably wouldn't be far enough! But an extra-heavy bag of gold is what you need to pay if you want to take Sir Christian's horse, weapons, armor, and equipment—or anything else, for that matter—far, far away from this inn. Your scourge of the fish gravy coupled with that other scourge you drug along—"

With a loud *crack*, he snapped his apron in the direction of Uncle Sir Cecil's good ear—and the archer snapped back a salute in the wrong direction. Sir Erbin shook his head and snapped once more at Britta. "Caused me a lot of damage! Therefore, I'm also making your quest knight pay for this"—he pointed his index finger at the wood and pottery splinters on the inn's porch—"and that"—he pointed at the freshly collapsed railing—"and I further insist on—" He pointed a serpentine finger at her.

Britta smacked that finger so hard, it resembled a serpent slithering away for its life. But for once, she didn't swing upward and whack Sir Erbin's head. She gently lowered the scroll as she leaned close enough to whisper into his ear. She then nodded toward Sir Christian in such a way that Sir Erbin stared at him as if he were a super-snake. A look of disbelief, shock, and a slight touch of horror spread across his face.

"Sir Christian de Galis and the serial bandit Sir Breuse sans Pitie," he muttered to himself. "Why, I had no idea."

Britta looked Sir Erbin straight in the eye. "The Knight of the Fish Gravy and the psychopathic Sir Breuse sans Pitie—why, it's possible that they're about to become just like—" Despite the scroll she was holding, and without completing the statement, Britta touched her two index fingers together.

Sir Erbin shuddered as if he were in an earthquake or an explosion in a small kitchen as he stared at Sir Christian standing below his porch. Sir Christian, on the other hand, stared at Britta touching her fingers. He started to ask Uncle Sir Cecil how she did it, when the archer yanked him behind the horses. Uncle Sir Cecil was thought by some to have more disabilities than arrows, but after long years of service with Britta, he sensed when she was up to something and needed help distracting someone like Sir Christian.

She told Sir Erbin, "Did you know that Sir Christian carries one of Sir Breuse's plumes in his baggage?"

"Really?" said Sir Erbin as his eyes grew large. "So Sir Breuse's savage raiders can identify him as one of their own?"

"It's totally possible and may explain why Sir Breuse was noticed in the crowd that was just outside your inn."

"Sir Breuse was here?" Sir Erbin shuddered even more. "I didn't notice him."

"I didn't notice him either, but it doesn't mean he wasn't noticed by someone."

The innkeeper shuddered even more. "What do you think Sir Breuse was doing in the crowd?"

"What does Sir Breuse ever do in a crowd? Looking for a wealthy person to kidnap, checking out a promising place to raid—that sort of thing."

"What qualifies a wealthy person or a promising place as 'that sort of thing'?"

"Low on sheriff's men, like your inn just became. It's totally possible. Now, let's assume he was in that crowd, where he carefully watched Sir Christian de Galis defeat all twelve of those Navarrese mercenaries."

"I carefully watched you and your archer defeat all twelve of those Navarrese mercenaries."

"Only after Sir Christian confused them."

"His spear tearing holes in my tree was confusing. And you say it was part of his strategy to defeat the Navarrese?"

"While possibly part of a secret, even-higher strategy. Did you notice how much it confused the Navarrese?"

"I noticed how much it confused everyone else."

"Sir Erbin, that's when you possibly witnessed, as part of a most skillfully choreographed subterfuge, the renowned Sir Sagramore side-step."

"I never heard of the renowned Sir Sagramore side-step, nor did I notice any other skillfully choreographed subterfuge when Sir Christian turned completely around."

"That's because that second maneuver was most skillfully choreographed with the equally famous Sir Bertholai-back-step. That's the one that goes one, two, three! One, two, three! Backstep, hop! One, two, three! One, two, three! Backstep, hop!"

"I never heard of that one either."

"As an innkeeper, you need to keep up with the new trends."

"I never saw Sir Christian keep up with the new trends, the old trends, or any in-between trends; nor did I see him step like Sir Sagramore while he hopped like Sir Bertholai!"

"That's because he stepped and hopped so fast that I barely saw it. To most people, it looked like he just stood around doing nothing— which was all part of his skillfully choreographed subterfuge."

Sir Erbin shook his head. "Which you say was also part of Sir Breuse's secret strategy to study the defenses of my inn?"

"While everyone else was busy studying everyone else— including Sir Christian—while he let them think he stood around doing nothing. It's totally possible."

"What does Sir Breuse look like?"

"Just like Sir Christian, when seen in a certain light, which means they may be related."

"So Sir Breuse also just stood around and looked like he was doing nothing?"

"It's totally possible. So if you know what's good for you and your inn, let me have Sir Christian's weapons, horse, armor, and other equipment in return for a modest shoe-latchet fee. Then I promise to take him on that quest far, far away from here and maybe even farther, especially if Sir Breuse comes back to your inn later looking for him. But long before then, I'll make sure Sir Breuse hears how generous you were toward Sir Christian. Then he might place your inn under his protection."

"I have never heard of Sir Breuse sans Pitie placing anything under his protection."

"Neither have I, but there's always a first time."

"You're guessing."

"As a benevolent friend to whom you owe a *big* favor, it's an educated guess."

"What if your educated guess is wrong?"

"What's the worst that could happen? You release Sir Christian's horse, armor, weapons, and equipment for a small fee, making it possible for him to go on a quest far, far away from your inn—and possibly even farther—with a lady who looks harmless."

"And I'm out of a lot of money!"

"That you used to benefit the local community, and for which you might even receive a decree of formal thanks from King Arthur. Wait until you hang a royally framed document containing an announcement like that in your dining room. Won't it attract some business! Travelers and pilgrims may come from all over Britain just to read it. Then they can hire *your* artists to draw their icon being seen with it—as they dine on patriotic cuisine next to sweet-smelling rushes placed daily over that famous hole in your dining room floor. Why, your inn could become a regular gold mine. It's totally possible. But what happens if you guess wrong the other way—and don't release Sir Christian's horse, weapons, and other equipment? Not only will you *not* benefit the local community, resulting in no decree from King Arthur, with all of the associated accolades and business opportunities, but if Sir Breuse hears that you offended his friend, who's possibly his long-lost cousin to whom he presented his plume, he might decide to burn down your inn!"

"Like Sir Christian almost did?"

"That was accidental, but Sir Breuse sans Pitie might do it on purpose!"

Sir Erbin swallowed hard. "You said *might*?"

"Possibly might. I'm not trying to scare you."

"You're not?" Then he asked, "If Sir Christian de Galis is so associated with Sir Breuse sans Pitie, why do you want him as your quest knight?"

She spoke closer to his ear. "It's part of a secret stratagem in which Sir Christian is actually the object of my quest. He just doesn't know it yet."

"So the knight of the quest is also the object of the quest, sort of like a dog chasing his tail. That sounds confusing."

"Everything about Sir Christian sounds confusing, which is all part of the secret stratagem. Meantime, beware of Sir Christian; under the current circumstances, he is more perilous than all of the other knights in Britain combined."

"Because most of them are sick?"

"Among other things."

"So you're telling me that all this time, Sir Christian was secretly a real killer?"

"Have you ever seen him kill time?"

"For two whole months."

"And that's when he didn't pay attention."

"He didn't pay his bill either."

"Now you know two ways he's perilous. And there's a lot more where that comes from—when one dares cross swords, spears, or even spatulas with the Knight of the Fish Gravy. Meanwhile, the fate of King Arthur, his kingdom, and possibly the entire known world, if not the universe, may depend upon—"

"Me helping Sir Christian de Galis! Every under-provisioned knight passing my inn tells me something like that. But after I give him a handout, he seldom saves King Arthur, his kingdom, the entire known world, or even the universe from anything except his presence. Meanwhile, he lives in a borrowed tent until he's broke again. However—"

Sir Erbin shuddered as if he were in an earthquake or an explosion in a small kitchen as he motioned for Britta to follow him.

On the ground below the porch, Sir Christian, whom Uncle Sir Cecil kept occupied with questions about fish gravy-enhanced archery, of all things, watched Sir Erbin and Britta disappear inside the inn. He said softly into the ancient archer's good ear, "Something certainly has changed." Uncle Sir Cecil smiled. In the meantime, the horses neighed as they looked for ways to do serious rubbing against Sir Christian's overly spiced cloak.

CHAPTER 13

Random Opponents

I creatively reinforce a knight like you by recruiting
random opponents—while they're still opponents.
—Wade the Scholar, *Chanson de Chrétien*

Sir Erbin didn't look easygoing when he reemerged on his front porch, and Britta de Brittany didn't look harmless when she reemerged beside him. For once, she looked tired as she brushed imaginary dust from her cloak, Sir Dagonet's scroll (which was almost as thick as Sir Christian's), and the splintered remains of the front porch rail still standing. She playfully considered Sir Erbin's split ends but restrained herself because she and he had struck a deal of sorts—after serious negotiations.

After they were inside, Britta initially made little progress convincing Sir Erbin to accept her shoe-latchet offer for Sir Christian's horse, weapons, armor, and equipment. Once the innkeeper could no longer see Sir Christian, Britta could no longer influence him with the knight's connection, including an uncanny resemblance, if seen in a certain light, to the serial bandit, kidnapper, and downright mischievous knight of terror Sir Breuse sans Pitie. (It was a clear case of out of sight, out of fright.) Sir Erbin only remembered what an inn-wrecking beggar knight his unwanted guest had become. He also remembered from his previous encounter with Britta that as harmless as she might appear, on this occasion, he might be on the verge of being had. Thus, he found easygoing courage to resist all initial shoe-latchet offers she made for anything concerning Sir Christian.

As things dragged on, Britta tried not to intimidate the innkeeper too much while she pleaded with him a little, twisted his arm behind his back a lot, and made one or two thinly veiled threats. She almost unloaded on Sir Erbin a mountainous dose of her most ferocious, bear-scaring, harmless-lady, leopard-claw-snarling, jester-frightening eyeful. After he collapsed, or fell through another hole like Sir Dagonet on her last visit, she would cheerfully collect Sir Christian's possessions—in the name of King Arthur—for the sake and survival of the inn, the kingdom, the entire known world, and possibly even the universe. However, someone somewhere must have said a simple, reasonable prayer, because the innkeeper unexpectedly and graciously gave in.

Sir Erbin breathed easygoing relief when Britta and her immediate retinue of modestly equipped, although not necessarily modest, heroes rode away from the inn, and he modestly prayed that it was for the last time.

But the three modestly equipped horses that Britta and company rode away on breathed something else in the air that suddenly blew past them from Sir Christian's heavily spice-soaked cloak. They looked ready to do the warhorse version of ruthless pleading, arm twisting, and veiled threats to get near it. Fortunately for our heroes, the horses, and everyone else in the kingdom, the known world, and possibly even the universe who still needed to be rescued from torture, captivity, or even unpleasant annihilation on this quest, it just as suddenly died down for the duration of this ride.

The activities of the Navarrese also died down for the duration of that day and most of the next, as they were once again laid out in their common room. But before they drove away more guests with moans, groans, and ugly shouted insults about Sir Christian, Britta, Uncle Sir Cecil the Steady, and the intelligence level of their complete list of friends, neighbors, and relatives, they were once more treated by the medical hermit, Meudwin. This was one of the conditions Britta negotiated with Sir Erbin.

The blessed hermit solemnly noted the not-so-blessed blue bruise borne by each Navarrese. The bruises were dead center on their foreheads, right between the eyes, making them resemble a new variety of Pyrenees mountain Cyclops. But the marks were not permanent. The aftereffects they still displayed from consuming fish gravy had him more concerned.

Sir Christian was unaware of this mercenary misery they left behind. He frequently looked over his shoulder for signs of red-eyed, bloodthirsty Navarrese pursuit, which Britta noticed while following her habit of observing everything and anything that occurred around them. When wielding a scroll up and down three times in the direction of Sir Christian's helmet eye slits produced nothing, Britta carefully moved her horse so that it couldn't bite larger holes in his scent-saturated cloak and banged the scroll's wooden end against Sir Christian's helmet. *Clang! Clang! Clang! Clang!*

"Sir Christian, hello in there!" Britta announced as she continued to swing the scroll like the battle hammer of a war goddess—which didn't really apply to her, because after all, that is a pagan notion. "There won't be any pursuit today! So let's relax and look immediately forward to the future!"

But the only thing Sir Christian now looked immediately forward to was the ground that he almost landed on as he reeled in the saddle. He painfully turned his head, recalling the last time it had gotten clobbered by Sir Lancelot during a hand-to-hand combat drill, as he attempted to focus on Britta. She stopped swinging and brushed more imaginary dust from the scroll, her cloak, and the fresh dents in the side of Sir Christian's helmet, in lieu of his split ends.

She said, "Uncle Sir Cecil's blunt-tipped arrows gave the Navarrese headaches that normally last twenty-four hours. Then, if I'm any judge of mercenary human nature, which I usually am, that's the optimal moment to look over your shoulder. That's when the Navarrese should begin pursuing you most vengefully for setting them up to be defeated and humiliated most publicly—by the Lady of the Youthful Hair, who looks harmless."

His reply echoed as if it came from the bottom of a gardé robe pit. "You mean the Lady of the Youthful Hair who looks like the Monster-of-Unheard-of-Savageness when she starts swinging one of those scrolls!"

"How do you know what a monster like that looks like? Have you ever seen one?"

Sir Christian refused to answer and for a moment felt like abandoning this quest for one involving the Monster-of-Unheard-of-Savageness, which suddenly seemed several helmet dents safer. But then he once again shrugged as he slowly and painfully removed his helmet and hung it from his saddlebow—on the side away from Britta. He rubbed his head to ease a twenty-four-hour headache of his own as he asked, "Britta, do we really want all twelve of those Navarrese mercenaries following us most vengefully?"

"Not *us*, Sir Christian—*you*. Also, I said *pursuing*, not *following*, to which there's a semantically strategic difference. Yes, we want all twelve of those Navarrese mercenaries pursuing *you* most vengefully, especially if we can keep them on your scent most scentfully"— Britta made a point of sniffing Sir Christian's reeking, arrow-shot cloak—"for as long as I decide that we most scentfully need them."

Sir Christian glared at her as she smiled back at him while she reached over and moved his helmet to her side of his saddle. She drummed on it with the scroll as she said, "Sir Christian, please consider. Do you think that you, I, and Uncle Sir Cecil, supported by only one squire and one girl servant in my remaining small retinue, can rescue my grandson—or anyone else, for that matter—from a sizable force of Saxon pirates? Even with my exhaustive knowledge of surprise military tactics, like I just demonstrated against the Navarrese, we might merely dent the Saxon numbers—"

"Like you *merely* dented my helmet!"

Britta pretended not to hear. "If Uncle Sir Cecil and I were forced to make *you* fight *them* single-handedly."

An outraged Sir Christian stopped glaring at the fresh dents in his helmet. "What do you mean if Uncle Sir Cecil and you were forced to make *me* fight *them* single-handedly? Is anyone else going to help?"

"Of course anyone else is going to help—if anyone else is available. Uncle Sir Cecil and I, assisted by the capable members of my small remaining retinue, will offer any and all help you require— if we happen to be available. But suppose something else unexpected shows up—the Monster-of-Unheard-of-Savageness, Sir Breuse sans Pitie, or an unforeseen world crisis. The universe contains more than one set of problems."

"I thought we were concentrating on your grandson's set of problems!"

"Of course we are! But just in case we're interrupted by other social needs, problems, and disasters, do note the fine calligraphy in your Round Table contract: 'You, as Official Quest Knight, temporarily reinstated, are legally and morally obligated to bear the brunt of any and all future fighting.' After all, that's how a Round Table quest contract is worded."

"That's very thoughtful of you and Uncle Sir Cecil to remind me."

Uncle Sir Cecil aimed his bad eyes, questionable nose, and good ear toward Sir Christian. "Why, thank you, my boy, but don't forget to listen closely to Britta if you're going to get along with us on this quest."

Sir Christian shook his head as he moved his helmet back to his side of his saddle. For the moment, he didn't care if he got along with anyone on this quest, particularly scroll-swinging Britta, the not-so-harmless-looking, bear-scaring, wild Christian lady, who distracted him with another swoosh of the scroll as she leaned over and shifted his helmet back to her side of his saddle. She drummed on it some more as she said, "Sir Christian, you have only begun to learn how thoughtful, helpful, and useful we can be—especially on a quest. In the meantime, let's face some Round Table reality. Before I left Caerleon, the right noble Neb de Seward, one of King Arthur's most loyal, faithful, and consistent coast watchers, informed me that this group of pirates you may be forced to fight single-handedly contains a force of seven hundred Saxons."

"A force of seven hundred Saxons! Against whom I may or may not have any help! How do I prepare for something like that?"

"Pray more effectively while you practice more efficiently."

"For doing what?"

"Fighting more than one bloodthirsty opponent at one time, like you did very well outside the castle."

"Because I didn't have six hundred ninety-eight of their friends standing around looking for ways to help!"

"On an imperfect quest, one must always allow for imperfect possibilities."

The thought of imperfect possibilities beyond what Sir Christian had already experienced on this so-called imperfect quest made his head suffer from a forty-eight-hour headache. He tried desperately to ignore it as he attempted with equal desperation to distract Britta with a stare. Then, with all the painful lightning he could muster in his fifty-year-plus Round Table–reinstated sword-swinging arm, he once more attempted to shift his helmet back to his side of his saddle as—*clang!* Britta's scroll blocked it. She gave him another smile as she drew back the scroll and said, "I learned that maneuver from Sir Lamorak de Galis. Did you know that at one time, he and I were about to become just like—"

When she saw his glaring frown, she drummed on his helmet, humming the opening bars of the popular alehouse march "The Knaves Pursue You Two by Two, Huzzah! Huzzah!" (whose music and lyrics were written by the Unknown Bard). Then she brushed more imaginary dust from her cloak, the scroll, and more fresh dents in his helmet. She gave the helmet a final soft *thud* as she said with another interesting smile, "Sir Christian, you look too tense, too tense, and also two-tenths of what you should be. Now, that's a little joke to help you feel loosened up."

Sir Christian neither laughed nor felt loosened up as he once more shifted his helmet to his side of his saddle.

Britta conceded the helmet-shifting contest—for the moment. She decided she had made her point in her usual scroll-banging manner. She now smiled semi-sweetly at Sir Christian as she said, "To further reassure you, let me explain something. Over the years, I have developed a series of successful stratagems to handle lopsided, unfair, and overwhelming odds that almost always seem to occur when I go on a quest with a knight like you."

"With a knight like me?" Sir Christian moaned as he rubbed his head, which now suffered from a ninety-six-hour headache.

"Yes, Sir Christian, I creatively reinforce a knight like you by recruiting random opponents—while they're still opponents! Under that inspiration, I come up with ways to keep opportune individuals like the Navarrese chasing lopsided knights like you all the way to the enemy encampment. Then, at the very best psychological moment, I maneuver them into the key watershed position, where their swords provide the most bang for the clang, as they will in your case, as they most valiantly, most vigorously, and most selflessly even your odds against the Saxons."

Sir Christian glared at her. "Britta, I acknowledge that you are a woman of military genius seldom seen in this realm, this dimension, or even this universe—"

"Ever hear of Sun Tzu?" Uncle Sir Cecil asked.

"Son who?"

"Wrote military scrolls Britta helped translate."

"After I corrected the mistakes," Britta added with a smile.

"Must not have been very good. What where they about?"

Britta shrugged. "Ten feet long apiece."

Uncle Sir Cecil said, "I thought Sun Tzu's scrolls would be much longer than that."

Britta said, "These were abridged copies."

Sir Christian shrugged some more, shook his head, and said, "What if at the very best psychological moment, those Navarrese mercenaries don't want to be maneuvered into the key watershed position, where their swords will provide the most bang for the clang, as they most valiantly, most vigorously, and most selflessly even my odds against the Saxons? Specifically, why should twelve Navarrese mercenaries *I don't like* take on seven hundred Saxon pirates *you don't like* after chasing the three of us, *whom they don't like*? That's ignoring mathematical odds of over forty-six to one in favor of the Saxons, and that's with you, me, Uncle Sir Cecil, and any small retinue you retain thrown into the mix."

Britta fluttered her eyes. "That small retinue I retain may surprise you with just how well, when thrown into the mix, they reduce the odds to a mere forty to one."

Sir Christian protested, "A retinue of two, of which one is a girl?"

"But a most polite and courteous girl," Uncle Sir Cecil said as he kept his good ear aimed like a pointed straight arrow, "if one also acts most polite and courteous to her. Otherwise, watch out!"

"Is that the same as 'run for your life'?"

When Uncle Sir Cecil merely smiled, Sir Christian said, "I'll make sure I do."

Britta gave him a knowing look that said, without words, *If you don't behave around her, you had better do both.* She said with words, "She's almost like an extra squire but much better at cooking, sewing, and making the beds. Yet congratulations are in order, Sir Christian. You just demonstrated one of my favorite adages: 'Outnumbered knights know how to count.' But don't worry. According to my plan, those Navarrese are as good as on *your* side. They just don't know it yet. And they also won't be turning back, because their contract with the local sheriff is as good as canceled. They don't know that yet either."

Sir Christian said, "And you do?"

Britta said, "I have the strangest feeling, because there are always more things to see on this quest than you think you see." Suddenly she rubbed her face. "Even if's there's strange particles blowing through the air from the castle."

"Especially after someone prays," added Uncle Sir Cecil ironically.

With the painful nod of a head now suffering from a one hundred ninety-two hour headache, Sir Christian didn't notice anything blowing from the castle, which like the inn was behind them, as he rested the center of Sir Pinel le Savage's second-favorite spear horizontally across the saddle. Meantime he muttered, "Prayer or no prayer, I definitely agree there are more things to see on this quest than I think I see."

"And we be two of them!" roared a Goliath-size voice.

CHAPTER 14

The Finest Demonstration

That was the finest demonstration of King
Arthur's secret spear ambush!
—Wade the Scholar, *Chanson de Chrétien*

"And we be two of them!" repeated the Goliath-size voice, giving Sir Christian a three hundred eighty-four hour headache as he saw two seven-foot warriors blocking the road ahead on equally mountainous mounts.

The speaker waved, not wielded—an important distinction—a sword the length of a spear in their direction as his voice shook small branches and leaves from the trees. "I be Maynard the Mangler, and he be called Pluto the Brutal. We be related, as in we be similar. Now, there be some that calls us too-small giants, and there be some that calls us too-tall dwarves—which I think may be wordplays. But we be most truly—"

"Opportune," said Britta as she positioned her horse behind Sir Christian's.

"Extra-size midgets," said Maynard the Mangler, "which lets us have it both ways. Although we be much gentler than our brethren—against whom we always try to appear more than correct. Therefore, not wishing to scare the lady—"

"With the youthful hair," said Sir Christian.

143

"Useful hair!" said Maynard with a puzzled roar.

"It helps her look uselessly harmless," said Sir Christian.

Maynard studied Britta for a moment and then roared with man-mountain laughter. "She looks as uselessly harmless as—"

Whack! His sword sliced a branch from the nearest tree.

"Have you ever thought of going on a quest to trim tree branches?" asked Sir Christian.

Maynard roared, "Not with so many humans to trim!" He shook his blade at Sir Christian like the fang of a giant snake. "Now, that be an object lesson to hold your attention. For times be hard, and opportunity be scarce for us whom some call dwarves of the taller variety—and others call giants of the smaller variety—but we being midgets of the seven-foot variety!"

"Seven foot makes you a midget?" asked Sir Christian.

"It be a matter of perspective! You should meet my eight-foot cousin, Plankford. He's considered tall for a midget!"

"Is it possible to meet your cousin?" asked Britta.

Sir Christian glared at her like the Monster-of-Unheard-of-Savageness as Maynard the Mangler roared again. "He be guarding banquets with lots of trimming—where no one's looking very well! But as I said, times be hard for midgets of any variety, especially guards who were caught and kicked out of banquets. So if we can collect—"

With his free hand, Maynard the Mangler produced a familiar-looking notice, whose contents he read: "A reward of one hundred fifty thousand groats—which I understand to be a fancy way of saying *shillings*—for Christian the Poisoner!"

Maynard's sword sliced off another tree branch so that it flew upward. When it descended—*whack!*—the flat of his blade batted it past Sir Christian's head. Maynard shoved the pointed fang back toward him like an even uglier snake. "Unless this icon be mistaken, it be ye!"

Britta asked quietly, "Where did you get that notice?"

"From a knave we left unconscious, which be the way we found him, next to other knaves we left unconscious, which be the way we found them, next to a spot where a castle once stood next to all kinds of knaves lying unconscious! According to a passing knave, before we left him unconscious, the castle disappeared with a sound that be something like *poof*!"

Maynard roared the last statement so loudly that Uncle Sir Cecil's bad ear felt the vibration. He rubbed it while asking, "A castle disappeared with a poof?"

"A loud poof! And in so doing created so many piles of poof that the castle garrison be digging themselves out for a week—once they be no longer unconscious!"

Uncle Sir Cecil asked Maynard, "What is poof?"

Maynard replied, "What be blowing in the wind?"

As Britta asked Sir Christian, "What is fish gravy?"

Sir Christian looked as if he suffered from a seven hundred sixty-eight hour headache as he stared at Maynard's spear-like sword and asked, "What is next?"

Maynard waved the note at Sir Christian. "This be next! We don't care about who makes poof! We don't care about who shovels poof! And we especially don't care about what is poof! But we do care about who will pay us groats—for you!"

He motioned to his accomplice, Pluto the Brutal, who produced a rock and, with a swooshing crack, batted it with a ball-and-chain-tipped club past Sir Christian. Meanwhile, Maynard's sword sliced an even larger limb from a tree as he glared at them with a ruthless, toothless look. "Now, that be a second object lesson of two examples to hold your attention! For here be instruction! If everyone comes along peaceable and tells us where to exchange the poisoner for the groats, we won't be crushing, crunching, or removing anything from any of ye! But if you tell us nothing—"

Maynard's blade smacked off another large branch as Pluto's ball-and-chain club belted another rock past them.

Maynard smiled at them wickedly. "It also depends how much we feel like not crushing, crunching, or removing. This, in turn, depends how much you feel like telling us what we want!"

Britta said, carefully leashing her eyes, "We found the poisoner first, so we have prior rights."

"Which must give way to higher rights—ours! That is, if you appreciate the larger sense of our higher humor! And if you also wish to be spared—"

Crack!

Pluto belted a small boulder past their heads.

"Or—"

Whack!

"Or even—"

Smack!

Maynard had sliced off two fresh tree branches and batted them past their heads.

"I get the crack and the whack and the smack," said Britta, eyeing the position of their opponents' horses.

"I don't," said Sir Christian.

"But you will!" roared Maynard the Mangler as—*ca-whack!*—he cleaved a tree from its trunk in such a way that when he gave it an additional smack, it soared over their heads like a scythe. Not to be outdone, Pluto the Brutal smacked a boulder that missed Sir Christian but not a medium-size tree, which it reduced to splinters.

"Lord Jesu, help!" cried Sir Christian as the two seven-footers clip-clopped their behemoth horses toward them, shaking the ground like an earthquake or an explosion in a small kitchen.

Maynard waved, not wielded—once again, an important distinction—his sword so that it dripped venom like the fang of a giant hydra. He sneered at Sir Christian, "Yes! Lord Jesu help you, me, and Pluto the Brutal become just like—"

There was a swoosh as a scroll smacked the rump of Sir Christian's horse. Bellowing a united "Aiieee!"—truly unusual on the part of the horse—they shot toward and then between the mounts of the gigantic midgets, where the horizontally held shaft of Sir Pinel le Savage's second-favorite spear swept Maynard and Pluto from their saddles. The super-size midgets hit the ground with a thud felt halfway to Navarre in one direction and all of the way across Ireland in the other.

When the ground, not the extra-large midgets, stopped moving, shaking, and stirring, Britta brushed twice as much imaginary dust off of her cloak, the scroll, and, with an amused look in her eyes, Uncle Sir Cecil's split ends. She commented, "That was the finest demonstration of King Arthur's secret spear ambush!"

Uncle Sir Cecil, with his good ear, jolted the wrong way answered, "What?"

Meantime, they caught up with Sir Christian, who looked as if he suffered from a fifteen hundred thirty-six hour headache. With an angry glare in their direction he wielded, not waved, the reward notice that had fluttered onto his saddle. Making sure they saw every word and the picture he shouted, "So this is motivation to perform a deed that is most useful!"

"And somewhat noble," Uncle Sir Cecil pointed out.

"For whom? People who don't like me! One hundred fifty thousand groats equals five thousand marks, which—"

"Equals something much more interesting than listing one hundred fifty thousand silver coins. Plus," Britta said toward Uncle Sir Cecil, "it's easy on the ink."

The archer replied again, "What?"

Britta tapped Uncle Sir Cecil's arm with a scroll. "Wrong ear again."

Sir Christian looked ready to smack Britta with Sir Pinel's second-favorite spear as he said, "You placed that notice in the armor—"

"Plate and chain mail," said Britta, who had carefully positioned herself beyond the reach of the spear.

Sir Christian said, "Of everyone you whacked."

"Mostly thunked," said Britta, her horse dancing and dodging in case Sir Christian moved closer.

"Or clunked, when done by my destrier," said Uncle Sir Cecil. He sensed the side of Sir Pinel's second-favorite spear and tapped it toward heaven.

Sir Christian gave in and moaned, "A reward notice of one hundred fifty thousand groats for me—*as a poisoner*?"

**"That was the finest demonstration of King
Arthur's secret spear ambush!"**

"The court scribes wouldn't copy it any other way," said Britta, carefully moving closer. "After the Christmas feast, they truly loathed you after your fish gravy caused them to be dragged screaming, pleading, and sobbing to help Ordericus and Hubert of Hereford clean out the castle gardé robe pits."

"That your fish gravy also helped overflow," said Uncle Sir Cecil.

Sir Christian's face turned fish gravy gray as he asked, "But who has one hundred fifty thousand groats?"

"The Saxon pirates," said Britta, "to whose camp everyone we tagged should persistently, passionately—"

"And possibly patriotically," said Uncle Sir Cecil.

"Pursue you with a vengeance," said Britta.

"Especially if no one gets lost in the pursuing," said Uncle Sir Cecil.

"Or catches up with you too early," said Britta.

"So let's keep moving," said Uncle Sir Cecil.

"Before someone else shows up prematurely with one of your notices," said Britta.

"And condemns you to fight seven hundred Saxons single-handedly," said Uncle Sir Cecil.

"After you first fight it out with whomever shows up." said Britta. "But first—"

She dismounted and attached fresh notices to moaning Maynard and plastered Pluto. She looked down on them. "Catch us if you can—and don't forget to bring Maynard's cousin!"

"And your friends!" added Uncle Sir Cecil.

"We don't have any friends!" moaned Maynard.

Britta shouted, "Then bring your enemies! I know you have lots of them!"

She leaped onto her horse, which was an amazing feat for a woman wearing her dress and cloak, and as her mount reared, she pulled a scroll and wielded it, not waved—an important distinction—toward the midgets.

She then sheathed the scroll and took off at a speed once again faster than most people and certain breeds of horses. Once again, Sir Christian and Uncle Sir Cecil had to catch up with her in what almost looked like a pursuit.

CHAPTER 15

A Pretty Long Name

A pretty long name takes a pretty long time to pronounce.
—Wade the Scholar, *Chanson de Chrétien*

A short time later, Uncle Sir Cecil's stallion turned its head toward his good ear and gave a neigh that resembled a horse version of, "Youuuuuu-heh-heh-heh!"

Without blinking a weak eye, Uncle Sir Cecil announced, "Britta, we're close to our camp."

"Good," Britta answered as she tapped Sir Christian's arm with a faster swoosh than normal. "Sir Christian, it's time you met the rest of my retinue."

"Consisting of one girl and one squire?" grumbled Sir Christian, vigorously rubbing the numbness in his arm.

Uncle Sir Cecil aimed his bad eyes, one good ear, and questionable nose at Sir Christian and said, "Britta's remaining retinue may be small, but the individuals are not, as you shall see."

"Or feel, if they hit like Britta," Sir Christian muttered as he continued to rub.

"They each have their own style, but in a most polite and courteous way," said Uncle Sir Cecil.

"Which you shall also see because they follow wherever Uncle Sir Cecil and I lead," said Britta.

"With little complaining," said Uncle Sir Cecil.

"Or questioning," said Britta.

"Because they're most courteously polite," reminded Uncle Sir Cecil.

"Much more so than you, Sir Knight of the Most-High Politeness," said Britta.

Then Uncle Sir Cecil asked politely, "Sir Christian, don't you have a small retinue?"

"Yes," said Britta. "Where is *your* squire?"

"We separated when I ran low on money."

"Low—or out?" asked Britta with one of her smiles.

"One thing led to another."

Uncle Sir Cecil said, "Low money or no money, a Round Table knight should be accompanied by his squire if he wants to impress the Saxons."

"I don't want to impress the Saxons."

"Oh, you want to impress the Saxons," Britta said. "You just don't know how much yet. Now then, where did your squire go?"

To move them on to still another painful point, Sir Christian said, "Sir Bertholai, King Leodegrance's old champion, saw him two weeks ago in the town square of Nauntes."

"What was he doing?" asked Britta.

"Interviewing peasants who thought they heard the Monster-of-Unheard-of-Savageness. Their hens stopped laying eggs, their cows stopped giving milk, and the wool on their sheep couldn't be sold, because it felt like wire. When the peasants threatened to stop paying their taxes, Prince Idris II recruited Sir Bertholai as one of the few remaining champions."

"You didn't put in the hospital," Uncle Sir Cecil observed.

"Sir Christian," Britta said as she smacked his arm harder, "what did Sir Bertholai see *your squire* doing in the town square of Nauntes?"

Sir Christian rubbed his arm where it almost felt sprained. "Sir Bertholai saw him in a stall with two other squires, surrounded by laundresses and washerwomen to whom they were selling laundry soap."

"Do you know what kind of laundry soap?"

"Sir Bertholai couldn't tell, because the women were yelling and screaming. He said he hadn't heard anything like that since the last time he visited a town while they were executing someone who was unpopular. Then the laundresses and washerwomen began pushing, shoving, and trampling each other in what looked like the start of a city-wide riot. In a grayish glob that resembled a flood of laundry-soap rinse water, they splashed against the sides of my squire's soap stall, shouting, 'Give us laundry soap or else!' They proceeded to tear down fixtures, woodwork, and even the overhead sign of a laundry-soap flask that said, 'Better clean than mean.'

"Sir Bertholai is an old-fashioned knight who thinks soap of any kind causes perilous results, especially when mixed with water. But he never saw anyone attempt total war over it like those laundresses and washerwomen. He retreated to one side of the square, where he saw one laundress wistfully inhaling fumes from her laundry-soap flask as she gasped, 'This not only makes my rags feel as soft as a baby lamb, but it also smells just like—'*Thud!*

"At that moment, a second laundress smacked her over the split ends with a laundry basket and grabbed the soap flask right out of her hands. The second laundress then dodged past a third as she ran out of the square with the first laundress and twenty others in hot pursuit."

Sir Christian noticed that Britta was listening with an unusual intensity, so he paused for a moment before he concluded with, "Sir Bertholai never heard what the laundry soap smelled like. So he shook his head in a baffled sort of way. Meantime, peasants he still needed to interview joined the commotion, some swinging barrel staves, table legs, and pitchforks. And it looked like the disturbance was growing severe enough to attract the local sheriff and his men. That's when an athletic laundress lobbed an empty soap flask right past his head as she yelled, 'Vile knave of an unwashed knight, don't even think of putting thy unclean hands upon my laundry soap!'

"He yelled back, 'Then why didst thou launch thy flask at me?'

"'That's the wrong answer!' she shouted, winding herself up like a catapult as she grabbed a flask the size of a boulder to pulverize him.

"'To the wrong question!' he replied. With a clink of his unwashed armor, which still smells like cinnamon sautéed with snake poison, plant poison, rock poison, dirty socks, rotten eggs, and sour milk, he leaped upon his horse and galloped out of Nauntes like the Monster-of-Unheard-of-Savageness was after him. Actually, it was the boulder-size flask that missed him and flattened a farmer's cart. On a whim, as well as breathing a sigh of relief over his escape from the dangerous world of laundry-soap advocates, he came by the inn to see me. Then he rode off to investigate safer monsters noises near Cadir Idris."

Britta said, "That confirms other news I received. Regarding your squire, the town of Nauntes is close enough to our camp and somewhat on our way. Let's ride by the town square, locate his stall—"

"And buy some laundry soap?"

She sniffed the air near his clothes and said, "That smells like a good idea."

"But does it smell like a safe idea?" asked Uncle Sir Cecil, thumping his nose in his ongoing search for his one good nostril.

Britta said, "Buying laundry soap used to be safer than chasing pirates. But to finish my statement, let's locate this squire and recruit him. We'll return him to laundry soap that helps people attack each other—"

"After he helps us attack seven hundred Saxons," Sir Christian said sarcastically.

"To rescue Adragain," Uncle Sir Cecil pointed out.

Sir Christian said, "What if we don't need his help, because Adragain doesn't need to be rescued?"

Britta whacked his other arm.

"If you do that again, I'll need to be rescued!"

"For the second time today?" Britta then asked, "Why do you think Adragain doesn't need to be rescued?"

"You seem much more concerned about—"

Clang!

"Learning something—"

Clang!

"Else!"

Clang! Clang! Clang! Clang!

Sir Christian rubbed a fresh row of dents on his helmet as he challenged Britta. "This Adragain doesn't sound like he needs to be rescued from anything. If he's been carefully—"

"And prayerfully," pointed out Uncle Sir Cecil."

Sir Christian nodded to move them on to the next painful point, "trained *by Britta* to keep track of everything and anything that goes on around him, how did he get captured in the first place?"

Britta said, "Even Sir Lancelot learned that on any given day, *anyone* can be captured by *anyone*."

Sir Christian replied, "Does that include anyone like you?"

"It includes anyone *like you*, so be thankful I came along."

"As an answer to all of your prayers," Uncle Sir Cecil pointed out.

"You're both so helpful!"

Britta resheathed her scroll as she said to Sir Christian, "Adragain needs all of us to be helpful as he is rescued from seven hundred Saxons—by you. Also, please remember there's a lot more to see than you think you see in this quest—and for a lot more reasons than just you and your squire. Of course, your squire will be required to sign and initial an attachment I prepared for your Round Table knight errantry contract. Will he only work for food and supplies?"

Sir Christian gave up rubbing his arm and said, "He won't work for fish gravy."

"He'll do."

At that point, they finally rode into Britta's camp. They were much farther away than Uncle Sir Cecil thought, thanks to his distracted horse.

Sir Christian saw two slender individuals watching them from the far side of the camp. The one on the right set down a shield and spear before removing a helmet with the doll-shaped figure of a girl on top. Sir Christian recognized it as similar to equipment once belonging to Merlin Ambrosias, King Arthur's first chief adviser, who had disappeared years earlier while visiting a cave with Nimue, the British Lady of the Lake.

The second person bore neither spear nor shield but wore a cap that looked like a helmet. It was bound with a long white scarf hanging down the back and had an equally long red plume fastened on top. The cap was pulled down completely over the hair.

As the two approached, Sir Christian saw that the first individual was a teenage girl, while the other was a slightly taller teenage boy. Sir Christian thought they acted like sister and brother, although they didn't display a clear family resemblance. The girl's spectacular blonde hair fell to her shoulders, where it draped over a long blue gown decorated in front with triangular groups of three white dots. Like Britta's garb, it was designed for easy comfort and rapid movement. A long sheath knife similar to Uncle Sir Cecil's hung from a leather belt near her right hand. She stopped in front of Sir Christian and curtsied.

Britta introduced her to Sir Christian as "My niece, who serves as my lady's maid, housemaid, horsemaid, handmaid, parlormaid, chambermaid, laundrymaid, milkmaid, kitchenmaid, trashmaid, camp superintendent, hair dresser, and assistant bodyguard."

"She must do the work of thirteen people," Sir Christian said.

"That's what she tells us when she needs money. You may address her by her first name, which is Sheena Unica Verena Antonia Serena Vivina Augustina Ruebena Serilda Athena Karmita Lalita Kairos."

"Why, I'm charmed to meet you," said Sir Christian, wrinkling his brow. "Sheena Unica Verena—hmm! Antonia Serena Vivina—hmm! Say, I never have been very good at remembering short names. How did yours go again?"

"Milord, Sir Christian," replied the tall girl with an impish smile. "It goes Sheena Unica Verena Antonia Serena Vivina Augustina Ruebena Serilda Athena Karmita Lalita Kairos."

"That's a pretty—*long*—name you have there. Have you ever thought of matching the different parts to your different jobs?"

"No, Sir Christian. That might make them hard to remember."

"What about using an acronym?"

"Is that like an acrobat?" the niece answered with another impish smile.

"That's my niece's first name," said Britta. "Her mother wanted a large family but went through a difficult first pregnancy. It was pretty long, like everything else that has to do with my niece. So her mother decided to have no more children and gave all of her favorite girl names to her one beloved daughter."

"Does her one beloved daughter have a middle name?"

"No one really knows. When she was born, the hospital scribe ran out of room on Myrddin's new birth certificates."

Sir Christian looked at the taller teenage boy. In addition to the helmet-like cap, he wore a blue tunic with a centered red cross above brown trousers with the legs tucked into black boots with gaudy red flaps. His double-wrapped belt supported a sheathed sword on the left hip and a long sheath knife, identical to those of the girl and Uncle Sir Cecil, near his right hand.

Sir Christian had a knack for knives, which was why his father had given him one forged by the great sword smith Trebuchet. One detail Sir Christian always observed about a person was where he placed his belt knife. He noted that only two persons on this quest weren't wearing one within easy reach of their right cutting hand: Britta and himself. Someone had lifted his at the inn when he wasn't looking very well. As he wondered where Britta's hung—

Swoosh!

She pulled another scroll like Sir Lancelot drawing a sword and handed it to her niece, saying, "Here's the supply list."

Her niece smiled and tucked it away with a sweeping swoosh of her own.

With his first smile in a long while, Sir Christian concluded that Britta was the only person on this quest, maybe even in the entire realm of King Arthur or even the entire known universe, who didn't need a belt knife within reach of one of her hands—and King Arthur help the bandit, pirate, or miscreant knight who attempted to draw his blade against one of her flying scrolls.

The boy also carried a brass-tipped horn bugle called an olifant[15] on a diagonal black leather strap that hung from his left shoulder. The boy's right hand brushed over it as it reached up to pull his cap farther down on his hair before he bowed politely to Sir Christian.

Britta said, "This is Uncle Sir Cecil's squire, Andred—"

Who clicked his heels together as he jerked straight up and shouted at the top of his lungs, "Huzzah!"[16]

A startled Sir Christian almost fell from his equally startled horse as it jumped high enough to clear the Monster-of-Unheard-of-Savageness, or so it was recorded. No one else present, including the other horses, noticed anything abnormal.

"*The Silent*. He's also very steady," said Britta.

"And polite," reminded Uncle Sir Cecil the Steady.

Sir Christian stared at Andred the same way he had first looked at Uncle Sir Cecil. Keeping one eye on Britta in case claws, scrolls, or even the Monster-of-Unheard-of-Savageness suddenly flew from her direction, he asked cautiously, "And what makes Andred so silent?"

Britta said, "Andred is actually diagnosed as *sort of silent*. That's because he suffered a severe shock as a small child. One night, he woke up and saw a giant she-bear watching him from a tree outside his chamber window. When he fearlessly watched right back, it became so excited it shook the tree like it was in a windstorm, an earthquake, or an explosion in a small kitchen. But instead of growling, it uttered a continuous string of two syllables that sounded like a deep-breathing form of 'Huffa! Huffa!' It became loud enough to eventually wake the entire manor house. The manor huntsman was summoned, and he initially tried to scare the she-bear away with fire and banging pots. Andred screamed when the huntsman threatened to shoot it with his hunting bow. When that didn't work, the huntsman accidentally cried, 'Hubba! Hubba!' That's when the she-bear ran off and was never seen near the manor house again. But

---

[15] Archaic for "elephant."

[16] Pronounced "huh-ZAH," with the accent on the second syllable, as with *the Shah* in the expression "the Shah of Iran."

since that night, Andred has never said more than one or two syllables between pauses, in addition to his own version of a single 'Huffa!' which comes out after an accented shift to the second syllable as—"

"Huzzah!" shouted Andred.

Sir Christian held on tightly as his horse jumped again before he asked, "How does *huzzah* sound like *huffa* or even"—he mouthed the word distastefully—"*hubba?*"

"No one really knows," Britta said, "but that's his mother's story, and she's sticking to it. Now, the word—"

"Huzzah!" shouted Andred as Sir Christian's horse jumped again.

"Is very positive because it derives from the Hebrew word *hosanna*, which, of course, means 'the Lord saves.'"

Uncle Sir Cecil said, "Whatever caused *hosanna* to become *huzzah* in Andred is also unknown, but Nimue, the British Lady of the Lake, who likes bears, thought this one may have been sent to watch over and protect Andred. But nobody knows from what or who."

Sir Christian said, "So besides—"

"Huzzah!" shouted Andred, making Sir Christian's horse jump again.

Britta said, "Andred says many other things but only in one, two, or three syllables between pauses."

Andred once more pulled his hat down tightly as he again bowed politely, clicked his heels together loudly, and, this time, stood straight up as he belted out an even louder "Huzzah!"

Sir Christian looked like a modern rodeo rider as he hung on to his mount and cried, "Aiieee!"

"Not aiieee—huzzah!" Andred announced proudly yet politely.

Sir Christian looked neither proud nor polite as he barely brought his horse under control again. Andred seemed not to notice as he explained in his unusual short-syllable format, "Yes—milord—Sir Christian. I am—Andred—the Silent—who can—say—many—other—things—as well as—"

"Nothing?" suggested Sir Christian.

"Yes—milord—Sir Christian. I can—also say—nothing!"

"Then please do," said Sir Christian.

"Nothing!" announced Andred cheerfully, which he prepared to follow with another equally loud and cheerful "Huzzah!"

"Andred!" ordered Britta, pointing down with a scroll for lower volume.

He politely responded with a softer and less-volatile "Huzzah!"

Thankful his horse didn't kill him before he was tempted to kill Andred, Sir Christian said softly, "So, uh, young squire, your name is Andred the—hmm—Silent. Now, could that possibly be Andred and anything more besides—"

"Huzzah!" said Andred, again more softly.

Britta gave Andred a soft nod, which was her way of keeping his *huzzah*s within the range of safety and reason. She said to Sir Christian, "His first name is just Andred, which means 'strong and manly.' By the time their mother got around to him, she was so tired of selecting names that she only came up with one. No one knows if he has a middle name either. Incidentally, he and his sister are twins. My niece, who was the only one their mother was expecting, was born first. Then Andred arrived, which was such a surprise that when the doctor first picked him up, all he could say was—"

"Huzzah!" shouted Andred.

Sir Christian, prayerfully thankful his horse appeared jumped out, said, "Andred's name minus—"

"Huzzah!" shouted Andred.

Sir Christian continued, "Seems just about right for addressing a squire."

Britta nodded in agreement as she hand-signaled Andred to check on the packhorses. He saluted her as he forgot himself and belted out an even louder "Huzzah!" Once again, Sir Christian's horse plunged, and he barely brought it under control.

"Huzzah!" Andred shouted from the packhorses.

Sir Christian breathed a sigh of relief as, once again, his horse appeared to be jumped out. He said to Britta, "Your niece's name— once again, just how does that go?"

"Sheena Unica Verena Antonia Serena Vivina Augustina Ruebena Serilda Athena Karmita Lalita Kairos," the girl repeated sweetly.

"Of course, but isn't that a little long for everyday use?"

Britta said, "The first time I heard it, I told her mother, who's my first cousin, that a pretty long name takes a pretty long time to pronounce. She agreed but couldn't decide which part of my niece's first names to get rid of. She finally decided to keep them all. As a special favor, Ordericus the scribe wrote them up for her in his most flowing calligraphy, along with their definitions on a small scroll she carried around on the end of a gold chain attached to her waist. That way, she never forgot what the names meant[17] or in what order she liked to hear them. She also directed the immediate family to address my niece by a different name on each day of the week. So in their family gatherings at the manor house, she was Sheena on Sunday, Unica on Monday, Verena on Tuesday, Antonia on Wednesday, Serena on Thursday, Vivina on Friday, and Augustina on Saturday. Her last six first names—Ruebena, Serilda, Athena, Karmita, Lalita, and Kairos—were rotated through the church holidays."

When Britta saw the blank look on Sir Christian's face, she added, "I only call her Sheena because it saves time when I need her in the morning."

---

[17]   The contents of the small scroll carried by the mother of Britta's maid:

1.	Sheena	Hebrew	God is gracious
2.	Unica	Latin	Only one
3.	Verena	Latin	Truthful
4.	Antonia	Latin	Praiseworthy
5.	Serena	Latin	Peaceful
6.	Vivina	Latin	Full of life
7.	Augustina	Latin	Majestic
8	Ruebena	Hebrew	Daughter
9.	Serilda	Greek	Armed warrior woman
10.	Athena	Greek	Wisdom; always defeats war god
11.	Karmita	Hebrew	Song
12.	Lalita	Greek	Talkative
13.	Kairos	Greek	Final; complete

Sheena added gleefully, "My thirteen jobs and thirteen first names further identify me as Lady Britta's prayer maid, or maid with prayer. Isn't that clever? My mother came up with that too. Now, Andred—"

"Huzzah!" Andred shouted from the packhorses.

"Is the prayer squire."

"Which makes you all one big happy answer to prayer," muttered Sir Christian as he prayed thanks that his horse stopped jumping.

"Huzzah!" erupted in agreement from the packhorses.

Sheena interrupted further thoughts Sir Christian might have had on those interesting yet eccentric subjects when she curtsied politely again and asked, "Sir Christian, why does your horse try to eat your cloak? He doesn't look as hungry as you. Also, it's so full of holes that I don't think it could fill him up."

Sir Christian looked hungry enough to eat anything that would fill him up, provided it didn't resemble the slobbery mess that had become his cloak. But he still found enough strength to pull his horse's reins, keeping its head from chomping on the remains—too much. The other two horses also looked ready to chomp, but Uncle Sir Cecil and Britta backed them away. Fortunately, all other horses in the camp were still upwind.

"Slow Silver, stop!" Sir Christian commanded his destrier. When it ignored him and stretched forth its neck for another chomping chunk of cloak, Sir Christian wheeled him around in another circle as he cried out to Britta, "What in the name of King Arthur was in that flask of spices you gave me?"

"Nothing that excites horses when used in moderation, which, in my youthful judgment, nowhere includes dumping half a flask of anything on one's clothes. That's even if one does smell like he spent a week screaming, pleading, and sobbing in the crew that cleans out the castle gardé robe pits. Sir Christian, I told you to anoint yourself with those spices, not take a bath!"

"I concede the point," Sir Christian said nervously as he watched the three horses watching his cloak, "but what is that stuff?"

"Its official name is the Oil of the Perfume Perilous."

"You are serious?"

"Is the archbishop of Canterbury Catholic? Let's cut to the joust. In situations like this, I am always serious; Sir Christian, the flask I gave you contained the latest blend of an absolutely necessary fragrance, developed to handle the ever-growing population of unwashed knights. Those slobs of the Round Table were beginning to smell more disgusting than Sir Bertholai of Cameliard, even sharing his delusion that soap is perilous. Therefore, scores of fair damsels complained to Queen Guinevere that they were tired of loathly smelling knights escorting them to an even more loathly series of evening feasts at the current castle.

"This came to a head the last time King Arthur came home from a hard day's quest with his loathly smelling comrade Sir Yvaine, the Knight of the Lion. Only King Arthur also smelled like the lion. That was the royal last straw—or, shall I say, aroma—for Queen Guinevere, for she immediately gave King Arthur a royal ultimatum. He could do something about his unknightly as well as loathly smell—or else! Well, ruler or no ruler, he knew better than to oppose his queen on that request. He may reign as high king over all the Britons, but he could still get locked out of the royal bedchamber. Then he might find himself sleeping in the royal courtyard with Sir Yvaine's lion.

"In a panic, he summoned Myrddin to a summit in the scriptorium. That's where he said a crisis had arisen between the outraged court damsels and the unwashed knights of Camelot. Arthur did not mention his personal problem with Guinevere, but Myrddin had nose enough to sniff around—and sense enough not to repeat what he sniffed. Based on looks Myrddin had seen unwashed knights of Camelot receive from the court damsels for some time, he wisely discerned this etiquette problem, as he diplomatically dubbed it, could kick off a bigger panic than the one between Sir Meranges des Portz, Sir Gauuaine le Franc, and the terrified scribes. He quickly assembled a team of master perfumers who once worked for Merlin. Drawing on Round Table discretionary funds to start things up, he assigned them a room near the laundry, plus adequate time and procurement money. There they carefully and skillfully developed the liquefied spices you have since excited, if not utterly astounded, our horses with—namely, the Oil of the Perfume Perilous."

"But why is it called an oil? It doesn't feel oily."

"It contains just the slightest hint of an aromatic oil to validate its name. Otherwise, it might not wash out of whatever clothes a knight of your aptitude might dump it on. Incidentally, due to the amount you did dump on your clothes, particularly your cloak, I'm sure you learned it's quite watery."

"As well as highly gaseous."

"That is correct, Sir Christian, but the word *oil* in the title is there to make it sound appealing. Don't you agree that the name Oil of the Perfume Perilous comes off better to a spear-thrusting, sword-swinging, monster-mashing man-at-arms than, say, Liquid of the Perfume Perilous or even Gas Cloud of the Perfume Perilous?"

Sir Christian didn't completely comprehend Britta's logic, but once again, he nodded to move them on to the next painful point as he kept Slow Silver moving in painfully slow circles.

Sheena noticed the resistance Slow Silver was giving to Sir Christian while moving in those circles, so she asked sweetly and innocently, "Sir Christian, why do you call your horse Slow Silver?"

Praying this question might lead to a safer and less eccentric subject, Sir Christian said, "My destrier's original name was just plain Silver. But his first owner, Sir Egglame de Moated, never liked to go anywhere fast, so he always commanded his horse, 'Slow, Silver!' Eventually, the horse heard the words *slow* and *silver* together so much he thought it was his real name. But the extra word stuck in an ironic way because Slow Silver never liked to go anywhere slow, no matter what his owner commanded. That's when Sir Egglame demoted him to second-favorite horse. When that didn't produce desired results, he sold him to me for a penny. Does that make sense?"

"No, Sir Christian."

"What's your horse's name?"

"Oh, Sir Christian, my horse is a wonderful mare I call Butterfly. Although she looked more like butter covered with flies when she was born. But even then, I could tell by looking into her deep, wistful eyes that she contained the right spirit to grow up wise, graceful, and beautiful—with buckskin-blonde-colored hair just like mine."

"Andred's dark horse is called Fountain, although he looks and sounds more like someone splashing through a mud puddle; however, he's a quiet, polite, and most courteous horse the same way Andred is a quiet, polite, and most courteous squire."

Sir Christian said, "Who likes to yell."

"Huzzah!" shouted Andred from the packhorses.

Sir Christian breathed another prayer of thanks when his horse didn't buck as he asked, "Does Fountain ever say the horse equivalent of—"

"Huzzah!" shouted Andred once more from the packhorses.

Sir Christian breathed an additional prayer of thanks over his horse's new nonbucking response.

"No one really knows," replied Sheen, "except maybe another horse—like Uncle Sir Cecil's. He's a mighty multicolored destrier called Rainbow. Oh, Sir Christian, I think that's a wonderful name for Uncle Sir Cecil's horse. He's ridden by the warrior who would easily be the most famous bowman in all of Britain—if he didn't have bad eyes, that is. He would also be one of the most interesting knights at the Round Table—if he could listen to the Round Table gossip better, that is. And then he might even have gotten his name entered at the bottom of King Arthur's Round Table Honor Roll—like you once did, that is. But that would only be if he wanted to, that is—and he wasn't needed to protect Britta traveling around the realm, attempting to look harmless."

Sir Christian thought someone needed to travel around and protect the realm from Britta and her retinue attempting to look harmless.

"Oh, Sir Christian," Sheena added as she folded her arms in an appealing way, "don't you agree that a name that contains the word *bow* is most appropriate for the horse of Uncle Sir Cecil, who is so, so steady and—"

"My horse is called Ice Water," said Britta. "Sheena, I am sure Sir Christian, as Knight of the Round Table in good standing, temporarily reinstated, found your explanation most interesting. But now you must help Andred—"

"Huzzah!" came from the packhorses.

"The Not So Silent," commented Sir Christian.

"Take down the tents, pack up the supplies, and put the campfire out before there's an accident prompting someone to yell an utterly enormous—"

"Huzzah!"

"Loud enough to cause a stampede?" Sir Christian snorted louder than his horse.

"Because ingredients for your fish gravy might explode?" Sheena asked sweetly, impishly, and perhaps a little too hopefully.

Britta gave everyone, especially Sir Christian, a knowing look that made even Uncle Sir Cecil smile. She said with the authority of one who is used to being obeyed—most of the time, "Sheena, help Andred. Uncle Sir Cecil and I will assist you shortly."

Britta turned to Sir Christian. "Speaking of fish gravy—you don't have ingredients for that stuff anywhere near you?"

Sir Christian gave her a grayish gravy look.

Britta said, "I thought so. Wherever you have it, puh-lease keep it away from the fire. Meanwhile, we must make your clothes less appealing to the horses, especially your cloak. Otherwise, it might be difficult for a master horse breaker to ride them. I also wish to locate your squire in the town square of Nauntes before nightfall. What did you say he was doing there?"

"Selling laundry soap."

"That causes riots," Uncle Sir Cecil reminded him.

Britta smiled at Sir Christian as she sniffed at his cloak. "You did mention buying some. If things in Nauntes have calmed down despite its proximity to rioters, robbers, pirates, and monsters, it might be time to get your overripe, overspiced clothes washed. Come to think of it, let's get enough soap to wash all of our overripe, overspiced clothes. When operating on a shoe-latchet budget, it never hurts to cut corners when one can."

"Britta, what if we can't afford that much soap?"

Britta replied with a smile, "Then your squire will make a generous donation. He just doesn't know it yet."

Britta then noticed a lean, hungry look on Sir Christian's face as he watched the smoldering campfire. She called to Andred and Sheena, who had started work nearby, "Give Sir Christian something to eat before he passes out. But first put that fire out—and find something in which to seal his cloak!"

CHAPTER 16

A Virtuous Woman

Worse, she's a virtuous woman who looks harmless.
—Wade the Scholar, *Chanson de Chrétien*

Miles to the east, in a private room at the Inn of the Knight Extravagant, a tall knight sat serenely yet painfully up in bed. He was known for his fair, curly hair, which, in a realm where most adults looked thirty years old for decades, had grayed early at the temple edges. His handsome face, marred by an evil expression, frowned as he listened to a battered squire. But his concentration was hindered by two things. The knight looked extremely pale and bleached like Captain Sarito's mercenaries, and the squire looked extremely brown and bruised and smelled like the wrong end of the wrong horse after it had grazed for a week at the wrong end of the wrong field growing the wrong onions.

The squire stood with his back to an open window through which a gracious wind blew away from him; his ungracious, disgusting clothes; and the interior of the room. Before the wind changed, the knight wrinkled his nose and asked impatiently, "Melehan, are you telling me that Lady Britta de Brittany, Myrddin's confidential kinswoman as well as chief liaison between him, King Arthur, and Nimue, the British Lady of the Lake, traveled all the way to the most blighted castle in the most blighted shire to find Sir Christian de Galis, the Round Table's most incompetent and blighted knight?"

"Yes, milord."

"The same Sir Christian de Galis who landed the entire Round Table in a Christmas feast hospital ward with his father's fish gravy?"

"Yes, milord, which also makes him the same Sir Christian de Galis you landed in a gardé robe pit runoff hole. That's after you dared him, on his honor as Knight of the Round Table in good standing, to charge on his horse through a thatch-walled cottage. It was merely misfortune and therefore no fault of yours, mine, or a host of others who had their servants drug screaming, pleading, and sobbing—at sword point, no less—to connect the hole in the cottage floor with the castle sewers, that Myrddin passed by at the exact moment that Sir Christian—if you excuse the expression—dropped in."

"Like a food cart going down a mudhole?"

"Why, yes, milord!" the squire answered in surprise. "You know that line too."

When the knight quietly nodded, the squire continued, "And Myrddin happened to be in conversation with the only engineer not in your pay who operated a crane strong enough to lift an armored knight and his horse out of twelve feet of castle sewage."

The knight nodded again, but frowned further as he brushed back his hair and said, "And now you tell me that Lady Britta de Brittany has gone out of her way to recruit the idiot of the fish gravy to rescue her annoying grandson, Adragain, from our allies, the Saxons?"

"Yes, milord."

"Melehan, I find that incredible knowing Lady Britta de Brittany the way I think I do."

"How well do you know her, milord?"

"Maybe not as well as I thought. Are you absolutely sure, with some kind of written proof, that Sir Christian de Galis is the Round Table knight—"

"Former Round Table knight, milord."

"Yes indeed, former Round Table knight that she came to Castle Perilous to recruit?"

"Yes, milord. I got the news from Sir Christian's innkeeper, a nervous old wreck known locally as Sir Erbin the Easygoing."

"Sir Erbin the what?"

"Easygoing, milord. His name is a local joke. Behind his back, everyone at his inn says he's just easy and seldom going, as in anywhere toward success. Thus, someone is always taking advantage of him, especially the sheriff of Castle Perilous. But he has one popular characteristic: he is always willing to return a favor. So when I visited his inn after Sir Christian left, I informed Sir Erbin, using extra small words so that I knew that he understood, that he owed me one. I explained that I was King Arthur's favorite grandson on a royal mission for the security of the realm, possibly the entire known world, if not the universe; therefore, I needed to see his copy of every contract he had recently notarized as an innkeeper."

"And he immediately complied?"

"Actually, milord, he immediately refused—and told me to look for a quest handout at someone else's inn."

At that moment, an evil gust of wind blew into the room with such force that the knight gagged and replied angrily while trying not to choke, "Surely that didn't help!" He fanned the air away from his nose with one hand as he pointed at the squire's disgusting clothes with the other.

Then the wind graciously reversed itself, which allowed the squire to reply meekly, "Uh, no, milord, the uh—hmm—easygoing innkeeper of what is now being called by some the uh—hmm—Inn of the Fish Gravy has sinus problems."

"Fortunately for you," the knight said as he took in a deep, gasping breath. He hoped he developed sinus problems before the wind shifted again.

Melehan, eager to shift the subject to anything besides the shifting wind, explained, "Sir Erbin swore that he had never heard of King Arthur having a son, much less a grandson; therefore, he owed me nothing. That's when I pleaded with the innkeeper a little, twisted his arm behind his back a lot, and made one or two thinly veiled threats. When that did nothing, I threatened to confiscate every contract on file at his inn in the name of the first Round Table knight I could think of. Since you asked me never to mention anyone associated with Orkney, I picked Sir Dagonet's name out of the air, of all people. But that's when Sir Erbin looked like he had just seen the Monster-of-Unheard-of-Savageness."

"Melehan, there is no Monster-of-Unheard-of-Savageness."

"I know, milord. It's a fictional character invented by a monk with too much time on his hands. But if it did exist, Sir Erbin looked like he had seen it. And he told me peasants living between Nauntes and Cadir Idris claimed that they had heard it. So had their hens that stopped laying eggs, their cows that stopped giving milk, and their sheep whose wool now felt like wire. Someone even swore it made a horse die of fright!"

"Melehan! Cut to the joust!"

"Yes, milord. When I mentioned Sir Dagonet, Sir Erbin looked like he had seen the Monster-of-Unheard-of-Savageness and let me see the documents."

The knight finally gave Melehan an approving nod but watched warily for another shift in the wind.

As Melehan tried to ignore the knight's disdain for his smell and his even more disgusting appearance, he replied with a skittish laugh, "Milord, he showed me all *one* of them. The only document he has notarized in the last six months is Sir Christian's quest contract."

"Why is that?"

"Most travelers consider Sir Erbin too easygoing and therefore too inept to notarize their documents properly. So they always wait until they reach the next inn, which is usually this one."

"That simplifies things for us, Melehan."

"Yes, milord."

The knight continued to watch the squire warily with one eye and the wind with the other as he said, "I overheard travelers at this inn speak of a battle that just took place at the other inn. What can you report?"

"Milord, this morning, I witnessed from a safe distance, because there was strange dust blowing in the air that gave off a sound that went something like *poof,*"—he didn't add that he had also kept his distance so that no one could smell *him*—"an archery skirmish at the other inn, where twelve Navarrese mercenaries were most painfully and, I must add, most embarrassingly defeated by Lady Britta de Brittany and her ancient archer, Uncle Sir Cecil the so-called Steady."

"Hmm, her half-blind relative they jokingly call the prayer archer—did she repeat her trick of feeding him arrows while she pointed him and his bow in the correct direction?"

"Yes, milord, and their combined archery was devastating."

"What triggered that debacle?"

"Milord, Sir Christian de Galis collected seven shillings twice over from those mercenaries after they advertised for a condiment to serve at a banquet. He persuaded them that his father's fish gravy tasted similar yet superior to garum, a popular food sauce they have consumed in Navarre since Roman times. But the only thing superior about this batch of fish gravy, if one can call such a thing superior, is that it laid up the mercenaries for only a week. That's after it set fire to the inn. The results may not have been as devastating as what happened at Caerleon or on the Humber, but they took the easygoing out of Sir Erbin the innkeeper. Also, the Navarrese mercenaries looked thin and bleached like you and the other Knights of the Round Table. For revenge, they planned to fasten Sir Christian to a splintered stake piled high with firewood as they taught him a long, painful, as well as heated lesson."

"Melehan, it seems they have good reason to share our disdain for Sir Christian de Galis and his father's so-called fish gravy."

"Yes, milord, but hopefully we're not inept enough to be soundly defeated like them by a middle-aged grandmother and her ancient archer uncle."

"Melehan," the knight said soberly, "that middle-aged grandmother and her ancient archer uncle, allied with something I still find unexplainable, helped defeat a well-equipped, well-organized, and well-supported Saxon invasion on the Humber."

"Yes, milord, but that something unexplainable included Britta's annoying grandson, Adragain, whom your Saxon allies now hold prisoner. Meanwhile"—Melehan couldn't hold back his laugh—"the defeated Navarrese find themselves dubbed the mercenaries-not-so-perilous. You should hear songs children are singing about them. The best one begins—"

"Melehan, cut to the joust!"

"Yes, milord!"

The knight waved his hand impatiently, partly to clear the air, which also started to contain small particles that had floated in through the window with a sound that went something like *poof.* He said, "The other inn appears to be a gathering place for the incompetently perilous."

"Yes, milord. It's a regular gardé robe pit full of them."

That you wallowed in yourself! the knight thought while giving the squire another disgusting sniff.

Melehan continued, "Now, that's despite the presence of Lady Britta and her uncle, who are just plain perilous—to men in black armor like us."

When this remark made the knight frown once more, Melehan quickly added, "The locals were astounded by Uncle Sir Cecil's archery. He can barely see the ground in front of him, much less down a well-lit road. Yet he hit twelve mercenaries with twelve arrows in less than twenty seconds. The innkeeper and his maids, knaves, guests, and neighbors had never seen anything like it."

"Not this side of Caerleon?"

"No, milord, not even this side of Camelot."

"Melehan, have you?"

"Yes, milord, a year ago, I saw Lady Britta de Brittany feed lightning-fast arrows to her uncle at the Lady of the Lake's annual archery shoot. They hit twenty-three targets in less than a minute. More than one competitor complained that it wasn't fair for Uncle Sir Cecil to compete with the aid of an assistant. But the tournament marshal was Sir Lancelot, who laughed so hard every time Uncle Sir Cecil swung his bow and made even the established atheists fall down on their knees and pray that he not only awarded them first prize but also gave Uncle Sir Cecil the Round Table Ribbon for Distinguished Citizenship."

The knight nodded grimly as he motioned for Melehan to continue.

"Yes, milord. Now, because Lady Britta and her uncle have provided so much interference to your recent plan of an early succession via the clobbered Saxon invasion, I ordered extensive research be conducted into their background. Thus, I learned that the speed of Sir Cecil's shooting style is based on the archery standard of the ancient Sarmatian cavalry. In fact, he's faster, as well as a direct descendant of a Sarmatian knight who came to Britain in the second century."

"Melehan, Lady Britta; her grandson, Adragain; and those nutty twins she travels with are all direct descendants of those Sarmatians."

"Milord, who is Sir Christian de Galis descended from?"

"A half-witted Celtic fish cook who disappeared years ago!"

Melehan was astonished by this venomous outpouring from the knight, who was normally so cold, calculating, and calmly evil. He stood quietly for a moment before he asked, "Milord, do you know anything about the disappearance of Sir Christian's father?"

"Melehan, have you learned something?"

"I may have, milord. I recently visited Great-Aunt Morgan le Fay at Castle Chariot, where she holds court with the Queen of Norgales, the Queen of Eastland, and the Queen of the Outer Isles. They chanted like an eerie choir as I entered their presence, 'Melehan, beware the Dolorous Stroke!'

"Milord, when your plans of an early succession vaporized via a volcanic blast on the Humber, I heard more than one older knight say that he was reminded of the Dolorous Stroke."

The knight said, "That happened way back in Merlin's time."

"Yes, milord. But I also heard you declare that the Humber debacle was caused by something on a dolorous camp stove used by Sir Christian. I therefore had Myrddin's scribe in our secret pay, Hubert of Hereford, search through every old scroll in Camelot's library. In particular, I directed him to look for any connections between Sir Christian's father and the original Dolorous Stroke. He sent word to me he was on the verge of a discovery, when he was dragged screaming, pleading, and sobbing to serve in the castle gardé robe pits."

"Was he caught working for us?"

"No, milord, he was caught playing cards while copying scrolls."

"Melehan, what are cards?"

"Milord, I'm not exactly sure. But a squire is said to be behind them. When I tried to find out which one, the other squires gave me an unfriendly look and pretended not to know. Meantime, further research by Hubert of Hereford must wait until he finishes cleaning out the castle sewers."

The knight thought with a shudder that anything Hubert of Hereford touched would smell like Melehan. He gave his squire a severe look in the eye. "Make sure he only sends his reports to you."

"Yes, milord."

"Did Hubert provide any hint of what he was on the verge of discovering?"

"I'm not sure, milord. He submitted to me the strangest report, which made me wonder at times if he took his assignment seriously. At the end of a long scroll containing rules for playing twenty-six variations of whatever card games are—as well as backgammon, chess, mumbly peg, jump rope, hopscotch, checkers, and the best way to pitch pennies when there's ice on the pavement—he mentioned in one final footnote that Sir Christian's father disappeared at the exact minute and hour as the original Dolorous Stroke. But he found nothing further to show it was more than a mere coincidence. Yet the warning of Great-Aunt Morgan's friends, who are accused by many of being broom-closet witches, haunts me."

"Melehan, Great-Aunt Morgan or not, beware of warnings from broom-closet witches."

"Yes, milord, which is something I often sweep through my mind."

The knight shook his head at the pun, but nodded as he thought back to the Humber campaign and its odd association with the

Dolorous Stroke. Ever since the sky above the Saxon camp had filled with fire and ashes, he had suffered from a recurring dream in which he saw himself trapped near the bottom of a fiery inferno. In the meantime, the poet Virgil climbed down next to him, discussing the best way to rhyme British poetry in three lines with an Italian exile named Dante. The knight violently shook his head to rid himself of that vision. When it wouldn't completely leave, he tried focusing on anything else.

The wind once more blew strongly into the room, and despite the presence of a growing amount of *poof* dust, caused the knight to focus on the even more nauseating way Melehan smelled. He was also covered with livid brown bruises. Once again, trying not to gag, choke, or throw up, the knight asked in an irritated way, "Melehan, did you participate in anything against my orders?"

"No, milord, my appearance was caused by a separate mishap, which I will explain in due time."

"I see," the knight said, struggling to speak between choking on dust and gagging on Melehan. Then the wind graciously switched again and once more blew out. He said without disguising a distinct sigh of relief, "Melehan, if Lady Britta de Brittany were a man, she would be more formidable than Sir Lancelot, Myrddin, and my father combined. But as a lady, she is scarier than Morgan le Fay, her three weird friends, and Nimue, the British Lady of the Lake, put together."

"Is she a witch, milord?"

"Worse, she's a virtuous woman who appears to look harmless. She also believes that the impossible is possible. For example, she thinks that the worst choice is sometimes the best choice, which is nonsense. Yet that thought provides her with unstoppable motivations that we must deal with. Have you ever seen a mouse placed inside a maze where it must find its way through dead ends and wrong turns to finally reach cheese at the other end? If Britta became that mouse, she wouldn't waste time figuring out a path through the maze. She would bare her teeth and eat nonstop straight through the walls. No witch of my mother's acquaintance wants to tangle with a woman like her. In fact, no witch of my mother's acquaintance will come within three miles of her. For one thing, Lady Britta de Brittany terrifies them with her stare. If she wasn't virtuous, I would be tempted to label her part cockatrice.[18] But that implies a male monster, doesn't it? She's no monster, male or otherwise, but she does seem to be more than a match for one."

"Milord, it's said her stare scared a bear off a mountain."

"Melehan, I wouldn't be surprised if her stare scared three bears off a mountain."

"Yes, milord."

The knight continued, "Yet Lady Britta de Brittany took my bait to seek her captured grandson among the Saxons."

"Yes, milord—but not before she sought Sir Christian de Galis among the last-place locals."

"Melehan, have you learned something further?"

"Yes, milord. For thirty-plus years, Sir Christian's been dubbed the absolute worst knight at King Arthur's Round Table. Hubert of Hereford showed me the following excerpt from Sir Christian's latest liaison review: 'Jesters told jokes about him. Heroes avoided him. Bullies humiliated him. King Arthur got real tired of having him around.' But somehow, milord, he located his father's long-lost secret, supposedly a substance of great power surpassing even Greek fire of the ancients. Disguised as a food condiment, it has the most innocent-sounding name—yet it blows up, burns up, or makes people sick, depending how you add sugar."

Sir Mordred looked skeptical and much more interested in whether the wind was going to change again. So Melehan quickly added, "Sir Christian has yet to discover its true use and magnitude. But his tampering with it so far has delayed your plans. Great-Aunt Morgan le Fay and her friends insist that there is a connection between it and the Dolorous Stroke. That was especially true after she noticed the

---

[18]   A cockatrice was a mythological creature that hatched from an egg. It had the head of a cock and the body of a reptile, and it could kill with a stare. The name was also used in the King James Bible for a certain type of viper.

quantity of her special healing ointment she was obligated to ship to the Humber field hospital."

"Melehan," the knight said with distracted disdain, as if a higher force were working hard to make him confused, "I was at the Humber and Caerleon. I don't completely understand what happened in either place, but any similarity between a food condiment called fish gravy and ancient Greek fire is surely nothing more than, if you'll excuse the expression, a fish story. For one thing, nothing blew up at Caerleon."

"All of those things happened at the inn, milord."

"Melehan, I'm seldom wrong, but in case I am this once, keep Great-Aunt Morgan le Fay's warning in mind and continue looking into secrets behind this so-called fish gravy. Meanwhile, I think Britta de Brittany remains our main threat. Therefore, we must continue to understand her better to defeat her. She's also well known for another quote: 'There are often more things to see than you think you see.' That surely contains the key to understanding her secret strategies and motives. It also may point to the real reason she recruited this blundering Sir Christian de Galis as her quest knight. It can't possibly be something silly sounding, like a condiment consisting of *gravy*. Let me repeat her quote one more time so you don't forget it: 'There are often more things to see than you think you see.'"

Melehan said, "Whenever Lady Britta uses that quote around Uncle Sir Cecil—"

"Melehan!" the knight interrupted. "Sir Cecil is not your uncle!"

"Yes, milord, put that way, it does have an odd sound. When Lady Britta—"

"And I question whether Lady Britta is a lady!"

"Yes, milord."

"But we'll keep calling her one for convenience."

"Yes, milord. When Lady Britta uses that quote near Sir Cecil's good ear, he likes to add, 'And someone prays.'"

The knight sneered, "The name Cecil doesn't mean 'blind' for nothing. Melehan, only actions help one see more than he thinks he sees. I suppose you'll be telling me next that prayer, not action, has been changing Sir Christian's luck."

"Milord, something has changed Sir Christian's luck."

The knight shook his head, more from annoyance than from Melehan's smell. He stared at his squire. "For the time being, let Lady Britta, the obnoxious, bear-scaring, wild woman from Brittany, travel with this Knight of the Fish Gravy. After all, he caused the Christmas debacle that helped make her grandson's capture possible. In the meantime, I'll think up ways to neutralize her half-blind, half-deaf, sinus-infected, over-confident, and over-the-hill prayer archer of an uncle. In the finale, Lady Britta's beloved Uncle Sir Cecil will not be decisive. Then, if she continues on her current collision course, she'll easily fall into the hands of my Saxon allies. They'll slip a hood over her scary little head like the notorious falcon she resembles—a female bird that thinks it was created to dominate male counterparts. Then we'll be rid of her, and at the same time, we will pull a key spoke out of Myrddin's influence. Then we will employ a plot I have long toyed with to compromise Sir Lancelot with Queen Guinevere. Lancelot is the last significant knight I need to dispose of before I once more call upon my Saxon allies to help transfer the kingdom from Arthur to myself. You know, Melehan, I hate that hypocritical hero who acts so self-righteous as the queen's personal champion. My plan will trap him with the queen in such a scandalous way that he will either be executed or exiled. But first, we must dispose of Lady Britta de Brittany!"

The tall knight was none other than King Arthur's illegitimate, backstabbing son, Sir Mordred the Murderous, half brother to the four sons of King Lot, known as Gawaine, Agravaine, Gaheris, and Gareth. He asked the squire, who was his oldest son, Melehan, "Where are Lady Britta and Sir Christian at this very moment?"

"Milord, they seek Sir Christian's squire, the unexceptional—"

Sir Mordred finished his sentence: "Wade the Scholar. Melehan, why do you call someone unexceptional who frequently shows himself more exceptional than you? Are you implying you are also unexceptional?"

"No, milord," Melehan mumbled with a frown.

Sir Mordred would have given him a knowing look, but he was still too annoyed and distracted by Melehan's smell and some of that dust, as he said, "We probably need to dispose of him too. I overheard my sister-in-law, Lady Lynette, say it's no accident his namesake is Sir Wade, whom she listed in prowess just below Sir Lancelot, Sir Tristram, and Sir Lamorak."

"Yes, milord, but Wade the Scholar willingly serves the bumbling Sir Christian de Galis. If he's really that high in prowess, why isn't he squire to someone like Sir Lancelot?"

"Melehan, this brings us back to 'There are often more things to see than one thinks he sees.'"

"Yes, milord."

"Melehan, regarding this Wade, right before the Humber campaign, I watched him defeat Sir Gawaine's three sons simultaneously on the practice field. While they moaned, groaned, and foamed, he hardly worked up a sweat."

"Yes, milord, yet this Wade attempts to hurt no one deliberately— even during the squire's portion of a pitched battle. He acts kind, polite, and courteous to opponents that I would threaten with a beheading. In my scroll—"

"It had better be written that something is very subtle about him," said Sir Mordred, "and don't forget that he's also known for clever sayings repeated all over Camelot."

"Yes, milord, like 'Sensational mistakes are more perilous than regular mistakes.'"

"Exactly," said Sir Mordred. "Thus, to paraphrase Lady Britta's saying, there are often more things to see than one thinks he sees regarding this squire."

"In that case, milord, you'll be pleased to know that at this very moment, Wade the Scholar should be seen as being tied up in the town of Nauntes. Maybe he's not as subtle as you think. Because he was out of money, I tricked him into selling a most interesting laundry soap I received from Morgan le Fay and her three friends. If you only knew how it makes people's clothes smell."

At that moment, the wind blew in the window so hard that it rattled every item in the room. Sir Mordred covered his nose desperately as he choked, gagged, and said angrily, "Hopefully not like you! Melehan, don't you have any other garments you could have reported to me in?"

"Milord, they were stolen off a clothesline."

"How did that happen?"

"I had them washed at the Inn of the Knight Perilous."

When the knight stared at him, the squire quickly explained, "Milord, it was right after Sir Christian's fish gravy caused a clothing shortage at the inn."

"Why didn't you have your clothes laundered in Nauntes—with that most interesting laundry soap?"

Melehan actually shuddered. "Milord, that wouldn't have been advisable. But let me say this: when Sir Christian de Galis and Lady Britta de Brittany attempt to contact Wade the Scholar in Nauntes, they're going to get a big surprise. Milord, listen to this plan." And Melehan, despite his loathly smell, came close enough to whisper into the tall knight's ear, after which he laughed wickedly.

His father approved of the plan and would have laughed wickedly too, but his oldest son, Melehan, smelled even more disgusting than his sensationally wicked plan. Thus, Sir Mordred desperately held his murderous, backstabbing nose while he frantically motioned for Melehan to move back and give him some sensationally less-wicked air.

CHAPTER 17

Riding in Front

Riding in front of the quest doesn't mean that you're
in charge of the quest, especially this quest.
    —Wade the Scholar, *Chanson de Chrétien*

Sir Christian's cloak was hermetically sealed for Arthurian times, and everything else was securely packed as Britta and her modestly equipped retinue, now numbering five, mounted three warhorses and two unusually large palfreys. Ice Water and Butterfly were warhorses too, but Britta directed her retinue to always refer to them as palfreys. It drew less attention when they were boarded overnight in a strange stable, especially when the stable hands received eccentric horse-care instructions from a lady who looked harmless attended by a niece who acted completely unpredictable.[19]

---

[19]   A brief note on the horses in this story—or, as equestrian punsters might say, a horse tail. During the historic Middle Ages, a knight rode his warhorse, also known as a destrier or charger, mostly during a tournament or battle. The rest of the time, it was led by a servant while the knight traveled around on a lesser-grade mount called a hackney or a palfrey. But our story occurs in the not-so-normal Arthurian Middle Ages, a time and place in a dimension slightly outside of regular time. Yet it was connected the same way a railroad siding joins the main track. Thus, it received occasional visitors and tourists from other times and locations. When these travelers eventually returned home, they frequently described their visits. But as an unspoken rule, they

Warhorses, in the delightful Arthurian time, location, and dimension, like the men who rode them, were extra tough and, when necessary, extra rough. The horse breeders must have been doing something right, because these noble steeds lived extra long as well as youthful-looking lives. This enabled them to be ridden constantly. One seldom, if ever, reads a story of an Arthurian knight riding one of the other horses. It was like the American cowboy movies in which the hero and his producer could only afford one mount. Thus, it was written into the script that these mounts were also tough enough, rough enough, and therefore obligated enough to carry their cowboy heroes through everything and anything that might kill a normal horse. This might be illustrated most clearly by the following quote by a descendent of Wade the Scholar who wrote western movie scripts, "Charge up that hill through those one hundred arrow-shooting Indians!"

Mounted on Fountain and Butterfly, Andred and Sheena, respectively, tended the reins of Silent and Whisper, the two Arthurian packhorses. These powerful beasts of burden were examples of a distinguished breed and possessed easygoing personalities that matched their names. Their historical equivalents easily transported four hundred properly distributed pounds twenty miles a day without breaking into horse sweat. But they, being Arthurian super packhorses, carried twice as much for twice as long. They were so dependable that they seldom broke anything, including their legs, even if their baggage was as fragile as an eggshell or packed in a hurry, which was important to Britta's retinue traveling on a shoe-latchet budget. In addition to modestly equipped tents that resembled small pavilions, they carried chosen gear, including a small cauldron, a frying pan, dishes, plates, saucers, glass cups, and a bread grater.

---

almost always made King Arthur's Britain resemble the time and dimension from where they originated. Thus, the Arthurian fifth and sixth centuries in story and song seldom resemble its historic Dark Age counterparts. Yet despite differences in century, location, or dimension, it was created by the same all-powerful living God; thus, prayer to him followed the same all-powerful living rules.

A medicine kit included laxatives, restoratives, saffron, pepper, and a variety of other spices, and there was a special case for makeup and cosmetics. Whenever Britta and her attendants needed to camp, their baggage ensured that everyone would stay dry, clean, and warm and hopefully not smell too much. Meanwhile, they had supplies to prepare a hot meal. Afterward, they even had a few camp games to play, such as trestle-top catapult, in which Sheena currently led Andred three games to one—but knew he could come back.

The carefully selected baggage also enabled Britta and her niece of multiple names and assignments to appear sensationally elegant and, even more important for Britta's main assignment as a liaison representative as well as royal messenger, to look harmless. This attitude was further emphasized by the way they rode out of a spotless campsite, something always insisted upon by Lady Britta de Brittany, who had attitudes and sensitivity toward nature and camping that would have made her a distinguished environmentalist in the modern historic era. It also simplified her approach to placing trail markers—or, as she called it, the stratagem of planting clues. She and Sheena made sure any object they positioned on a trail, road, or bridge crossing not only looked natural but also was easy to find, such as a tattered strip of lace hanging from a lower tree branch, a scarf fragment fluttering in a thorn bush, or an old glove lying on the gravel beside a stream crossing—always with missing fingers and with a large stone inside so that it wouldn't float away. This minimized any chance Britta's pursuers of choice would get lost. She made a special point of informing Sir Christian as they clip-clopped down the trail, "You can never be too careful when you must organize your own pursuit. Furthermore, you must pay close attention at all times, or—"

Clang!

A scroll smacked his helmet, which she had shifted to her side of his saddle. Sir Christian angrily jerked it back to his side as she finished. "Someone might whack you with a war club!"

He looked ready to whack her with Sir Pinel le Savage's second-favorite spear. Which didn't faze her as she nonchalantly sang early lyrics to "Men of Harlech," by the Unknown Bard: "Knights of Arthur ride to glory. Make sure things are hunky-dory." She interjected with a smile, "Similar in meaning to okeydokey."

Sir Christian's hand turned white holding the spear as he asked, "Okey what?"

"Not okey what!" Britta exclaimed. "Okey where! As in right there over your head!"

"What's right there over my head?"

"Most things when I try to get your attention as—"

Thunk!

She swung the scroll over his head, clobbering a club-swinging three-foot warrior preparing to leap on him from a tree.

At Andred's "Huzzah!" Slow Silver leaped aside allowing the small warrior to thud into the ground between Sir Christian and Britta. Meantime Sheena leaned out of her saddle and snagged the notice that blew upward from his hand. Peering at it closely she said, "Sir Christian, did you know there's a reward for a poisoner who looks just like you?"

Andred, looking over her shoulder, said, "Huzzah! And he—even has—the same—first name!"

Sir Christian looked tempted to whack Britta harder than she whacked the warrior, but she nonchalantly dismounted beyond the reach of Sir Pinel le Savage's second-favorite spear. Humming additional lyrics by the Unknown Bard, she fastened a fresh notice to the latest lump of chain mail lying on the ground. Its tiny voice moaned upward in response, "I am Griffith ap Griffin—the giant!"

"Among midgets?" asked Sir Christian as he brought Slow Silver under enough control to look down at him.

"Don't confuse me with Maynard the Mangler!"

Sir Christian thought that unlikely as he added, "Are you a small giant or a tall giant?"

"Where I come from, I'm a gigantic giant!"

Sir Christian said, "Where you come from, I shudder to think what the small giants are like!"

"They come large enough to spear a fish like you!" threatened the little voice between moans. "I'm warning you! When I get up, I'm going to—"

Clang!

Britta tossed an additional notice wrapped rock into the giant's tiny helmet lying next to him on the ground. Still out of reach of Sir Pinel le Savage's second-favorite spear, she leaped onto her saddle as she blew the little giant a kiss and added, "Catch us if you can, and don't forget to bring your gigantic friends!"

"And don't forget to look for gigantic clues!" announced Sheena.

"And when you—find them—don't—forget—to yell—huzzah!" Andred shouted.

"Huh-what?" asked the little voice.

But the retinue was already riding around the next bend. Britta then rode patiently until Sir Christian had brought his horse, and his desire to spear-smack her under slightly more control. When she finally noticed that Sir Pinel le Savage's second-favorite spear was nonviolently pointed toward heaven, and Sir Christian's eyes were nonviolently pointed toward her, she said with another smile, "This is a good day to catch pursuers."

Uncle Sir Cecil with his right ear pointed to the conversation once more like an arrow said, "They do seem to be running our way."

Sir Christian said sarcastically, "The last one seemed under the size limit. Why didn't you throw him back?"

Britta said patiently, "When operating on a shoe-latchet budget—"

Uncle Sir Cecil finished, "Never turn down a volunteer!"

"Huzzah!" said Andred as Sheena nodded in agreement.

Sir Christian snarled, "Even when he jumps on one of us with a club?"

"Not us—*you!*" said Britta. "Besides, the ones who are aggressive make the best keepers."

Sir Christian said, "And does this aggressive little keeper know what he's a volunteer for?"

Britta said, "He'll find out soon enough. Besides, if we turn him down, it might hurt his feelings."

"He tried to hurt mine!"

"It was nothing personal. He just wants a share of your reward money."

"That you also offered to all of those other thugs!"

"Volunteers!" Britta corrected him.

"Whatever you call that eclectic gang you coerced—"

"Creatively recruited!" Britta corrected him again.

"Into pursuing me."

Britta smiled.

Sir Christian didn't as he pointed to the trail ahead. "Does that little giant also know he's *volunteering* to eclectically collect that reward from seven hundred Saxon pirates?"

Andred said, "Cherry! Berry! Apple pie!"

Sheena said, "He's going to get a big surprise!"

"It won't be that big of a surprise," Britta said, "if he can get seven hundred of his little gigantic friends to come along and help."

"If they're as little gigantic as him, I can hear the Saxons now: 'Look out, kneecaps—here they come!'"

"But until they do, please pay closer attention as I explain important features of what I consider successful questing!"

"Britta, I have—"

"Thirty-plus years of merely satisfactory experience," she reminded him. "It's neither exceptional nor legendary, which is why you're questing for me—and not me for you—Sir Knight of the Most-High Politeness."

Clang! Her scroll gave his helmet one more dent. Then she sheathed it with a spectacular star-circle cloud-burst swoosh she learned from Sir Ywaine, the Knight of the Lion, with whom, despite his lion-like smell, she was at one time about to become just like— well, never mind. She nonchalantly brushed more imaginary dust from her cloak, his helmet, and, as he shifted it back to his side of his saddle, a previously untouched section of his split ends.

Britta blew more imaginary dust off her free hand as she said, "On a shoe-latchet budget, one must always travel with three things: food for your followers, money for your friends, and clues for your pursuers. Whenever possible, also throw in shiny scrap metal for the barbarian hordes. But never forget the first three."

Sir Christian nodded to move them on to the next painful point, but he secretly hoped Britta was traveling as low on clues as she seemed to be on everything else, including certain levels of intelligence. Then she might run out, and those twelve Navarrese mercenaries—and any other thugs she attached those reward notices to—would get lost or, better yet, find someone else to vengefully, or even eclectically, pursue.

In the meantime, Britta informed Sir Christian that he was now questing under an official and legally notarized contract.

"Since when?"

"Since Sir Erbin notarized it."

"Since when did he do that?"

"Since when you weren't looking very well." With another signature swoosh she produced his worn-out pouch and hung it on his saddle. She blew more imaginary dust off her free hand as she said, "You dropped this while trimming the inn's tree."

With the fingers on his free hand he lifted the pouch to open it and glare at the tip of the contract, which was too rolled up to read. Then he closed the pouch and violently shook it as if it were in an earthquake or an explosion in a small kitchen. When he didn't hear the ca-ching of money inside, he glared at her. "What happened to my seven shillings?"

Britta replied. "What happened to the bill for your damages?"

Sir Christian stuffed the pouch inside his hanging helmet as he grumbled. "I went to a lot of trouble to collect those shillings from those mercenaries!"

"And we went to a lot trouble to keep those mercenaries from collecting you!" Britta smiled at him semi-sweetly. "As an alternative to death by flaming torture with splinters sticking out of you am I not a better answer to your prayers than seven shillings?"

Like a well-aimed boar spear, Britta knew she had pinned him again, except there wasn't anything to pin him to this time besides his saddle. So with another interesting smile she now calmly went over his first assignment. As his official quest employer, she informed him that he, as Knight of the Round Table in good standing, even if only temporarily reinstated, would normally ride in the vanguard of the quest, as he was doing now.

"However," she informed him, "riding in front of the quest doesn't mean that you're in charge of the quest, especially this quest."

"Then why must I normally ride first?" answered Sir Christian sarcastically, still smarting from the loss of his seven shillings.

"Because that's what Knights of the Round Table normally do," said Britta. "It is so stated in the fine calligraphy of your quest document. You will lead in such fashion that you diligently scan the road ahead for giants, midgets, knaves, braves, bandits, pirates, runaway slaves, and underpaid soldiers, especially if they're unshaved—which is always a bad sign—and also unsupervised domestic animals, including horses, camels, quarry elephants, and oxen as well as wild beasts, such as bears, wolves, lions, and serpents, followed by monsters, including dragons, ogres, gryphons, cockatrices, bonnacons, satyrs, sirens, the serra, the monoceros, the manticore, the basilisk, the questing beast, but most important of all, the Monster-of-Unheard-of-Savageness. No one has ever encountered anything in the third category, especially the Monster-of-Unheard-of-Savageness, whom most scholars think is a rumor concocted by a monk with too much time on his hands. But if one of *my* quest knights ever does sight him, or any of those other creatures, it will be great publicity."

"For who?"

"For *whom*, which doesn't mean you, unless specified in your contract—which it isn't. Let's cut to the joust. In the event you do perceive any of the above, stop and call back to Uncle Sir Cecil and myself. Then await further—"

"Clangs!" Sir Christian sneered

"When appropriate, but not without proper instructions!" Britta emphasized. "Furthermore, *do not*, and I repeat, *do not* follow the first instinct of one newly accolated quest knight—"

"Which was?"

189

She shifted his helmet back to her side of his saddle, where she tapped out a funeral dirge by the Unknown Bard, climaxing with a bang twice as loud as any earlier ones. She said, "Don't exchange challenges with them, after which you utter a loud—"

"Huzzah!" shouted Andred, making Sir Christian's horse buck.

Britta once again politely signaled Andred to adjust his volume. He politely nodded as she continued. "And wildly charge into them. That newly accoladed knight, who also never learned to see very well, did just that on a high-profile quest last summer. After his memorial service, in which we wrapped him in an extra-thick shroud to hide the beating he got from the athletic laundry lady he mistook for the Monster-of-Unheard-of-Savageness, it took us three whole weeks to find a suitable replacement. Meanwhile, the princess we were tasked to rescue languished in one of the dampest dungeons of the late Sir Meliagrance. This did not go over well with her grandfather, King Brandegoris of Stranggore, when we finally rode into his castle with his granddaughter coughing and wheezing while shedding hair, losing teeth, and peeling skin. That's when King Brandegoris threatened to throw us into his dampest dungeon. So I repeat: if you see anything unusual up ahead, stop first, call back second, and, above all, third, listen for instructions. Uncle Sir Cecil and I are always on the alert, and—"

"What?" asked Sir Christian.

"Usually know what to do."

"Not always?" asked Sir Christian.

"Not even Sir Lancelot always knows what to do on a quest. But do remember that I hold you under notarized quest contract; therefore, you receive food and supplies only if I decide you are fulfilling its conditions."

Those somber words gave Sir Christian much to think about as he attempted to shove his helmet back on his head—and smacked himself with his scrip.

In Britta's role as a special liaison between King Arthur, Myrddin, and Nimue, the British Lady of the Lake—or, as she called them, the Big Three—she assumed command of any quest she attended. Any questioning of her authority, as far as she was concerned, was not open for discussion. During day-to-day operations, she originated the plans and personally took charge of all quest documents. These included knight errantry contracts, fact-finding parchments, and copies of active Round Table personnel scrolls that she was responsible for. She delegated food and supplies to Sheena. Security, surveillance, and scouting were nominally covered by Uncle Sir Cecil, but he sub delegated most visual responsibilities to Andred, who proved reliable despite his tendency to unexpectedly blurt a loud "Huzzah!" Because of what this shouting might cause, attract, or instigate, including stampedes of wild and domestic animals, although so far no legendary monsters, Britta always provided backup surveillance.

Thanks to Andred's help as his substitute squire, when his shouts weren't waking the dead or those who thought they were about to be dead when trampled by an agitated herd, Sir Christian once more wore his father's armor. When he recovered it with the rest of his equipment at the inn, he decided not to wear it at that time, because he always needed help with the fasteners, or they never fit and frequently poked him. With Uncle Sir Cecil's eyesight such that it was; Britta's bear-scaring attitude such that it was; the horses' interest in his clothes, particularly his cloak, such that it was; and his desire to put as much space as possible between himself and the Navarrese mercenaries such that it was, he stuffed his gear into his baggage until he reached Britta's camp.

Just before they rode out of the camp, he had once more buckled on his father's sword, with the sword maker's name mysteriously blacked out near the hilt; hung his father's shield from his neck, with the shield maker's name mysteriously blacked out on the metal rim; and rested Sir Pinel le Savage's second-favorite spear on top of his father's right stirrup, with the stirrup maker's name mysteriously blacked out wherever the craftsman engraved such a thing, considering what got wiped on it. He pointed Sir Pinel's second-favorite spear upright, as in the direction of heaven, where he didn't want to accidentally send someone, especially the next time—

Andred yelled, "Huzzah!"

"Lord Jesu, save and protect us all!" Sir Christian cried as his horse reared, making Sir Pinel's second-favorite spear slice a branch from the nearest tree. It crashed to the ground with two green warriors clinging to the top.

One of them moaned, "I am the Knight of the Stripes."

The other groaned, "And I am the Knight of the Spots."

Sir Christian peered down at them after he once more brought Slow Silver under control, and observed, "But you each only wear one color."

The first answered, "Times are so bad that I can only afford one green stripe, and my brother can only afford one green spot—unless we collect this reward."

He feebly held up one of Britta's notices, which she snagged as she dismounted, and refastened it to his arm.

"Catch us if you can," she said as she remounted, "and bring lots of little green friends."

"But only after you stop moaning and groaning," Sheena said solemnly.

"Enough—to yell—huzzah!" Andred added loudly enough to make Sir Christian's horse jump again. Fortunately, the nearest trees weren't laden with any more armed men clutching his reward notice.

After they clip-clopped around the next bend, Britta said, "Isn't it promising how many mercenaries, bandits, and knights—"

"Not to mention midgets and giants," said Uncle Sir Cecil.

Sheena said, "And maybe even a few monsters."

"Who might—even yell—huzzah!" Andred announced.

Britta smiled toward Andred as she said, "Have seen Sir Christian's picture and—hope to make a killing!"

"Can we use a different phrase?" suggested Sir Christian.

Sheena said, "Does 'collect a lot of money for Sir Christian' sound more positive?"

But the latter brought no response as the cavalcade began traveling in a wild goose *V.* Sir Christian rode at center-front vanguard, where he could hopefully see the best; Uncle Sir Cecil was slightly behind at left front, where he could hopefully hear the best while still finding time to check his nose; Britta positioned herself slightly behind at right front, where she could, from her perspective, bang on Sir Christian's helmet the best; Sheena was at right rear, where she could, from her inclination, talk the best; and Andred rode at left rear, where he could belt out his loudest and most unexpected "Huzzah!"

There was one particularly loud "Huzzah!" followed by an equally annoying sequence of *Clang! Clang! Clang! Clang!* Sir Christian angrily shifted his helmet again as he turned to Britta, whom he found riding at his elbow. "Aren't you and Andred telling every perilous person, place, or thing on this road exactly where we are?"

Using a lightning swoosh she learned from the Knight of the War Clubs, Britta gave his helmet an extra loud *clang* as she said with another of her interesting smiles, "Let's hope so."

Sir Christian looked west and prayed, "Lord Jesu, deliver us from evil!"

Andred prayerfully pulled his cap down farther over his hair as he belted his most-deafening-to-date "Huzzah!"

This was followed by crashes, bangs, and thuds in all directions. Also, on a road less taken somewhere behind them came a loud *splat* as a mounted Saxon scout was thrown into one of the local sheriff's road pits, where he disappeared like a food cart going down a mudhole.

CHAPTER 18

Uncle Myrddin

Some people think Uncle Myrddin and Merlin are the same person.
—Wade the Scholar, *Chanson de Chrétien*

Britta's retinue continued south toward the large city of Nauntes to locate Sir Christian's squire, known to some as the mysterious Wade the Scholar. His name, reference, and reputation were truly a mystery to the squires who tangled with him on the practice field. Following one of last fall's training exercises, when he smacked multiple opponents in consecutive duels, then brushed imaginary dust off his cloak, his sword hilt, and a scroll he was simultaneously reading for fun, some declared him a future Lancelot. But he was so polite and courteous about the way he ran over rivals who threatened to behead him when he pretended not to look very well, some thought he jested. Others swore he was a show-off. A few jealous knaves thought he wasn't ruthless enough, and an additional group couldn't comprehend his loyalty in serving Sir Christian when he could have attached himself to a famous champion at the Round Table, such as Sir Lancelot. Eyes were also raised by rumors he preferred poking through scrolls with the point of his stylus rather than less fortunate fighters with the point of his sword.

The cavalcade had proceeded halfway, when an unexpected wind, at a moment when there was no wind, suddenly blew down from the north. Almost like a pair of prayerful hands, it snatched Andred's pulled-down cap and sent it sailing past Britta. With her usual alertness for everything and anything going on around her, out of the corner of her eye she saw it coming. Thus, at the very best psychological moment, with her right hand in the key watershed position, she snagged it faster than Sir Lancelot seizing his sword.

To Andred, Sheena, and especially Sir Christian, who had removed his helmet to better watch for Saxons, bandits, mercenaries, the Monster-of Unheard-of Savageness, or another one of Britta's scrolls, she resembled a mantis snatching a fly. This action, of course, went unseen by Uncle Sir Cecil, but he sensed it in his steady-as-a-rock fashion.

"Ha!" Britta announced with a swoosh of her hand. "I captured it as smooth as Sir Lancelot spearing the ring at the tournament! Will someone award me my prize?"

But an unusual silence had fallen on the group. With an amused yet thoughtful look, Britta turned to hand Andred his cap, but she almost dropped it when she saw the condition of his once long, wavy blond hair. His cap had been hiding the fact that his hair was now an astonishing shade of green—with a hint of orange!

"Andred!" Britta called out in one of her rare moments of sensational surprise. "What in the name of King Arthur, the Lady of the Lake, and anything that could go wrong in a war, a dining room, or even a hair salon happened to your hair? That color would look ugly on a Pictish pig!"

Everyone stared at Andred's hair until he looked so embarrassed that he truly lived up to his suffix, the Silent. His face slowly acquired the same hint of orange that accented the heavy green dye that permeated most of his hair. He muttered his lowest possible "Huzzah!" and then paused. Then, in an even lower voice, he muttered, "Dye arrow."

"Dye arrow?" said Britta as she directed everyone to dismount in an abandoned village. She was so distracted by this development that for once, she didn't notice everything and anything going on around her, including a bed of mildly warm coals where someone had recently camped.

Andred, who, as stated earlier, seldom made observations longer than two or three syllables delimited with pauses, muttered another low "Huzzah." This was followed by another pause and then an even lower utterance of "Dye arrow."

His sister, Sheena, whose observations were seldom shorter than the New Testament concatenated with King Arthur's latest legal-code revisions, interceded.

"Milady, while you and Uncle Sir Cecil searched for Sir Christian, a troop of archers passed our camp, wearing the livery of Castle Abblasoure. That's the fortress Sir Galahad visited during the Grail Quest where no one says *mass*. Now, milady, before I speak further on Andred's hair, let me put in a few words about that castle. Did you know it was recently occupied by Sir Arthfrel the Awful and his collection of equally awful bears? Stories have since circulated about visitors to Abblasoure being forced to wrestle those bears, with none ever being seen again."

Britta interrupted Sheena with a wave of Andred's cap. It fell under her duty as a special liaison to investigate stories like Sir Arthfrel and his castle of potentially awful bears. Thus, she had already submitted a scroll-length report to Myrddin, along with a plan for confrontation if the stories were indeed true. But that was for another day. To deal with the current business, she looked at Sheena and said, "Tell me about Andred's hair."

"Yes, milady, I am telling you about Andred's hair the way I tell you about anything. Hmm—now, where was I?"

"The archers of Castle Abblasoure," said Uncle Sir Cecil, aiming his good ear, bad eyes, and optional nose in her direction. He found Sheena's digressions entertaining and told Britta that they lit up conversations like a volcano whenever things appeared dull during one of their quests. But like all tried and true philosophical warriors, he knew to save a good digression to fill in time for when enemy swords, spears, knives, and arrows weren't filling it.

Sheena smiled at him and said, "The archers of Castle Abblasoure were so impressed when they saw Andred make a difficult bow shot that they invited him to join their troop that was on its way to that new type of archery tournament. But when I told them I just made the very same shot, they only smiled—even though they saw me do it as they approached our camp. Then their leader had the gall to ask if I would cook dinner for them if they stopped by on the way back."

Sir Christian said, "Sheena Unica Verena—I mean, just Sheena— you can shoot a bow and arrow as well as do all of those other jobs? But you're just—"

"A damosel!" Sheena declared defiantly. "As in a girl!"

Britta said while providing a gleaming hint of the leopard-claw look, "That's right, Sir Knight of the Most-High Politeness, Sheena is just a damosel, as in a girl. Yet in addition to all of her other jobs, she shoots the bow and arrow quite well and, I have very good reason to believe, quite superior to you."

Uncle Sir Cecil, as master quest archer, team diplomat, spiritual adviser, and occasional discussion group facilitator, politely asked Sheena, "Little niece"—he affectionately called her that even though she was an inch taller than he was—"what difficult shots did you and Andred make that attracted such professional attention?"

"Dear Uncle Sir Cecil the *Most* Steady"—she emphasized the word *most* so sweetly that it put a glow in Uncle Sir Cecil's ancient face, as well as a small tear in the corner of each visually challenged eye—"we practiced that technique *you* recently taught, where I fired an arrow at half speed across the road by our camp while Andred took a split second to estimate its path before he knocked it down with a lightning-speed snapshot. Together, those two shots, as you coached us so sensationally, are tricky—but worth knowing how to do."

More tears appeared in the corners of Uncle Sir Cecil's poor eyes.

"Then we switched. It was much more interesting than shooting tree branches and definitely kinder than killing small birds we won't eat."

She concluded with another sweet smile in Uncle Sir Cecil's direction, causing additional tears in his eyes.

She looked back at Britta, who acknowledged her with a warm nod and said, "Pray, continue."

"Yes, milady," Sheena answered. "Andred declined the invitation of the Abblasoure archers with a wave of his cap—which he could still take off—and a disinterested *huzzah*. That's because you told us to watch the camp, and he is especially trustworthy in following your orders. So neither he nor I would have gone with them anyway, but they still could have invited us both.

"Andred then turned his back on them with an additional disinterested *huzzah*. That's because he didn't appreciate their superior attitude toward me. He is so supportive." At that point, she gave Andred an enormous smile that turned his face an even darker shade of orange.

"Milady, those Abblasoure archers grunted sullenly as they shouldered their bows and went on their way to the tournament. But who do you think showed up next? Why, it was Uncle Myrddin."

"Uncle Myrddin?" Sir Christian started to say more but stopped when he noticed an even sharper hint of Britta's leopard-claw look.

"Yes, milady, it was indeed Uncle Myrddin. Andred and I watched alertly, but he slipped into the middle of our camp, dressed as an old forester pretending to be an animal artist. But he didn't fool *me* with that disguise. I'd know Uncle Myrddin anywhere. But I let him *think* he fooled me. That's because it puts him in such a good mood that he tells Andred and me some of the most interesting things going on at King Arthur's court. As you know, milady, he has access to some of the most sensational stories. That's also because when he's not advising King Arthur in the current court city, he roams around the forests and outer towns, looking for things that are honorable, edifying, and interesting. Now, some people say Uncle Myrddin appeared out of the very cave where Merlin disappeared while traveling with Nimue, which means—"

"Some people think Uncle Myrddin and Merlin are the same person," Britta said, cutting Sheena off with another wave of Andred's cap. She knew exactly what, why, when, where, how, and who Myrddin was. She also knew it wasn't open for discussion and added firmly, "Sheena, cut to the joust."

"Yes, milady. Myrddin asked us if we knew about the archery tournament about to begin south of camp. It was one of those new events he developed from a popular sport in his home country. He's using it to recruit bowmen for King Arthur."

Britta nodded as one who knew all about Myrddin's new archery tournaments. Instead of contestants shooting regular arrows at still targets, they shot special arrows at each other—after they shot one qualifying round with regular arrows at a variety of still targets, which might include butts, wands, and nosegays. The best archers were divided into two small armies, which were each assigned a battlefield umpire who ushered them to opposite ends of a roped-off field. The umpire in each group selected one archer to serve as the commander. Then the armies were given one turn of an hourglass to plan their strategies. When a trumpet blew, each battlefield umpire told the leader of his respective army to form up. Then they advanced to any point where they could shoot the special arrows at the opposing army. These were similar to hollow cane-shaft fire arrows, except that they were filled with washable dyes instead of incendiaries and were designed to burst apart when they hit opponents. Contact made the dye splatter over a large area of the person and his clothes, providing a clear indicator to the heralds and umpires that the victim had been wounded or slain.

Sheena said, "Myrddin told me his tournaments are catching on in the local shires, where archers are experimenting with that new longbow."

Sheena paused for a minute before she observed, "Milady, I don't know if that longbow will ever catch on. It only allows the archer to shoot twelve arrows a minute. The Sarmatian composite bows that Uncle Sir Cecil trained Andred and me on are eight arrows faster. Milady, that Sarmatian bow is a real weapon."

Britta motioned to her with another wave of Andred's cap to continue.

"Milady, for reasons he chose not to reveal, Myrddin decided not to be seen at this tournament. So he turned its operation over to the local citizens. However, there were a few things about the way they chose to operate that he didn't agree with, such as charging admission and not allowing damosels to participate. As you know, milady, Uncle Myrddin won't recruit females to fight in the army, but he doesn't mind if they participate in any kind of tournament, provided that they can do it. He said that the average damosel could instinctively teach the average man-at-arms a few things about the bow and arrow. That includes how to hit a man who is running away from you because he—hmm—is running away from you. Milady, I didn't completely understand that running-away part, but Uncle Myrddin smiled and said that I would someday. He added that it was a joke. When I told him I had heard better jokes, he only smiled again. But I'm sure he meant well."

"He has always meant well," Britta said as she motioned to her with still another wave of Andred's cap to cut to the joust and continue.

"Milady, once Myrddin turns a tournament over to someone else, he never interferes with how things are done. However, he still wanted to know how that tournament would come out. So he offered to watch the camp if we would participate. All he asked in return was a verbal report to him, on his request only, if anything unusual happened. He then gave us a look that said he should be obeyed without question. That sounded simple enough. Yet I suspected there was something more than simple behind his motive."

Britta replied, "There is always something more than simple behind one of Myrddin's motives. In that way, he resembles his predecessor, Merlin."

"Yes, milady. He then gave me the cut half of one of those silver pennies he identifies his assistants with. He said I should show this to you if we needed to explain anything later, because you carry the other half in your scrip. Otherwise, he told us to say nothing. But if it came up, he added that you would understand such instructions."

Britta handed Andred his cap as Sheena handed Britta the half coin she pulled from her belt pouch. Britta momentarily balanced it in her left hand as she judged its weight. Then she held it up to the sunlight as her right hand opened her belt pouch and pulled out the coin's other half. She matched the halves for all to see. Then she returned her half to her pouch and the other half to Sheena, to whom she said, "This is now *your* halfpenny. Carry it to remember that Myrddin found you worthy of this interesting assignment."

"Yes, milady. Shall I also carry it for luck?"

"A coin is never the source of luck, but it may be a token for good memories."

Sheena politely nodded as she turned and showed the half coin to Sir Christian.

He took it and noticed how it was cut vertically. He saw half an image of King Arthur on the heads side, and when he turned it over, he saw half the bird of prey known as a merlin on the tails side. This latter device was stamped in honor of Myrddin's predecessor, Merlin Ambrosias. It also represented, in symbolic language, a messenger from afar. The silver in the coin had been mined from deposits on the southern coast of Britain, in the shire of Devon, at a place that would later be called in regular historical times Beer Alston.

When Merlin disappeared early in King Arthur's reign while traveling with Nimue, the British Lady of the Lake, rumors circulated she had trapped him in a cave, possibly with a cave-in. These stories were soon followed by prophetic rumors that Merlin would return from wherever Nimue had left him, but only in Britain's time of greatest need. Apparently, that time wasn't yet, because Nimue had returned to her lake without him. If anyone asked Nimue about the fate of Merlin, she responded casually but with the hint of a stare more ferocious than Britta's that the matter wasn't open for discussion.

A short time later, Nimue arrived in Camelot with a stranger who in many ways resembled the vanished Merlin, except he spoke with a faraway accent and used unusual phrases, such as *hunky-dory*, *okeydokey*, *hot dog*, and *cat's meow*. In private, she introduced him to King Arthur as Myrddin, a distant kinsman of their liaison, Lady Britta de Brittany. When Nimue endorsed Myrddin to succeed Merlin as the king's main adviser, he was immediately accepted, as though Arthur had been expecting him.

Myrddin quickly confirmed his appointment by demonstrating an economical method to extract the silver at Beer Alston. That grabbed King Arthur's attention because it stabilized the kingdom's money supply and national economy. It also provided leeway for Myrddin to implement other innovative ideas, including everything from hiring experts to mix up the Oil of the Perfume Perilous to medicine to new archery techniques.[20] He introduced even more slang and musical shows to entertain military personnel, and he experimented with an alphabet for a language he called pseudo Arthurian.[21]

Sir Christian returned the halfpenny to Sheena, who returned it to her belt pouch.

With a swoosh, Britta snatched Andred's cap back out of his hands, once again like a mantis snatching a fly, and used it to brush his greenish split ends. He softly muttered, "Huzzah."

Britta motioned with Andred's cap for Sheena to continue.

---

[20] Note: The knowledge of Myrddin's mining techniques never reappeared outside the age of Arthur, although in regular historical times, King Edward I tried unsuccessfully to mine that same silver at a profit in the 1290s.

[21] Pseudo Arthurian sounded similar to what one hears at a modern Renaissance festival.

CHAPTER 19

A Big Stave and a Big Brother

A damosel with a big stave and a big brother is not to be despised.
—Wade the Scholar, *Chanson de Chrétien*

"With your pardon, milady," said Sheena, "I borrowed some of Andred's clothes to wear to this tournament because Uncle Myrddin emphasized that the head marshal, Sir Brutus de Augusta, would only allow males to participate. His assistant, Sir Ogier the Greedy, said that damosels were welcome to watch—after they paid his varlet a copper halfpenny, twice what he charged the male spectators. But he added with a sly wink that he would enjoy showing the damosels a nice viewing spot along the sidelines. Yet a really good spot in the shady pavilion near him, complete with drinks and salted turnip chips, which must be an acquired taste, cost a silver penny. In defiance to these unfair male attitudes, I decided this tournament provided me with an excellent target of opportunity—if you excuse the pun, milady—"

Britta excused it with a smile and another wave of Andred's cap.

"To test military strategy and subterfuge you have taught me."

"Britta," Sir Christian said, "you taught *your maid* military strategy and subterfuge?"

Britta replied firmly, "Sir Christian, I teach members of my retinue many useful things, as you shall learn."

"But—"

"Sir Christian, but me no *buts*!"

"Unless they be archery butts,"[22] said Uncle Sir Cecil, attempting a wink with one of his visually challenged eyes.

"Sir Christian," Britta continued, "according to Ordericus the scribe, main keeper of the Arthurian Court Chronicles until someone's scholarly squire got him dragged screaming, pleading, and sobbing to clean out the castle gardé robe pits, this kingdom contains more than its share of thuggish bandits, callously careless men-at-arms, and grossly incompetent knights. Thus, it doesn't hurt for its damosels to learn a little military strategy and subterfuge."

"But—"

"Once again, but me no *buts*!"

"Unless they be archery butts," Uncle Sir Cecil repeated.

Sir Christian omitted the *but*. "Britta, doesn't that make a damosel's life more perilous?"

"Sir Christian, in this kingdom, a damosel's life already is more perilous with knights like you on the loose, and by your own admission, you're the most polite one."

She addressed her niece. "Sheena, let's hear what my tutorage of my maid in military strategy and subterfuge has turned loose on the world of unsympathetic men."

"Yes, milady. Andred and I went to the neighboring meadow and registered for the dye-arrow tournament. Because it was Wednesday,[23] I signed the entry scroll as Antony, short for my fourth first name, Antonia. Isn't that clever, milady? When someone at the tournament hears me called Antony, he'll never guess it's your lady's maid, housemaid, horsemaid, handmaid, parlormaid,

---

22 *Butts*, in this case, refer to targets and their supports on an archery practice field. Those who served in the military should recall that *butts* also refer to the targets and their supports on a modern rifle range.

23 March 7, AD 535.

chambermaid, laundrymaid, milkmaid, kitchenmaid, trashmaid, camp superintendent, hair dresser, and assistant bodyguard, more formally known as Sheena Unica Verena Antonia Serena Vivina Augustina Ruebena Serilda Athena Karmita Lalita Kairos."

"We wouldn't want you giving all of that away," said Sir Christian.

"Who did people think you really were?" asked Uncle Sir Cecil.

"Some thought I was Andred's brother. Others asked if I was his cousin. I neither answered nor acknowledged anything to anyone, but kept quiet—"

"For once?" asked Sir Christian.

Sheena smiled. "And let other people say *and think* what they wished."

Britta smiled. "You get a plus on your scroll for that one."

"Yes, milady, my scroll could use some. Andred and I may have earned a few more when we entered the qualifying archery shoot-off and were judged for speed, accuracy, and distance. We can't match records you and Uncle Sir Cecil set, but between us, we shot nineteen arrows a minute with ninety percent accuracy at two hundred fifty yards. That was more than adequate for each of us to qualify.[24]

"When the tournament umpires separated the finalists into two teams of twenty-four archers, they tied a red ribbon to the right arm of one group and a green ribbon to the left arm of the other. Because they thought that Andred and I were related, they assigned us both to the red team."

Sheena suddenly paused and then asked, "Andred and I are related, aren't we, milady?"

Sir Christian later recalled that this was one moment when Britta made no response.

Sheena said, "The judges especially decided to keep us together after I demonstrated that Andred and I are just like this!" With a swoosh, she drew the bow stave from her saddle sheath and, holding it steady, touched both index fingers together.

---

[24] This speed and distance might seem unusual, if not amazing, in regular history, but it was not necessarily so in Sir Christian's Arthurian Britain.

"How did you do that?" exclaimed Sir Christian as he attempted to touch his index fingers together. But once again, he held Sir Pinel le Savage's second-favorite spear in such a way that his fingers stayed apart.

"Oh no, Sir Christian," said Sheena. "It's not like just like *that*." She pointed to the way he held his fingers. "It's just like *this*!" She once more pressed her index fingers together while holding her bow stave. "Why, even Uncle Sir Cecil—"

"Can do it another time!" said Britta as she motioned with Andred's cap for Sheena to continue.

"Yes, milady. Well, guess what? Three archers from Castle Abblasoure also qualified for the red team, but only three. Most of the bowmen from that bear castle are nowhere as good as anyone Uncle Sir Ceil trained. I think they spend more time feeding visitors to their bears than arrows to their bows—or even something more worthwhile, like words to their prayers."

"That's not known for certain," said Britta.

"Yes, milady, but it's almost known for certain. I heard one of those bears was recently seen kneeling with a visitor's cap between its paws—and it wasn't praying!"

"Not even—grace," muttered Andred.

Britta used the cap to brush imaginary dust off Sheena's and Andred's split ends as she said, "Sheena, cut to the joust!"

"Yes, milady. The three most competent Abblasoure archers looked surprised when they recognized Andred, and even acknowledged his presence with a nod. But they had no idea who I was and paid no attention to me—at first.

"A trumpet blared as the head herald mounted his horse and rode out before both teams with a large scroll, which he drew from his cloak with a lightning-fast swoosh!"

Britta nodded. "How else would a good herald draw a good scroll?"

"The same way a good archer draws a bow," Uncle Sir Cecil said, listening with his good ear, and agreeing with a smile.

"Milady," continued Sheena, "this was followed by shouts of 'Huzzah!' which grew even louder as Andred joined in, and I am proud to say that he quickly out-huzzahed everyone present—that is, until he got the head herald thrown from his horse. This halted all further huzzahing, especially Andred's after I punched him. Attendants rushed onto the field to assist the head herald in remounting, as he looked sprained over every inch of his body. He also looked ready to feed Andred to the Monster-of-Unheard-of-Savageness. But he was in so much pain that he barely held the scroll as he read, between chalk-board screeching moans and body-shaking spasms, the three commandments of dye-arrow archery battles.

"Commandment number one: 'Thou mayest not smite thy foe with thine dye arrow in his eye.' Milady, I thought that might be tricky for the field umpires to enforce; they encouraged us to aim at the head directly above—or even between—the eyes.

"Commandment number two: 'Thou mayest not smite thy foe with thine dye arrow below his sword belt.' Milady, this commandment was obviously written by a knight; not all archers own a sword belt. Correct, Uncle Sir Cecil?

"Commandment number three: 'Thou mayest not smite thy foe with thine dye arrow after thou hast been announced slain by a herald.' Figuratively, of course, milady; nobody is really slain in one of these battles, I think.

"Now, for some reason, the herald said nothing at all about the unwritten fourth commandment of this particular tournament: 'Thou mayest not smite thy foe with thine dye arrow if thou be-eth a damosel.'

"The head herald rolled up the scroll before rolling right off his horse, hitting the ground with a *thud*. Attendants with a stretcher rushed him off of the field as a replacement head herald rode out, giving Andred looks that could kill, while I poked him in the ribs to prevent more *huzzah*s that might kill the new head herald. The new head herald cautiously kept one eye on Andred as he directed the battlefield umpires to escort each team to their end of the battlefield, from where they could barely see and hear each other.

"It was now time for each umpire to select someone on each team to serve as its battlefield captain. But before anyone else could speak"—everyone smiled, including Andred—"I petitioned our umpire to give me the command. Before he had too much time to think it over, draw the wrong conclusion, and miss out on a truly ground-breaking opportunity, I resolved to sensationally dazzle him in ad hoc fashion. I therefore unloaded, for the amazement of his astonished ears, my exhaustive and analytical dissertation on the archers who fought in the ancient battle of Cannae, Italy.

"I filled his ears with little-known, illuminating details of how Hannibal Barca, the Carthaginian field commander, hid his North African composite bow archers in the middle of his cavalry, heavy infantry, and war elephants. And he did it so cleverly that the opposing eighty-thousand-man Roman army—and every ancient historian I checked—didn't know they were there. Then I told him the really good part—namely, how the clever North African composite bow-archery sergeants resupplied their men with fresh arrow quivers delivered on the backs of rare Middle Eastern racing camels. These crafty creatures of Carthaginian procurement scooted around the battlefield so fast that, once again, neither the eighty-thousand-man Roman army nor every ancient historian of note that I checked knew that they were present either.

"That's when I realized how much I had truly impressed the battlefield umpire assigned to the red team. He clamped my mouth firmly shut with his strong right hand and declared, 'Young squire, peace—be silent!' But he next sighed deeply as he commented softly, 'Squire Antony, I, uh, hereby appoint you captain of the red archery army!' Then he did the strangest thing, milady. He took his hand off of my mouth and completely covered his face with both of his hands. He was so moved by my presentation that he began to cry.

"Now, milady, please don't be offended by what may seem to be his rudeness to me, for I don't think he said, 'Peace—be silent!' in a derogatory way. Rather, he said 'Peace—be silent!' in a protective way, because he realized that in my enthusiasm to educate and illuminate, with no critical information left behind or forgotten, I might accidentally give away important military discoveries. Therefore, he was helping me protect them, which was so understanding of him. Someday I must return and look him up. Maybe I can reveal myself as a damosel and lend him one or two—or how about several dozen—of your carrier pigeons. He could send messages to me—I mean us—at our castle."

Britta raised her eyes at that remark, but Uncle Sir Cecil only smiled.

"And what did Andred say during this dissertation?" asked Sir Christian.

Andred muttered a low and embarrassed "Huzzah."

Uncle Sir Cecil, who had worked hard to hear all of this with his good ear, said, "Andred seldom says more than one *huzzah* followed by one or two other syllables. And that's just as well for me, because I have trouble hearing anything he says, right, Andred? Huzzah yourself!"

This was not one of Uncle Sir Cecil's sensationally humorous lines, so Andred only replied with another soft-spoken and highly embarrassed "Huzzah."

After another moment of forced politeness, Britta waved Andred's cap again and said, "Sheena, cut to the joust!"

"Yes, milady. Now, as I said, both teams had been escorted by a battlefield umpire to their end of the dye-arrow battlefield, which was a rectangular area of trees, bushes, tall grass, and holes. It was one hundred yards long by fifty yards wide and surrounded by a rope attached to yard-high stakes. In the middle was a log-filled ravine, and at each end stood a battle standard for the defenders to protect and the attackers to capture. As the green army organized itself on the north end, I did the same with the red army on the south end. Each army was allowed so much time to plan strategy, after which the heralds would signal another trumpet to sound that would start the dye-arrow archery battle.

"I am proud to say that he quickly out-
huzzahed everyone present."

"Milady, this is where things got awkward and disappointing. As I took command of my army, I divided it into six four-man archery teams, and I directed each unit to move forward like a diamond. Each formation consisted of a point archer, two flank archers, and a rear archer who would steer his men as archer team leader. I positioned each of my leaders slightly offset to prevent him from shooting down his point archer. But believe it or not, milady, while I explained this, one of my loutish leaders released an arrow that nearly splattered his point archer before the battle began. This was one of those obnoxious louts from Abblasoure, whose point man was his first cousin from Abblasoure's nearest neighbor, the Castle of Maidens. They had been feuding over something that was surely a sword, a bow, a knife, or a horse. One of his fellow Abblasoure archers whispered it was over one of those maidens, but I find that hard to believe."

Sheena looked firmly at Britta and said, "Milady, I reversed the feuding archers and then positioned the strongest team in front of the flag. I centered the remaining five as an inverted *V* on the battlefield ten yards farther up. Andred served as point archer, and I positioned myself as archer team leader in the rearmost diamond of the inverted *V*. From there, I could best see developments and shout changes to my battle orders.

"I told my teams, 'When the head herald signals the trumpet to sound and the tournament begins, we will advance in such a way as to funnel the enemy into our inverted *V*, where we will hit them with enfilade flights of arrows. Are there any questions?'

"That's when the Abblasoure archer I demoted took a good, long look at me from the first diamond on my left. Unfortunately, I had just turned sidewise, providing an unexpected glimpse of what I sometimes looked like from the—uh—hmm—side. I thought I had disguised myself very well, but apparently not well enough. He shouted to the rest of my teams, 'Antony is the girl from the nearby camp!'

"He turned to me in the most boorish manner possible and said, 'I didn't understand a single word you uttered. But if you had been a real warrior—that is, a *male* warrior—I would have pretended otherwise. But since you're just a loudmouthed Amazon girl, I refuse to serve under you!' Then my teams disintegrated as the rest of my army sided with this nitwit. Every one of those louts aimed the palm of his right hand over his head backwards, yelling, 'Puh-cheer!' That is with the exception of Andred, who stayed loyally by my side, shouting a defiant but not too loud, 'Huzzah!' My mutinous dogs—I mean rebel archers—now ignored Andred and me as they huddled in a mob near our flag and began yelping over who should now be the lead dog in their whining pack.

"Our battlefield umpire hadn't heard any of this, because he went to the left side of midfield to meet with the remaining heralds and other battlefield umpires. The new head herald finally gave a hand signal, and the main trumpeter blew his call on a bugle similar to the one Andred usually carries. This was the official start of the dye-arrow archery battle that Uncle Myrddin sent us to.

"The other army was captained by an efficient-looking squire who appeared capable of leading a lot more than a handful of tournament archers. I could see from the distance how he authoritatively ordered his army to knock arrows. Then they advanced toward us as they efficiently maneuvered around trees, holes, and bushes. I also noticed that each of their lines operated in a zone containing three archers closely supporting each other. It reminded me of a maneuver I had recently witnessed in that sport called soccer.[25]

"'Andred,' I said as I pointed at the advancing team.

"He had become so intensely focused that he forgot himself and belted out such a horrendous 'Huzzah!' that it was followed by an equally horrendous *thud* as the second head herald was thrown from his horse. After emergency knaves carted him off the field, a second replacement head herald took over from the stands, where he absolutely refused to get near a horse. He also looked ready to feed

---

[25] Although some refer to this sport as football, most readers in my audience will likely know it by its North American name. In the historic Middle Ages, it was once outlawed when it became so popular that it interfered with archery practice.

Andred to the Monster-of-Unheard-of-Savageness as I gave him more jabs to suppress his killer *huzzah*s.

"When Andred stopped rubbing his ribs after I jabbed him as hard as the Monster-of-Unheard-of-Savageness, combined with a kick from Uncle Sir Cecil's horse, we shrugged off the third head herald's unfriendly look. Then we exchanged our brother–sister battle look, followed by our brother–sister battle nod."

"How many brother–sister things do you do?" asked Sir Christian.

"Enough," Sheena said. "We're very close."

"Huzzah," murmured Andred.

"Cut to the joust!" ordered Britta.

"Yes, milady, which brings us to the finale, where we uttered our brother–sister battle rhyme."

"'First we pray, and then they pay'?" asked Uncle Sir Cecil.

"We don't mean it quite the way it sounds. Who told you?" asked Sheena.

"Ad—dragain," muttered Andred.

"Nothing gets by Adragain," said Uncle Sir Cecil.

"Except maybe the Saxons," muttered Sir Christian.

Britta announced, "Everyone, please cut to the joust!

"Yes, milady," continued Sheena. "Then we defiantly knocked arrows and advanced to the midfield ravine. That's where Andred unfortunately lost his first arrow exchange with the squire leading the green team. This individual, who was addressed by his team as the Scholar, crouched like lightning behind a well-placed tree in the middle of his front line, which positioned him on the higher ground. Nevertheless, from our lower ground near the ravine, Andred almost nailed him, but an unexpected gust of wind deflected Andred's arrow at the last minute. And that was the only strong wind I remember seeing around here until Andred's cap blew off. Andred dropped to the ground to avoid the opposing squire's shot. But when he got back up, a field herald assisting the battlefield umpire on our side pointed at Andred's once beautiful blond hair, now covered from top to split ends with green dye containing that nasty hint of orange. He announced, 'Young squire, I declare thee slain!'

"Andred responded with a most humble—what else?—'Huzzah.'"

"Meantime, I splattered my first opponent with red dye that contained a hint of yellow. Unfortunately, this was not the squire who shot Andred but one immediately on his left who squirmed around like he suffered from a horrible itch. I now prepared to rapid-shoot as many opponents as possible, when I inadvertently turned sidewise again. Andred's clothes once again didn't disguise me as the herald pointed a serpentine finger at me, declaring angrily and, in my opinion, most impolitely, 'You are a damosel! Remove thyself from this field!'"

"If he had only told me politely and courteously and had refrained from pointing his finger at me like a viper! Right then and there, I was tempted to unstring my bow and, adapting one of your favorite scroll swings, smack his finger into the next field."

"That's when the squire commanding the other team rushed up with his front line—minus the archer I hit. He halted within reach of my bow stave, which, for some reason, he appeared too distracted to see very well. Seeming slightly dazed, he still had the gall to say, 'Milord, herald, your suspicions were correct. This is no awkward-shaped knave but truly is—'"

"He froze for a moment with wide eyes and his mouth even wider before he finished, 'A damosel! You have caught her bow-handed and have declared her status true!'"

"Ooooh, milady, the words of this knavish, low-life soccer squire were much more insulting than the herald's finger. For one thing, that squire had talked about me—in front of me—as though I wasn't there. Then he dug his hole into the gardé robe pits deeper when he said, 'War belongs to men, so unless you're willing to become my captive—just teasing, ha-ha—you had better do as the herald says and remove thyself from this field.'"

"But when I stood there and stared at him, that knavish lout of a soccer squire dared to amend his words by adding in a sickly sweet tone, 'Damosel, I think you should be going.'"

"Milady, then he did a most funny thing that I still don't understand. He took a truly long look at me in a way that almost made him as immovable as a statue. He just stood there and stared at me. His mouth especially became truly wide open, and I saw everything inside: his tongue, his tonsils, and the fact that he really did have nice teeth.

"Meanwhile, his archers, minus him and the one I plastered, continued to advance. They made short work of my mutinous dogs, who were still fighting, barking, yelping, and growling over who was going to replace me as leader. And this happened because my archers, especially those louts from Castle Abblasoure, where no one says *mass*, because they'd rather play with bears than say their prayers, were too proud, too inflexible, too stupid, and simply too arrogant to be led by a teenage girl with true military know-how.

"Milady, I might have restrained myself and quietly left the battlefield containing those clown clods of a herald and a squire. But that winning squire did have the supreme gall to address me as 'my captive.' That was unacceptable to me even as a joke. I shouted back to him, 'I'll show you how much war only belongs to men and who truly deserves to be someone's captive!'

"Milady, I'm sorry if I disappoint you when you hear what I did next, but that squire's comment poked deeper than the herald's finger. I grabbed my bow stave after the fashion Uncle Sir Cecil showed me and unstrung it with a swoosh. Winding up with a swing around my head, I lunged forward to smack that squire across the shoulders like the wrath of God. Unfortunately, milady, I quickly learned that aiming a bow like a quarterstaff is not quite the same as aiming it like a bow. That means that in this case, I, uh, aimed too high and hit his head more like an elephant tusk than anything to do with God. It left a bruise that looked like Andred's bugle.

"Fortunately, it didn't break my bow—because Uncle Sir Cecil made sure our composite weapons were constructed with extra strength wood, bone, and bronze.

"I also hoped it didn't break anything on the squire. But it was hard to tell, as he slid into the nearest ditch like a food cart going down a mudhole!"

Sir Christian said, "You know that line too?"

Sheena said, "Sir Christian, everyone knows that line. Except maybe the squire after his head hit the boulder at the bottom of the mudhole. That really made me feel sad, because he truly was nice looking, before I smacked him, that is. Maybe if the right person had come along and helped him with his attitude."—she suddenly stopped as she noticed that everyone, including Andred was giving her an interesting look, possibly about her attitude—so she coughed and continued, "But he did call me that awful word: *captive.*"

Britta politely nodded in agreement, and said, "Cut to the joust."

"Yes, milady. From the safety of the stands, the third head herald looked ready to feed me to the Monster-of-Unheard-of-Savageness. He screamed at the battlefield umpires, who yelled at the emergency armed guards. They in turn bellowed like the marauding Saxons as they rushed to my end of the battlefield, waving enough swords, spears, pikes, clubs, and battle-axes to engage the army of Attila the Hun. And that was just to deal with one lone damosel that you and Uncle Sir Cecil taught how to swing an unstrung bow stave faster than Sir Lancelot swooshing his sword."

Britta nodded politely again as Uncle Sir Cecil smiled.

"The guards swarmed around me—outside bow stave smacking range, that is. But they were in no real danger, for I had quieted down just as you taught me. I was behaving politely and courteously as I prepared to permit them, impolitely and discourteously, but not too closely, to escort me from the dye-arrow battlefield."

"So that's how Andred got his greenish hair with the ugly hint of orange," said Britta thoughtfully. "Before you left the battlefield, did anything else unusual happen?"

"Yes, milady, there was one other thing. As the heavily armed guards surrounded me from a safe distance, a different squire on the opposing team opened his dog trap yap and yelped his way into a gardé robe pit. 'Look at who gets to be the captive after all! Ha! Ha! Ha! Why don't you damosel savages learn to quit when you're behind?'

"Milady, guess what happened then. Faster than Uncle Sir Cecil's war arrow can pick off a Saxon, my younger brother, Andred, who had also been surrounded by the guards, ran over the largest two. He shouted, 'Huzzah!' so loud that horses threw four trumpeters, three merchants, two traveling musicians, Sir Brutus de Augusta, Sir Ogier the Greedy, and the third head herald, who had finally gotten enough nerve to climb onto his horse. It took a small army of knaves to carry them from the field. But no one remembered them until after we were finally gone. In the meantime, everyone watched in amazement as Andred lifted the loudmouthed squire high, at arm's length, straight up over his head. Milady, I always thought Andred was as strong as a bear, but I didn't realize just how strong until then. Did you know that Andred was that strong?"

Britta politely nodded as Andre politely mumbled, "Huzzah."

Sheena continued, "Milady, Andred shook that squire so hard that enough money fell out of his clothes to cause a fight among the guards. While they smacked each other around trying to collect it, Andred made the squire smack the ground on the other side of the battlefield's nearest rope boundary. That's where he landed with a gooey splat after Andred wound up and launched him like catapult ammunition. Andred then looked over the rope at that loudmouth as out of my brother's mouth proceeded one of the loudest and sweetest collections of two and three syllable phrases I had ever heard him say in his whole life: 'Hear me—thou churl—and lowlife—varlet! Absolutely—nobody calls—my sister—a behind!' This was followed by one final sensational huzzah that fortunately got no one launched from a horse.

"Milady, I recognized that sneering, loudmouthed squire as Melehan, oldest son of backstabbing Sir Mordred the Murderous. And I had the satisfaction of seeing him spit gooey globs of whatever he landed in out of that gardé robe pit he uses for a mouth. Andred then turned his back on Melehan and moved to my side as we watched the guards finish collecting Melehan's money. Then they once more collected around us, but from a safe distance, as we allowed them to hustle us off the dye-arrow battlefield."

"Well," said Britta, "there was certainly more to see here than we think we see. Although even before we met Meudwin, I suspected

Melehan was haunting this shire. According to information I received, his father, Sir Mordred, who appears on the verge of becoming even more backstabbing and murderous, should be nearby as well, which is what we want. Otherwise, I wouldn't have been as free to seek Sir Christian. Sheena, did you get into any other trouble we may have to account for?"

"Oh no, milady," Sheena said gleefully. "Several of the uninjured heralds as well as battlefield umpires and a few of the guards had come with Myrddin from Caerleon. Others were from Camelot. Several of them recognized Andred as the squire of Uncle Sir Cecil, whom they all know, respect, and definitely don't want any trouble with. On the other hand, none of them were completely sure who I was, although one guard studied me thoughtfully for a moment. Then he gave me a sly look as he asked if I had once attended a certain convent school. He said he was called out to it one night after the visiting five hundred squires of Castle Canguin started a riot. But before he said anything further, I gave him a dose of that stare you taught me, the one that makes a girl seem to have claws in her eyes like a she-leopard. He turned white as a ghost and almost fainted before he was half carried, half dragged from the field by another equally terrified guard.

"The remaining guards surrounding Andred and me, still at a safe distance, led us not only away from that field but several long Sarmatian bow shots past the next two. The guard captain then commanded us not to return to this tournament on pain of death!"

"Of course," agreed Britta. "What became of Myrddin?"

"When we returned to camp, Uncle Myrddin was waiting for us with everything in order. He had even cooked something for us—and a guest—to eat. But when he didn't see whomever he was expecting, he just smiled in his mysterious way and said he would ask us another time about the tournament. He picked up his staff, sword, and bow and said he would be on the forest trails between Nauntes and Cadir Idris. He then disappeared from our camp as mysteriously as he entered."

"Typical Myrddin," mused Britta as she once again handed Andred his cap. "Keep wearing this until we obtain one of those new shampoos being brewed by Myrddin's assistants. Hopefully there's one powerful enough to remove that dye without making your hair look twice as bad as that on a Pictish pig. Now, let's leave this vicinity. I can't chance you meeting more disgruntled archers who are tempted to make you prove that a damosel with a big stave and a big brother is not to be despised."

As Andred started to respond with his loudest and most sensational huzzah—*thud!*—he was felled by a war club. This was followed by a swoosh as a hood dropped over Britta's head, while a noose trapped her arms to her side.

Battle cries filled the air as Saxons surrounded them. They had been lying in wait, well-hidden, while listening near their last night's campfire in the abandoned village.

A gigantic Saxon saluted the sword-swinging commander with the swoosh of an equally gigantic ax as he reported, "Heretoga, look what has fallen into our net."

"Excellent, Sarlic. Let's examine the catch."

CHAPTER 20

Eighty-seven to Five

Is eighty-seven to five worse than forty to one?
—Wade the Scholar, *Chanson de Chrétien*

Andred's cap cushioned a glancing blow from the war club as he slowly regained his feet. But the Saxons ignored him.

Clang! Clang! Clang! Clang!

Their leader, Heretoga, banged the flat of his sword on the helmet of Sir Christian, who attempted to move it to the other side of Slow Silver's saddle. But Heretoga blocked him with a move he learned from Sir Mordred the Murderous, with whom he was about to become just like—never mind. He contemptuously ignored Sir Christian.

"Hello in there!" the Saxon chief said to Britta, who stood strangely silent with her head and arms—but not her feet—bound inside the rope and hood. He clanged another dent into Sir Christian's long-suffering helmet and addressed her again. "It seems that someone wasn't looking very well when we *were* looking very well—but what could have distracted someone like you?"

Thud!

The ax of Sarlic, Heretoga's right-hand Saxon giant, pinned Andred's cap to the nearest tree.

The Saxon leader took a long look at the squire's hair, which resembled a sea monster growing out of an onion and shook his head.

220

He said to Sarlic, "Return his cap before someone mistakes him for the Vegetable-of-Unheard-of-Savageness."

With a crack like the breaking up of spring river ice, Sarlic yanked the ax free, along with the cap full of splinters that he contemptuously threw at Andred. Still hurting from the blow, the squire managed to catch the cap and before he put it back on, he emptied it on Sarlic's boots when the Saxon wasn't looking very well.

Unaware of why Andred's face now had a quirky smirk, Heretoga glared at the squire. "If you feel like yelling—"

"Huzzah!" shouted Sheena, filling in for Andred.

Sarlic's ax sheared off a branch over Sheena's head, which she dodged while sticking out her tongue, shoving both thumbs in her ears, and waving her palms defiantly as she asked, "Can you read lips?"

Sarlic wasn't sure, which threw off his next ax swing, making him sever a branch from the tree next to Sheena. A green-clad warrior fell out of it and just missed landing on Sarlic as the Saxon jumped back and yelled, "The tree bears bad fruit!"

Sheena said, "It takes bad fruit to know bad fruit!" And she spit a day-old cherry stem in his face.

Thunk!

This made Sarlic's ax wedge itself into another tree. He tugged away on it as he glared at Sheena.

She sweetly pointed at the newcomer. "It's the Knight of the Green Apples—who can only afford to look like one green apple. Would you like to know why?"

"No!" Sarlic roared, finally ripping his ax from one of the few trees in the area in which no one was hiding.

Heretoga stepped between Sarlic and Sheena, giving Britta's maid an interesting look. He motioned Sarlic away from her as he pointed his sword at the new arrival and commanded his men, "Cut to the raid!"

The newcomer jumped to his feet in clothing covered with mold, shouting, "Without weapons, horse, armor, or even a safe place to wash my clothes, I can't cut to anything but this!" He waved one of

Britta's notices at Heretoga, as a Saxon named Drefan ripped it from his hands. But the knight thunked Drefan with the fallen branch as he ran past two other Saxons, yelling, "Times are hard!"

Sir Christian spoke into Uncle Sir Cecil's good ear, "They'll be a lot harder if he doesn't find a good place to wash his clothes."

A Saxon named Ator said, "I never find a good place to wash my clothes."

Heretoga's sword struck sparks from Ator's helmet rim as he shouted, "Silence! We have the ones we want, including—"

He signaled Sarlic, whose pointed ax-spike nailed Andred's cap to another tree. As the giant removed the nasty weapon in such a way that he gave Heretoga a mouthful of cap yarn, the Saxon leader spat it out declaring, "The human celery stick!"

A Saxon named Abeodan stared at Andred's fully exposed hair, which in the light looked fungus green with a hint of moldy orange. "Captain Heretoga, what if we catch something from him?"

The flat of Heretoga's sword just missed smacking Abeodan as the Saxon leader growled. "Make sure you don't first catch something from me!"

Uncle Sir Cecil asked Sir Christian, "How much do they outnumber us?"

"Eighty-seven to five!" announced Heretoga, whose ears were as sharp as Britta's.

Uncle Sir Cecil said to Sir Christian, "Say something distracting."

Sir Christian shouted, "Ouch! Who kicked me?"

Uncle Sir Cecil said, "Not distracting enough!"

Sir Christian thought Britta's feet were distracting enough as he yelled, "Fire!"

Heretoga asked Abeodan, "Did you put out the campfire?"

Abeodan shrugged as Sir Christian said, "I meant wire—"

"As in chain mail wire?" asked Abeodan.

Clang! Heretoga's sword smacked sparks from the helmet of the Saxon next to Abeodan as Sir Christian clarified, "As in why are you not outnumbering us one hundred to five?"

Abeodan volunteered, "We left four men on hut detail, four men on cook detail, four men on guard detail, and Thongor the Mighty was locked up for breaking into the mighty strong captured ale."

"That makes one hundred," Sir Christian said.

A whispered voice reminded him, "Outnumbered knights know how to count."

Heretoga roared, "Silence!" His sword finally struck sparks from the rim of Abeodan's helmet as he warned his henchman, "Before we outnumber these dogs eighty-six to five!"

Sir Christian asked, "Can you smack your henchmen on the helmet somewhere else?"

"Silence!" Heretoga roared.

Sir Christian said, "That's the loudest silence I have ever heard."

"Since the last time someone ignored you?" whispered that same voice.

"Silence!" Heretoga roared once more.

Sir Christian addressed Uncle Sir Cecil's good ear, "Is eighty-seven to five worse than forty to one?"

The archer replied, "If we're five, they're eighty-seven, and forty to one doesn't show up."

"What about Britta's reinforcements, who, at the best psychological moment, will appear in the key watershed position to provide the most bang for the clang as they most valiantly, most vigorously, and most selfishly—Ouch! Who kicked me again?"

"Selflessly," corrected Uncle Sir Cecil.

"I wasn't kicked selflessly," said Sir Christian, rubbing his leg. Then he muttered, "What was I thinking?"

"Selfishly," whispered the voice.

Sir Christian tried to ignore the voice. "Help us even the odds against these eighty-six—"

"Eighty-seven!" insisted Abeodan. He jumped out of reach of his captain's sword as he asked Sir Christian, "Were you just praying?"

Sir Christian said, "Why, does it scare pirates?"

Abeodan shrugged as Sir Christian added, "What was I thinking?"

"That you had better surrender!" commanded Heretoga.

A Saxon named Acwel pointed at Sir Christian. "Captain, beware! After Lord Cheldric was defeated on the Humber, this was the knight who was given a parade and several rich rewards, after which his name was added—"

"To the bottom of King Arthur's Round Table Honor Roll! Surely a ruse to trick us Saxons, for this is the Round Table's absolute worst knight."

"According to whom?" asked Acwel's twin brother, Acwellen. "Since we began raiding these shires, I heard this knight is most perilous—a true killer!"

Heretoga sneered, "I only heard he's been killing time!"

Acwel said, "Captain, he travels with the woman we were sent to capture, who appears to be harmless—when she isn't. Is it possible he also is not what he appears?"

"Yes," answered Heretoga sarcastically, "just as he appears to get decisive help when he prays to God. I heard those stories and assure you that they're rubbish! True warriors like us rely on actions when we need to change our luck!"

The warrior named Drefin handed Heretoga Britta's notice that he grabbed from the Knight of the Green Apples. "Captain, is this a change of luck caused by our actions? The likeness on this captured sheet appears to be of this knight."

Heretoga roared with laughter as he read the notice and said, "A reward of one hundred fifty thousand groats!"

"That's another way of saying *shillings*," said Drefin.

Heretoga nodded as he laughed even harder before he choked out, "For Christian the Poisoner!" He added with sarcasm, "That is the funniest joke I've read this year!"

Sheena said, "You mean *this* is the funniest joke you've read this year."

Andred added, "Written—by someone—who's good at—"
Thunk!
Sarlic removed another branch from over Andred's head.

"Silence!" Heretoga roared as he studied the notice thoughtfully. "Besides the plunder in our main camp, I don't think there are that many groats in this part of Britain!"

Heretoga showed the notice to Uncle Sir Cecil, loudly addressing his good ear. "Were you trying to collect this reward?"

The archer answered, "In a manner of speaking—at the last Christmas feast, this knight poisoned all able-bodied Knights of the Round Table."

"In that case," Heretoga sneered, "Lord Cheldric should reward *him*—as a way of saying thank you."

Uncle Sir Cecil smiled ironically.

Heretoga smiled even more sarcastically. "So surrender—or say your prayers, which I believe will only make things worse—so why bother?"

Uncle Sir Cecil said, "We'll bother."

The archer nudged Sir Christian, who cried out, "Lord Jesu! Help and protect us all!"

Uh-ruuu! Uh-ruuu! A horn bugle announced the arrival of more Saxons.

Heretoga said, "That's Offa's raiding party, which means we now outnumber you one hundred seventy-four to five."

Abeodan volunteered, "Offa also left four men on hut detail, four men on cook detail, four men on guard detail, and Cedric of the Saxes, who never misses with his axes, got locked up for using them to break into the mighty captured ale with Thongor."

"Silence!" roared Heretoga.

Sir Christian said to Uncle Sir Cecil, "The odds just got higher—and the silence just got louder."

"They're short twenty-six pirates," said Uncle Sir Cecil.

Sir Christian whispered, "What do we do with the one hundred seventy-four pirates they aren't short? Is this where I fight them single-handedly while you and your retinue decide if I need some of your help?"

"You'll need some of our help, but first, I would recommend that you request a little more help from Jesu."

225

"Because the help Jesu sent me last time as an answer to all of my prayers, namely you, Britta, and that zany pair of whatever they are, aren't doing that well—ouch! Someone kicked me again!"

"You were referring to our retinue," said Uncle Sir Cecil, "which now also includes you!"

"Most reassuring. Ouch! Kicked again!"

A voice whispered, "You know what to do."

Rubbing his leg, he nodded to bring them to the next painful point as he prayed, "Lord Jesu!" Then, almost like a man drowning, he cried twice as loud, "Help!"

A heavy breeze, at another moment when there had been no breeze, blew through Sheena's hair, causing her to turn sidewise to brush it from her eyes. That was when every Saxon in the two raiding crews saw her profile—and gasped. Rypan of Offa's Saxons said, "Did you see that damosel? She's going to be my captive!"

Crunch! Tobrytan of Heretoga's Saxons clubbed him, saying, "No, she's going to be my captive!"

Whack! Gilfre of Offa's Saxons belted Tobrytan with his sword hilt, saying, "No, she's going to be my captive!"

Thump! Earh of Heretoga's Saxons laid him out with a spear shaft, saying, "No, she's going to be my captive!"

An utterly amazed Sir Christian spoke into Uncle Sir Cecil's good ear. "If this keeps up long enough, we'll outnumber the Saxons. Is Sheena always this good at reducing the odds?"

"She has her days when someone prays. But it doesn't work with everyone. So with Britta tied up—"

Thud! Uncle Sir Cecil leaped into the side of Rainbow's saddle, instead of onto it. As he bounced off, Sir Christian said, "You need someone else to aim you?"

"For the moment, just onto my horse."

With a mighty heave, Sir Christian fired the archer onto the saddle. Seizing the reins, Uncle Sir Cecil reared Rainbow and opened his mouth to shout—

"Huzzah!" Andred out-shouted him, stampeding a mixed herd of captured livestock. Uncle Sir Cecil saluted Andred in the wrong direction as his horse charged through the commotion into the right direction. This caused a stampede among the Saxons as his destrier's hooves launched warriors who were screaming, pleading, and sobbing onto thatch rooftops and tree branches as well as into doorways and the local well.

"They don't—call—Uncle—Sir Cecil's—Rainbow—a warhorse—for nothing!" Andred called to Sir Christian.

Meantime, Heretoga and Offa called to their men who weren't trampled, launched, or running for their lives from Rainbow to start fighting someone besides each other.

In the middle of this mayhem, Sheena's bow stave smacked Earh of Heretoga's Saxons as she proclaimed to the battling mobs, "No one calls me their captive!"

One of Offa's Saxons asked, "What should they call you?"

"Sheena Unica Verena Antonia Serena Vivina Augustina Ruebena Serilda Athena Karmita Lalita Kairos!" As she prepared to smack him, she said, "You were thinking—"

Thunk!

Wulf of Heretoga's Saxons belted him first.

Wulf, in turn, was clobbered by Andred as the squire freed Britta, who immediately tripped Huff, who was Offa's nearest Saxon. Planting her foot on the middle of his spear, she gave him a stare that made him shudder as if he were in an earthquake or an explosion in a small kitchen. Huff abandoned the spear as he struggled to his feet, complaining, "It not be fitting for a woman to fight like a man!"

"That's why I fight like a woman! Surrender before I knock thee silly with documentation!"

"How?"

Kapow! Britta stared down at the limp, scaly lump of Huff as she said, "My scroll is mightier than your sword!" This was followed by her double *thunk* of two more warriors, who wished to remain anonymous, as her liaison messenger footwork helped her avoid their Saxon blows while swinging scrolls in either hand.

Pearce of Offa's Saxons snaked a finger at her. "Beware of a lady who looks harmless!"

Whack! Whack!

As two more warriors collapsed in front of Britta, Pearce added, "And hits with both hands!" He swung his spear to hold Britta back as she gave him a bear-scaring, harmless-lady eyeful.

Pearce scowled. "My woman knows how to look like that!"

"But does she also know how to look like *this*?" Britta gave him a wild woman day-of-judgment stare. She advanced with the twin scrolls cleaving the air in an attack she'd learned from the Knight of the Two Swords when they were about to become just like—never mind.

The Saxon backed up until—

Splat!

He disappeared into one of the sheriff's road pits. "Like a—food cart—going down—a mudhole," said Andred as he thunked a second Saxon right on top of him.

This exchange was followed by a nearby *clunk* as Sir Christian caught Sir Pinel le Savage's second-favorite spear in Sarlic's chain mail.

"Unsnag me," the Saxon snarled as he struggled to reach Sir Christian with his ax blade, which was so far dripping only tree sap, "and spear fight me like a Saxon!"

"You're ax fighting me like a Saxon!" Sir Christian yanked Sir Pinel le Savage's second-favorite spear free with such force that he spun around, knocking Tredan of Heretoga's Saxons over a rock, and Tolucan of Offa's Saxons into a doorway.

Sir Christian grabbed the spear by the middle and ran forward, mowing down a warrior on either side. Then he swung it over his head—and got caught in a tree. Leaving the spear for later, he drew his sword, which Sarlic's ax whacked from his hands. But the ax also cut the cords attaching the flask on Sir Christian's belt, which contained, of all things, the Oil of the Perfume Perilous. Sir Christian caught the flask, popped the cork, and as the Saxon wound up an ax swing that would knock Sir Christian through the walls of the nearest hut—*splash!*

Sarlic received a bath—not an anointing—that disoriented him so much he crashed over a wall by the nearest hut. His "Aiieee!" echoed as he stood enveloped by a dark cloud from which he was seen slashing at the edges—until his ax got caught in a tree. Then the wind, at still another moment when there was no wind, blew fumes from the cloud into the stampeding horses and cattle as Sir Christian jumped under an abandoned cart.

Neighs and moos were heard halfway to Navarre in one direction and all the way across Ireland in the other as mixed livestock crashed through huts, walls, and fences to reach the source of what, to them, were exciting and addicting fumes. Sarlic shrieked an even louder "Aiieee!" as horses and cows, led by elephant-size oxen, pursued him out of the village, down the road, and over the horizon.

Sir Christian said, "That's ox fighting like a Saxon!"

"That's awful fighting like a Saxon!" hollered Heretoga. He and Offa reformed their remaining men behind a shield wall from which they couldn't see Sheena, Britta, Andred, who looked like a killer vegetable, and Uncle Sir Cecil's horse, whose hooves launched a straggler into the air so that he landed behind Heretoga with a climactic *thud*!

Peeking through a gap between the two large shield rims, Heretoga caught Britta's latest wild-lady look as she cried, "Youuuuuu-heh-heh-heh!"

Heretoga covered his eyes and pointed his sword—in the wrong direction—as he roared, "Seize these dogs!"

Britta replied, "It takes a dog to catch a dog! Here, Toga! Toga! Toga!"

But the tide was turning as most of the remaining Saxons also covered their eyes. Offa managed to point everyone, including Heretoga, in the right direction, and the shield wall advanced, forming a murderous wedge.

Thump! Thump! Thump! Thump!

Sir Christian threw a pouch from his horse's saddle toward the campfire that Abeodan hadn't put out. But another unexpected wind blew its contents onto a wall whose stones disappeared with a small unexpected *poof.*

The Saxons noticed it with amazement but not fear as Sir Christian said, "Wrong mixture." He once more prayed, "Lord Jesu! Help!" and tossed another pouch from his saddle into the middle of the Saxons' smoldering campfire.

Kawoom! Kaboom! Fortunately for our story, our heroes, and the inhabitants of that immediate shire, it was not as strong as the batch Sir Christian had heated up on the Humber. Nevertheless, it shot a blast skyward like a small volcano—which for once wasn't felt halfway to Navarre in one direction and all of the way across Ireland in the other.

But it was enough to chase off the Saxons. Sometime after the last one regained consciousness and fled, which included everyone not on hut detail, cook detail, guard detail, or locked up with Cedric and Thongor, Britta's now even more modestly equipped retinue once more clip-clopped down the trail.

As they passed beneath a hill with a high overlook, Andred once again shouted a loud and unexpected, "Huzzah!"

Sir Christian, relieved that his horse was growing more and more used to Andred, shook his head as he muttered, "One prayer page, one prayer archer, one prayer maid—"

"One maid with prayer!" corrected Sheena.

"I'm sure you were," said Sir Christian. "Nothing else explains it, as well as one exceptionally loud prayer—"

"Huzzah!" Andred shouted.

Sir Christian said, "Nothing else explains him either."

"And I'm an answer to all your prayers," Britta reminded him.

"How can I forget?"

"Pray that you don't," Britta said.

"I still want to hear the other answers," Sir Christian said soberly.

"They're not available today, and if they become available enough to distract you tomorrow, you may never see your squire again. Now, that's just a feeling, but I'm seldom wrong," Britta said with a smile.

Sir Christian glanced at Uncle Sir Cecil, who reminded him, "In my condition, I don't feel much of anything."

Sheena said, "I have a feeling—"

"That you can tell Sir Christian all about after we camp." Britta now drew a short, sheathed object from her cloak and presented it to the knight.

"My stolen knife!" he exclaimed as he pulled it from its key-engraved sheath.

"Supplies I deem necessary to provide," said Britta, "unless someone else steals it when you aren't looking very well. Meudwin recovered it from the Navarrese while I negotiated with Sir Erbin. Do you think they noticed the message engraved on each side of the blade?"

Sir Christian showed everyone the words inscribed on the left side of the blade: "And lean not unto thine own understanding." Next, he showed them the words on the right: "The effectual fervant prayer of a righteous man availeth much."

"When did you first notice them?" asked Britta.

Sir Christian didn't answer as he shrugged, resheathed the knife, and attached it to his belt within easy reach of his hand. Instead, he looked south and called out, "Lord Jesu, help and protect us all!"

Behind him came the swoosh of a scroll swinging through the air before being sheathed like Sir Lancelot's sword.

CHAPTER 21

Who Will Really Be Pursuing Whom

Before this so-called quest of Sir Christian is over,
I wonder who will really be pursuing whom.
—Wade the Scholar, *Chanson de Chrétien*

From an overlooking hill, Melehan watched Sir Christian de Galis; Uncle Sir Cecil the Steady; Lady Britta de Brittany; Sheena Unica Verena, etcetera; and Andred the Silent not so silently clip-clop south toward the city of Nauntes. He turned to his younger brother, who was still smothered in Sheena's dye-arrow dye. "They're traveling fast. I wonder if it has anything to do with the recent tournament."

When his brother didn't answer, he mused, "Or does it have anything to do with our raiding Saxons?"

When his brother still didn't answer, he said, "I also wonder what forces we must face—besides them—to replace King Arthur with our father."

This time, his brother responded. "I wonder what forces we must face—besides them—just to replace our clothes!"

Melehan smacked the back of his brother's head and then ducked his return swing. His frustrated brother retorted, "Your clothes look *and smell* like you crawled out of a gardé robe pit. But mine make me feel like I've been clawed by the Monster-of-Unheard-of-Savageness!"

"There is no Monster-of-Unheard-of-Savageness!"

"How do you know? Have you ever seen it?"

"Have you?"

"I read about it in a scroll that Hubert of Hereford showed me before he was dragged screaming, pleading, and sobbing to clean out the castle gardé robe pits. He said the author was not the kind of knave who sat around a monastery making up things like that."

Melehan sniffed but not as much as his brother, when he wasn't holding his nose or scratching. "Hubert of Hereford also claims if a scroll gets copied, it must be true. With a mind like that, he belongs in the gardé robe pits. On the other hand, dear brother, I'm sure that time will tell what's truly fact and what's truly fiction, just like everything else dealing with King Arthur and his wonderful Knights of the Round Table—soon to be replaced, I might add, by King Mordred and his even more wonderful Knights of the Hierarchical Table. That's where location, location, location, especially at the head of the new table will mean everything. Just be thankful your clothes smell fresh. According to Great-Aunt Morgan le Fay, that clawed-by-a-monster skin itch won't last forever."

His brother painfully replied, "The time it has lasted so far feels like forever. Is our plot to assist our father's early succession to our grandfather's throne worth an early case of eternal punishment? What if this is an indication of worse things to come?"

That thought bothered Melehan too, but he tried not to think about it as he took another pecking-order swing at his younger brother. However, his sibling, becoming more sensitive to worse things to come, this time ducked out of reach. He glared at Melehan. "I would much rather be in your clothes—despite the smell."

"Why?"

Melehan's brother pointed at bugs buzzing around his clothes until they landed, dropped dead, and flaked off like dandruff. "Whatever Andred not so silently planted you in, it kills insects!"

All of a sudden, they heard a plop.

"And birds flying too close."

The younger brother's foot prodded feathers still fluttering on the ground. "It's not a total loss; your clothing just nailed a game bird. I wonder if that makes it safe to eat. Also"—he pointed a viperish finger at his brother's hair—"that's the best I have ever seen your split ends. It's almost an improvement."

Melehan drew a scroll from his cloak, not as quickly as Britta or even an ancient knight touching his sword hilt, and attempted to smack his brother. But once again, he ducked. Humming an off-key tune, Melehan then held the scroll in one hand as the other produced half of a cut penny. He tossed it into the air, and when it descended—*swoosh!*

"A swing and a miss!" his brother announced as the scroll fanned the air.

A red-faced Melehan dug the coin out of a pile of goo and tried to wipe it clean on his brother's cloak, but his sibling once again dodged. Becoming red-faced with a hint of raging orange, Melehan wiped the coin on the edge of his own cloak before he slid it back inside.

His brother said, "Whatever you tried to prove, you *almost* did it. But remember, that only counts in horse shoes, hail storms, Greek fire, flash floods, catapult boulders, and a whole lot of arrows."

Melehan said, "You know a lot about things that come in second."

"That's because I came in second—as your brother."

"Add to your list of second-best place-holders something called fish gravy!"

"What's fish gravy?" asked his brother.

"I'm not sure."

"So what makes it second best?"

"I'm not sure about that either, but we need to learn if we're going to assist our father's early succession to King Arthur."

Melehan resheathed the scroll, once again not as quickly as Britta or even a mediocre knight fumbling with his sword. He scowled at his brother. "I was demonstrating how my scroll is about to become mightier than the sword!"

His brother sneered, "I wouldn't draw against one of those mighty swords that's sharper than the words on your scroll. Why don't you try again on a day when your clothes don't smell like—"

Smack!

Melehan's scroll-less hand had nailed his brother's nose. "How do my clothes smell now?"

His brother held his nose as he shook his head and mumbled, "Where did you learn that scroll-swinging trick—from Sir Christian's squire?"

"No, I didn't learn that scroll-swinging trick from Sir Christian's squire! Dear brother, please note that Wade the so-called Scholar isn't the only squire who thinks he's on fire in the shire!"

His brother moaned, "The itch in my clothes make me feel like I'm on fire in the shire!"

Melehan ignored his brother's discomfort as he said, "For one thing, Wade still handles a scroll on the primary level."

"Which is?" his brother moaned.

"He primarily reads them. I, on the other hand—" Melehan redrew the scroll, took another swing, and got it caught in a bush. With a red face once again, he pulled it loose covered with leaves, branches, and more bugs that dropped dead when they brushed against his clothes. He quietly resheathed it.

"On the other hand—why don't you try using the other hand?" suggested his brother during a lull in his pain. "Maybe that side works better."

Melehan tried using his other hand to smack his brother, who once again dodged. Melehan insisted, "I'm still cleverer, more subtle, and sensationally more ruthless than Wade the so-called Scholar. For one thing, he gives allegiance to the idiotic Knight of the Fish Gravy."

"Once again, what is fish gravy?"

"When I find out, I'll tell you! Meantime, my personal cleverness has guaranteed that the wonderful Wade the Scholar is about to get his."

"I hope your personal cleverness doesn't guarantee that we're about to get ours along with him."

"Brother," Melehan said softly, "that has only happened to you so far."

"That's very generous of you. Meantime, we have a clothes problem, and thanks to the latest scheme you cooked up with Great-Aunt Morgan le Fay, we're running out of places to get replacements."

Melehan glared at his brother, who glared back as he asked, "Why are you learning that scroll swing?"

"At father's suggestion, I always study the tactics of our opponents. The Corps of Liaison, for instance, a female messenger spy ring, staffed by damosels and little old ladies who like to think that they're still damosels, know some useful tricks. Besides blending into the castle woodwork while they watch everyone, everything, and every place, they learn to handle scrolls like Sir Lancelot swinging his sword. It doesn't look possible at first, until one discovers the trick is all in the wrist as well as knowing which side of the scroll makes the calligraphy unroll. The resulting technique may come in handy at banquets, where all sharp weapons are checked at the door with the seneschal."

His brother frowned. "What good will a tricky scroll swing do if Sir Kay has *you* checked at the door for imitating a sewer? Court damosels have turned in numerous complaints about knaves who smell and look much less worse than you."

Melehan again tried to smack his brother, who once more successfully ducked. He said with a glare, "Forget our clothes, and let's think about what's really important! Namely, what forces we must face—besides them riding down below—to assist our father in winning his early succession to King Arthur's throne."

With most Round Table knights on hazardous quests or lying on even more hazardous hospital beds, exactly what forces were Sir Mordred and his sons facing besides those riding down below? To the south, near the summit of the twenty-nine-hundred-foot mountain called Cadir Idris, a formerly famous but now greatly disfigured bard leaned against a tree. He was careful how he opened his mouth, partly due to Saxon war wounds and partly due to something yet to be explained as he paused and looked over his shoulder for signs of pursuit.

In the nearby city of Nauntes, a scholarly squire who'd recently returned from the nearby archery tournament with a face that looked whacked by an elephant tusk paused and looked over his shoulder for signs of pursuit.

To the north, near the latest lair of the notorious bandit Sir Breuse sans Pitie, a reclusive wise woman wearing a cloak full of scrolls that supposedly—but not actually—made her look more harmless than Lady Britta de Brittany paused and looked over her shoulder for signs of pursuit.

Finally, in the valley below, Sir Christian de Galis, when he wasn't praying for deliverance from whatever quest he was actually on, looked over his shoulder for signs of pursuit.

Melehan, looking down on Sir Christian de Galis, pondered how someone that inept could be such a threat to his father's plans of an early succession. A thought suddenly struck him like the thud of an arrow: What if Sir Christian de Galis wasn't inept after all? How else had he survived thirty-plus years as the absolute worst knight at King Arthur's Round Table? Most knights acting half as inept as Sir Christian de Galis would have been picked off by a mediocre man-at-arms years ago.

Melehan reviewed his glimpse of Sir Christian's liaison review, when he remembered with a shudder who had written it—the one lady in the Corps of Liaison who worked harder at appearing harmless than Lady Britta de Brittany. So why wouldn't she work just as hard at making someone else look harmless as well as exceptionally inept when he wasn't? What if she were part of a master plot disguising the fact that the absolute worst knight at King Arthur's Round Table was one of the best as well as one of the most subtle and even the most perilous. He had been held in secret reserve yet plain sight by underground forces loyal to King Arthur in the event of an emergency. It would explain how he had just happened to foil a superb Saxon invasion plot on the Humber. But what explained Sir Christian's many mediocre mistakes stretched out over thirty-plus years? Was that also part of a cosmic design? Melehan shuddered as he once again wondered what forces they really faced as they plotted to topple King Arthur.

As Melehan and his brother mounted freshly acquired horses, his brother nudged him and pointed downward at Sheena. She momentarily brought up the rear of Britta's retinue, leaning from the saddle while carefully planting a clue that looked natural and easy to find. Melehan said thoughtfully, "That bow-swinging damosel plants objects on the trail like a fisherman worming his hook."

"Or a hunter baiting a trap," observed his brother.

Melehan said, "Before this so-called quest of Sir Christian is over, I wonder who will really be pursuing whom."

"I wonder if planting bait for pursuers is the only trick they'll use," said Melehan's brother. Despite his painful itch, he drew his bow to coldly shoot Sheena with an arrow that wasn't dye filled.

They were too far away for Melehan to hear Sir Christian's latest prayer as he said, "What else do you think they'll do?"

A thunderous "Huzzah!" heard halfway to Navarre in one direction and all the way across Ireland in the other made Melehan's horse slam him into the branches of the nearest tree. There was a *thud* as his brother's arrow pinned his cap to one of the branches and a *splash* as his brother was tossed over the back of his horse, where he rolled backwards head over heels twice before he disappeared into one of the sheriff's road pits like a food cart going down a mudhole.

Below them, an eerie-sounding voice announced, "Cherrrry! Berrrry! Apple piiiie! There's going to be a big surprise!"

The big surprise (actually several) along with more sensational mistakes, venomous villains, hilarious heroes, and a little more prayer will be continued in volume 2, *Raiders of the Lost Gravy.*

CHAPTER 1

The Worst Answer

The worst answer is sometimes the best answer.
—Wade the Scholar, *Chanson de Chrétien*[26]

"The worst answer is sometimes the best answer."

Sir Christian de Galis, Knight of King Arthur's Round Table, temporarily reinstated, removed a helmet that felt glued to his face and hung it from his saddle away from the speaker, muttering, "According to who—"

"According to *whom*," corrected Britta de Brittany, a cloaked lady who looked harmless until, with a swoosh faster than most knights could touch their sword hilts, she shifted the helmet—despite a disgusting stickiness—to her side of the knight's saddle.

Refusing to touch the helmet further, Sir Christian said, "The king of—"

Thunk!

"Divine intervention kept you from finishing a sentence with 'fools,'" Britta said with a smirk.

"What do you know about divine intervention?"

"I'm an answer to all your prayers."

"I want to see the other answers!"

"Wouldn't you rather hear them?"

His reply was stifled by a *clang*, followed by a *crash*.

"That may be one of them now!" replied Britta, even smirkier.

---

[26]   *The Ballad of Chrétien.*

The equally smirky, modestly equipped, and extremely quirky retinue led by Sir Christian and Lady Britta included Uncle Sir Cecil the Steady, an ancient archer with more disabilities than arrows; a loquacious niece with the realm's longest first name, whom Britta called Sheena to save time when she needed her in the morning; and a nephew with a speech defect and bad hair designated Andred the Silent, who was also Uncle Sir Cecil's squire. Riding three destriers and two destrier-disguised palfreys and leading two packhorses, they clip-clopped into the presence of an athletic laundry lady.

The woman yanked a spear from a laundry basket faster than most knights could touch their sword hilts and wielded, not waved— an important distinction—its fanged warhead in a manner perilous to anyone she found annoying. With an equally swift swoosh, she jabbed the bottom tip into the ribs of a chain mail lump lying pinned beneath a soap flask the size of a boulder. She informed the new arrivals, "He thought I was the Monster-of-Unheard-of-Savageness, and all I said was 'Blood stain, mud stain, light starch, or heavy?'— which is how I advertise!"

Britta looked down at the chain mail lump for signs of life as the laundry lady added, "Hope I didn't hurt him—too much. I never quite got over the newly accoladed knight I pounded last summer. He interrupted me right after I said, 'Bloodstain, mud stain,' with a loud—"

"Huzzah!" shouted Andred.

The laundry lady looked ready to pound Andred as Sheena jabbed his ribs.

Author's Notes (also Known as an Afterword)

As I completed volume 1 in the hysterical historical prayer adventures of Sir Christian de Galis, I felt obligated to reveal some—but not all—of my sources. My copy of *The Arthurian Companion* by Phyllis Ann Karr, now as tattered as Sir Christian's cloak, contains a map of King Arthur's Britain (pages 492–93) that is extensively used by Lady Britta and myself, when it isn't falling out of its cover.

John Leyland's *Assertion of King Arthure*, which lists both Merangis des Portz and Gauuaine le Franc as number fifty-two on a roster of Round Table knights, appears on page 105 of *Merlin* by Norma Lorre Goodrich.

Blunt-tipped arrows can be seen in the old Richard Greene *The Adventures of Robin Hood* episode "The Apple and the Archer."

The one hundred bungling knights of Castle Cameliard were suggested by an unscrupulous regiment of children and old men whom the Duke of Brunswick raised for the British army during the American Revolution. According to Robert Graves in *Sergeant Lamb's America*, this dubious fighting force didn't help General Burgoyne win the Battle of Saratoga.

The price of gravy and Britta's list of traveling supplies were taken from *English Wayfaring Life in the Middle Ages* by J. J. Jusserand. One of my main sources for information regarding money, contracts, and other odds and ends was *Daily Life in Medieval Times* by Frances and Joseph Gies. Coins cut in half were used as identification. The idea caught on in the movies, as evidenced by two halves of a one-hundred-pound note being used as pirate identification in the Clark Gable film *China Seas.*

Sir Mordred's plight in the afterlife—as well as other characters of the Round Table, with Queen Guinevere heading the list—is mentioned in *The Divine Comedy* by Dante Alighieri. Sir Mordred suffers at the second-lowest level of the Inferno.

The utterly delightful and somewhat overlooked Monster-of-Unheard-Savageness originated in *The History of the Kings of Britain* by Geoffrey of Monmouth, definitely a monk sitting around with too much time on his hands.

REVIEW REQUEST

Reviews are important to the success of books on Amazon.com and Kindle. If you enjoyed this yarn and were equally impressed by the sneak preview of volume 2, please note that more fish gravy is cooking and will be served even quicker if you leave a positive review. To do so, go to the *Sir Christian de Galis and the Fish Gravy* Amazon page. You'll see a big button that says "Write a Customer Review." Click there, and share your thoughts.

You are also invited to stop by and view fifty-four-millimeter models used in the development of Sir Christian's story, as well as the latest artwork developed by my good friend Paul Dillon. One of my model suppliers in the UK liked photos of his products I assembled and used so much that he asked me to discuss three autographed copies of Sir Christian's first book. The Facebook page is https://www.facebook.com/pages/Knight-of-the-Fish-Gravy-LLC/1420460441523299.

I also recommend a visit to illustrator Paul Dillon's website, https://www.PAULDILLONCARTOONS.com, where Sir Christian illustrations, as well as his other work may be purchased on coffee cups. T-shirts and posters of his cartoons are also available. My favorites are the stagecoach banjo bandit and the downsized crew of Roman galley slaves. As the son of World War II B-17 ball turret gunner hero and POW Richmond "Red" Dillon, he also specializes in military art.

As a side note, if you are interested in American heroes, I do a daily history tweet on Twitter as @Carl_Ramsey06.

Carl E. Ramsey,
a Missouri Yankee who drove
through Connecticut once on business

The Tenth is an outstanding pro-life novel by former military officer, active medical professional, and page-turning author Joanne E. Moudy. Check out her website, www.gatedcreative.com, for further information.